THE MUSIC OF
WHAT HAPPENS

A tale of heartbreak, resilience and a young girl's search for love

Shiloh Willis
Alaskan Author of Grit, Love, Triumph, and Determination

PO Box 221974 Anchorage, Alaska 99522-1974
books@publicationconsultants.com, www.publicationconsultants.com

ISBN Number: 978-1-63747-101-2
eBook ISBN Number: 978-1-63747-102-9

Library of Congress Number: 2022936450

Copyright © 2022 Shiloh Willis
—First Edition—

All rights reserved, including the right of reproduction in any form, or by any mechanical or electronic means including photocopying or recording, or by any information storage or retrieval system, in whole or in part in any form, and in any case not without the written permission of the author and publisher.

Manufactured in the United States of America

CHAPTER 1

To Take Pride in Our Name

Kicking at a pebble in her path, Celina Zagoradniy-Montoya trudged down the dusty, wooded path on her way home from school. She swiped at her eyes with the sleeve of her faded, oversized, sweat jacket. It had been nearly nine months since Papi died. Would this terrible sadness never end? She crouched down on her heels in the middle of the path.

I miss you so much, Papi. I like can't believe I'll never see you again. It doesn't feel real.

At the fork in the path, Celina hesitated. She had not been back to Papi's grave since the Requiem, but she knew Mama was expecting her home.

I'll only stay a couple of minutes.

When she arrived at the cemetery, Celina slung her denim bookbag over a fence post and glanced around, warily. *I hate cemeteries. They always give me the creeps.*

She searched for several minutes before she found the plain, flat stone etched with her father's name and dates. Sinking to her knees in the warm, dusty grass, she absently brushed away the masses of brownish grass and dead yellow and purple wildflowers from the stone. She traced her fingers over the name **Giacamo Montoya** as tears filled her eyes.

I miss you so much, Papi. Nothing's the same with you gone. It's not fair, it's not right. Again, she wiped tears from her cheeks with her sleeve.

The Music of What Happens

Sitting back, gazing up at the dusky, purple sky, she sighed, closing her eyes as memories nearly one-year-old took over.

That evening, it had been her turn to care for her ill father and youngest brother, Immanuel, called Little Man, while Mama and the others were working.

"Papi, please eat. Your meds will make you sick if you don't. It's just cabbage soup, you can keep it down." Twelve-year-old Celina's heart pounded as she offered a spoonful of cabbage water. She blinked back threatening tears. *"Por favor* eat something. Just a little?"

Giacamo Montoya, face pale and gaunt, wide, dark eyes faded and exhausted, was silent for a moment. He inhaled thickly. Celina winced at the desperate sound.

"I'll try, *nena,*" he managed, hoarsely. After rearranging his pillows, a relieved Celina offered a spoonful of broth. After several sips, Papi was simply too worn out to eat more. Leaning back against his pillows, he exhaled, heavily, and Celina thought he had fallen asleep until he opened his eyes and motioned for her to join him on the bed. His hand trembled as he stroked unruly curls out of her eyes. He wrapped his arms around her, and Celina leaned into his chest, his sweat-soaked t-shirt pressing against her cheek.

I don't even care. Just stay, Papi, just don't go. I don't care if you're sick, I don't care that we have to take care of you. Please just stay.

"My little Lina. I'm so sorry I never could give you and the others a good life. You deserved better. But you're smart and you're strong, and you're gonna be somebody someday. I absolutely know that. *Por favor* don't ever change; I love my little girl, I'm *so* proud of my little girl." He gasped for breath, coughs shaking his frail body.

"Don't talk, Papi. You're okay. Just rest. Mama would want you to rest."

"No, Lina, you gotta hear me. I need you to listen. I don't have much time. Oh, Baby," he stroked her cheek, tenderly, "from the moment I met you, I should've known you'd do me good someday. You work too hard for a child. Never had much chance just to be a little girl." He inhaled hard, closing his eyes in pain. "Lina, you know I've taught

4

you, and you've taught me but— Giacamo fell back against the pillows, perspiration glistening on his gaunt face. He reached for her hand and gripped it, with surprising strength. "I never taught you how to say goodbye, did I?"

Celina pressed her face into his t-shirt, gulping back sobs as she did. *No. Not goodbye! I don't wanna say goodbye. Not now. Not yet.*

Papi leaned back away from her and gently wiped the tears from her cheeks. "Listen to me, my warrior princess." His eyes glistened with tears. "Please remember the things I've taught you. Remember to always be kind, be proud; proud of who you are, proud of our Montoya name. And remember, don't ever take charity. Remember to help your mama as best you can. And *por favor,* Evangelo and Little Man, they won't remember well. Make-make sure they remember love; make sure they remember how much their papi loved them. Never forget . . . never let them forget what I always tell you all— one can be happy just by loving people . . . and being loved. Always remember that, my princess."

"I promise."

"Now listen," Giacamo gasped hard, "about the children. Chaim will try to take my place. Let him. But help him. Help him look after your mama and the little ones. You're all each other has. Don't fight among yourselves. You're all as strong-willed as they come, except maybe Yacque and Elian. Love each other; protect each other. Don't leave each other behind. Remember we're family."

Unwanted tears again filling her eyes, Celina swiped them away angrily and squeezed her father's hand. "I promise," she whispered, inhaling raggedly. "I promise, Papi." Still holding her father's hand, Celina glanced at the other bed where Little Man, her youngest brother, was napping, blissfully. His faded *Mickey Mouse* t-shirt, too small for him now, was soaked in perspiration and drool. Little Man was not yet three. *Papi's right, he won't remember unless we help him. He must remember love, oh, he must."* She sighed as she switched on the box fan and turned it toward her little brother.

Leaning back against her father, Celina laced her fingers through his and laid her head on his chest, albeit gently, as his breathing became more and more labored. His cheeks and forehead glistened, Giacamo coughed violently, and Celina tried to give him more medication.

"No," he gasped, raising on his elbow, desperate for air, "it-it can't do me any good anymore. J-just lay with me. Let me hug my baby girl. You-you know, I'll always be lonesome for my Lina, even when I'm with God. I'll never forget how you always took such good care of your old papi."

"But I—but you're—

"*Yo sé*. But I was born this way, like Elian. Nothing you could have done would have-have changed that. I mean, God has us all down in his book for something. We mustn't question; we must accept. But don't ever think it's your fault. God wants me with him; he calls my name. No other reason than he calls my name. Just know I'll be watching over you from heaven for-for always. Love doesn't die, Lina, time cannot kill it, nor many miles or even death. Remember that my girl. Remember it always."

For the next hour, Celina lay with her father as he drifted in and out of fitful sleep, punctuated by violent coughing. He was too exhausted to speak, but he held her close and each time he kissed the top of her curly head, she felt his tears wet her hair.

Celina had known for a while that her father didn't have much time left, but he had defied doctor's expectations all his life. Before Javier was born, a doctor told Giacamo that he had maybe two years to live at most. Javier was now ten.

"*Can't he-can't he do that again, Holy Mother?*" Celina remembered fervently praying. "*Papi can get well. Please don't take him from us. Dear God, please don't let my Papi die!*

As her heart prayed, desperately, Celina could no longer stop the steady flow of tears that ran down her cheeks like summer rain. She reached down and again took her father's hand. She held it gently but firmly as if, by holding onto his hand, she could help him hold onto life.

He took a walk with me just two weeks ago. Almost half a mile. He was better then. What happened?

"Lina?"

Celina turned to see her mother standing in the doorway, Elian by her side. Mama smiled, but her smile did not reach her eyes.

"*Malaynkia,* there are quarters in my bag and the Red Rider's outside. *Puzhalsta* take the laundry to the laundromat. Take Little Man with you."

Celina tilted her chin almost defiantly, "I'm not leaving Papi. I don't care what you say."

"Lina—

"I said no!"

"Lina," Papi reached up weakly to touch her hair, "d-don't be disrespectful. Please do as your mother says." When Celina hesitated, he whispered, "I'll be all right. I love you, my Lina. Even from heaven, I'll always love you."

"Alexei," Giacamo gagged hard on phlegm after the door closed behind their daughter, "I-I didn't-didn't want her to see me die. She'll take it the hardest, my love." He paused, exhausted. "You gotta make sure she knows it's not her fault; she took care of me almost as well as you always have, and-and she's just a little girl. *Por favor* make sure she knows it's not her fault."

Alexei's eyes filled with tears as she stroked her husband's flowing dark hair, contrasting starkly with the white pillow. "I promise, my angel. I promise." Taking Giacamo's hand, she pressed it to her breast. "My heart beats for you. *V'segda y navsegda.* Always and forever."

Dark eyes fading to gray, Giacamo clutched his wife's hand with surprising strength as she cradled him close in her arms. His trembling hand reached up to caress her cheek. "E-even now, my-my heart beats for you."

As her husband's eyes closed and his limp body became dead weight in her arms, Alexei wept into his hair. "I love you."

Pulling the Red Rider behind her, Little Man toddled along beside her, three wildflowers in his sticky, chubby fingers. His cheeks and mouth were still dripping from the red popsicle Celina had bought to keep him occupied while she did the family's laundry. She could not help but smile back as the toddler stared up at her with his large, laughing, brown eyes.

He's lucky. He don't know enough to hurt like the rest of us do.

As Celina lugged the laundry basket into the shack, she halted in the doorway. Mama was holding Papi close in her arms, weeping into his flowing hair. "Oh, Giac," she whispered, through tears, "Giac, I love you."

Celina's eyes widened in horror, and she dropped the laundry basket in front of her on the concrete floor.

"Mama?" she barely managed, her breath coming in gasps. "Mama, he's-is he . . . her voice trailed off.

Alexei looked up just then. She wiped her eyes with the back of her hand and reached out to her daughter. "Lina, come here, *malaynkia*. It's okay. He-he's with God now. *Puzhalste*—

Celina could barely breathe. *His skin's almost white! He's*— Pushing Little Man towards their mother, she turned and ran from the *dacha* and down the dusty path into the woods. Pushing away tree branches as angrily as she brushed away now free-flowing tears, Celina ran until she could not run any further. She halted, panting.

Throwing her head back, she screamed at the sky. "I hate you! I hate you, God! I hate you! Why did you do this to me, to us? Why'd you do this to our mama? What's wrong with you?" She reached up around her neck where she wore a Jerusalem cross, representing the Jewish faith of Mama and Papi's, Christian faith. All the Montoya children wore one. Celina yanked it hard, breaking the chain, then threw it as far as she could. She fell on her hands and knees on the bed of soft dried leaves on the forest floor and sobbed into the ground so hard she gagged over and over, vomiting on the ground between her hands.

In the days that followed, nothing felt real. After the Requiem Mass and the burial, Celina busied herself caring for Little Man and Elian. Elian was five. He was Celina's favorite little brother, and she was protective of him. Elian had been born with the same congenital heart condition that had taken their father's life.

He's next. I don't know when, but if it's left up to God, he's next.

The Montoya's had almost no furniture save one queen and one king-sized bed the family shared. Because of this, when family and people from church stopped by with food or other condolences, the children sat quietly on the edge of the beds. Celina sat beside her siblings, squirming. Elian lay next to her, resting his head in her lap. She hated his labored breathing.

God, don't. Please don't.

Celina could not stop squirming, trying not to scratch. Mama had borrowed dresses for her, Yacqueline and Soledad to wear for the funeral Mass. She knew Mama would be embarrassed if she sat, scratching at the itchy red taffeta and stiff lace on the ugly, too-small, Christmassy dress that she could not wait to be rid of. All Celina could remember wearing were denim cut-offs and old t-shirts that her younger brother, Chaim, had outgrown. Despite being the second oldest, Chaim was the biggest and tallest of the children, stocky and a head taller than his petite sister. Celina glanced at Chaim who sat beside her in a borrowed suit that he was about to split the buttons on. She barely suppressed a giggle. He was also squirming.

"Who'd this thing belong to, a midget?" he muttered to Celina.

His sister, despite the current state of her emotions, could not help but snicker.

"Shhh," Yacqueline gently scolded her siblings, "the grown-ups are talking, remember?"

Celina sighed. *I could just rip this thing to pieces right now. Papi wouldn't have made me wear this itchy, ugly thing. I bet he wouldn't have.*

Celina's ears perked up at the words. ". . . we'd be happy to adopt them. I mean, you could still see them occasionally. You know we only live three blocks from here."

The Music of What Happens

"Adopt *who?*" She blurted out.

"Lina, shhh!" Mama turned to her, a finger on her lips.

Ignoring her, Celina stood and came to stand by her mother's side. She glared at Alvarado, one of her father's many half-brothers, and his wife, Marisa. "Adopt *who?*" she demanded, "none of us are going anywhere with you!"

"Lina, *nena, por favor* try to see reason," Tía Marisa turned to her. "You're a big girl. You know how poor you all are. There are just too many of you for your mother to care for. Your tío and I want to adopt Yacqueline and Little Man."

"Like hell you are!"

"Lina, your language!" Mama broke in, sternly. With her hands on her daughter's shoulders, she turned her in the direction of the big bed where the children were all sitting. "Go sit back down."

"But Mama—

"Sit. Now."

Celina said no more, but she sat, shooting daggers, with her eyes, at Tío Alvarado and Tío Marisa until the pair departed.

They can't have my brother and sister. Papi said we're all each other has now. I promised him I'd look after them all. Besides, that would be charity! And who'd be taken away from us next? Mama can shut me up all she wants, but it ain't right!

"Oh, Alexei," Mrs. Bass, the church busybody, cooed as she pressed a small casserole dish into Mama's hand and patted her shoulder. "It was time, wasn't it? Mr. Montoya is finally where he belongs, poor man. Healed and well, walking the crystal streets with our dear Savior. Exactly as it should be. We mustn't grieve; we must thank the Lord that Mr. Montoya is in the very best place he could be, and his sufferings have finally ceased. He-he *did* make his last confession, didn't he? We certainly want to see him in heaven, now, don't we?"

"What the—

Mama shot her a warning glance, and Celina glared hard at Mrs. Bass.

I could just punch her right in those humungous teeth and knock that witchy smile off her nasty mug! Who does she think she is? Of course, Papi's in heaven. He was always a good person. I bet she won't make it to heaven with her witchy ways! Always shooting off her mouth!

When Mama cast a disapproving look in her direction, Celina looked down at the black, patent leather, dress shoes that were a size too big and hard to walk in.

When the last visitor had departed, Mama allowed the children to change into their everyday clothes and took the borrowed items to wash and iron before returning them.

Good riddance to this nasty dress! Celina thought as she handed it back to Mama from behind the curtain.

Yacqueline put her hand on Celina's shoulder, "You okay, Lina?" she asked, softly.

"No, I'm *not* okay!" Celina snapped, immediately regretting her tone. "This isn't what Papi would've wanted at all. Father Domingo droning on and on about death! Saying it's not the end but the beginning. What in the heck does that mean? And these awful, borrowed clothes— Papi never would have made us wear them, he loved us the way we are. And he wouldn't have liked those lying hypocrites like that old bat, Mrs. Bass, that have always looked at us sideways in church, coming by and pretending to be sorry for us. He never liked fake people, and neither do I!"

"Oh, sis, I'm sure they mean well," Yacqueline patted Celina's shoulder, "Papi even said that people make mistakes. Because we're not God. We do wrong things. But if we're smart, we say we're sorry and do better. Maybe these people are trying to do better."

Celina did not answer. It was pointless to argue with Yacqueline who was nothing but gentle, and peaceful and saw only the best in everyone. "Little Tranquility" Papi had always called her. *I know she's only nine but she's like-like a little nun. She's never done a wrong thing in her life—*

Like a clearing fog, Celina started as her mind returned to the present. Fishing her broken watch out of her pocket, her eyes widened, horrified at the time. She had been in the churchyard for nearly an hour! Mama would be home from work by now and worried! She sprang to her feet and bounded from the cemetery, taking a shortcut through the woods to where the Montoya family lived in an abandoned garage that Mama sometimes called a *dacha*. Celina smiled at the sight of her brothers and sisters sitting in a circle in the small, dirt yard next to their home, adding up the money they had earned from their various jobs.

Cross-legged in the dirt, eleven-year-old Javier turned and waved to his sister. Celina hurried to join them. She plopped down in the dust, sitting cross-legged, chin in hand, as she mentally counted the money that lay on the ground in the circle.

"Where you been, Sis?" eight-year-old Giacamo Jr. known as 'Jackie' asked her. "Mama's asked where you are twice. She was about to send Chaim and Javier to find you."

Celina sighed. "Nowhere," she mumbled sullenly. "I wasn't nowhere."

"Did you work today?" five-year-old Evangelo piped up. "Do you got any money today? I got five bucks helping Señor Boggs with weeding his flower beds." He held out both hands filled with quarters.

"Good job, *hermano*. That's really good."

"Well, did you get any money?" nine-year-old Soledad asked.

Celina shrugged, "Naw, got kept after school by that old fool, Mrs. Chavez. Just cuz' I couldn't do all the words on my spelling test. What a total B."

"Aw, that's crap, sis," twelve-year-old Chaim sympathized. "Papi always said you were smart, but that woman acts like you're dumb or something."

"Yeah, I don't wanna talk about it anymore. How much did we bring in today?"

The others looked on while ten-year-old Yacqueline recounted the coins and cash out in the middle of the circle. "Would you look at this haul—we did great today! $56.27! Geez, if only Lina had been able to get over to the store, we'd have had at least $75 with all the tips she gets."

"My winning personality," Celina replied, sarcastically. "But don't worry, I'll be at Tío Aleman's store tomorrow after school, no excuses. And Javier, I heard about a big office party over by Johnson's place last night. There's gotta be tons of—"

"Booze bottles!" Javier exclaimed, "Perfect! I'll head out there before school. That should bring in *mucho dinero.*"

"What's this about booze bottles?"

The children started and turned to see Mama standing there, hands on her hips. "Well? Speak up."

"Just a big drinking party they had at the Johnson Building over on Creekside. Javier's gonna' collect the bottles tomorrow."

"Oh. Glad that's all you meant. Was wondering if my children might be getting too big for their britches." Alexei's stern expression changed to a laugh as she reached down to take Elian, age six, by the hand. "Time for your meds, Sunbeam. I made supper this evening, so let's all eat, and get the evening work done before bed."

Four-year-old Little Man riding on her back, Celina followed her siblings into the house. A large, wooden, wire reel served as a table. A small hotplate and microwave cooked their food, and a large wooden box under the bigger of the two beds served as a dresser for their clothes. A small cupboard, usually quite bare, stored their food. On either side of the biggest bed where Chaim, Yacqueline, Soledad, and Jackie slept was an army cot. Because they struggled with bedwetting, Celina and Javier each slept alone on those cots. The youngest Montoya children, Elian, Evangelo, and Little Man, slept with their mother on the smaller of the two, big beds. A curtain for dressing privacy separated the two beds. The family hauled water for washing and cleaning as the residence had no indoor plumbing. As the children sat on the floor and the edge of Mama's bed, Mama dished up bowls of watery bean soup. Celina sighed to herself as she finished her bowl and then filled her stomach with cold water from the cooler.

I'm glad I lifted those cigarettes from Aleman's office.

The Music of What Happens

While Yacqueline heated water to do the washing up and Soledad put sheets, fresh from the wash, onto the beds, Celina discreetly motioned for Chaim and Javier to follow her outside and behind the shanty. While she scrubbed and rinsed their honey buckets, she lit a cigarette from her pocket and took a long drag before passing it to Javier and then Chaim. Not long thereafter, their sisters and Jackie joined them, and Celina lit one more.

"What's with the cancer sticks?"

The children started and looked up, fearfully.

"Tío!" Jackie exclaimed, hiding the cigarette behind his back as he put it out in the sand.

Marcos Gonzalez, Giacamo Montoya's best friend, and "Tío" to the children, smiled as he squatted in the sand in front of them. "So?" he held out his hand and Celina reluctantly handed him the pack of Marlboros.

Marcos stared at the pack in his hand then, to the surprise of the children, he pulled one out and lit it with a silver lighter.

The one with the Chinese letters, Celina remembered as he handed the pack back to her.

"Listen, I just brought some groceries; I hope your mama will take them this time."

"No sir, she won't,' Soledad interjected, stoutly, "Montoya's don't take charity. You know that. Our papi made that a strict rule."

At the nods of the other children, Marcos sighed, deeply, as he stood and finished his cigarette. "Just don't let Eli, Evangelo, and Little Man have any."

Celina giggled. "W-what do you think I am, stupid?"

Marcos Gonzalez, a brilliant lawyer, and partner at the firm of Dugan and Gonzalez in downtown Santa Fe had been best friends with Giacamo Montoya since childhood. When the boys were Celina's age, Marcos' family and Giacamo's single mother and six half-brothers had immigrated to the United States from Mexico. Marcos Gonzalez was considered one of Santa Fe's, most eligible bachelors. Thirty-five, he stood six feet tall with a slender build, thick, wavy, black hair and wide mocha eyes behind thick, wire-rimmed glasses.

Marcos had been married previously. His wife, concert pianist, Elessa de la Vega succumbed, unexpectedly to cancer. Their newly adopted baby daughter, Katherine, whom Marcos had lovingly nicknamed "Kitty-Cat" died of SIDS just days following her mother's death. Marcos had been devastated and, although it had been fifteen years since that tragedy, he had never fully recovered. Only when he was with the Montoya children did Marcos' old love of life seem to reappear. He loved his best friend's children as if they were his own, and they, in turn, thought of him as a second father.

"Children? Children!"

"That's Mama! Come on, Tío."

Before they rounded the shack, Marcos touched Celina's shoulder. The children halted and quickly partook of the Altoid tin he offered them.

"Come, children," Mama motioned them into the house. "Hello, Marc." With obvious reluctance, Alexei handed him the two, paper bags filled with groceries. "I'm sorry, friend. We can't."

Marcos sighed and looked at the ground for a moment. "Not offering charity. I need my house cleaned tomorrow and cleaned well. Was hoping Yacque and Sol might be up for that?"

Alexei smiled and nodded. "Yacque and Sol are needed at the house after school, but Lina and Chaim will be there at three-thirty. Thank you so much."

As Marcos drove away, Mama wrapped an arm around Celina's shoulder as she stared after the clouds of dust following his truck. "Always such a good friend. Now you two," she leveled Celina and Chaim with a stern look as she led the children inside to prepare for bed, "make sure you earn those groceries. I won't have anyone saying our family took something for free."

As the children climbed into bed, Mama sat down in the old rocker between the two beds and listened to their prayers. Though the Montoya children had been baptized Catholic, the children studied and recited prayers not just from the Catholic church but from Jewish prayer books, as well, as their parents had agreed that they would also honor their Jewish heritage. When they were finished with prayers, Mama read to them from the *Tanakh*, a Jewish book of prayers and conduct. Because her grasp of Hebrew was passable at best, Alexei haltingly read the passage in Hebrew and then re-read it in Russian.

Laying on her stomach on her cot, Celina pretended to listen to the nightly devotion, however, her thoughts were much too distracted. She glanced to her left at the two, brown paper grocery bags on the counter.

I wonder if he brought blueberry pop tarts. I'm so hungry.

As though Mama had read her mind, she closed the devotional and reached over for the first grocery bag. The children watched, hopeful. As Alexei dug through it, she smiled. "Rice, beans, cream of wheat and milk for the ice chest. And look at this," she pulled out a package of pop tarts.

Soledad squealed, "Apple cinnamon, my favorite!"

As she lay, nibbling her pop tart and sipping her Capri Sun, Celina stared contentedly at the ceiling as Mama began to softly sing *Cossack Lullaby*, the same song she had sung to her children since they were babies. Celina closed her eyes on the haunting sound of Mama's gorgeous contralto. By the time the song ended, she was nearly asleep. Mama paused and then sang *Rozhinkes Mit Mandlen*, an old Jewish lullaby she had also sung since her children were small.

Despite the sleep that was close to claiming her, Celina glanced to the left and briefly studied her mother's silhouette, framed against the crack of light coming from the left-hand corner of the ceiling.

Though her family was from Israel, Mama had been born in what was now St. Petersburg, Russia. Although she grew up speaking the language of her adopted country, Alexei Zagoradniy Montoya and her older brother, Menachem had been raised strictly in the Orthodox Jewish faith. At the age of sixteen, Alexei moved to the United States with an aunt. A striking, Middle Eastern beauty, just five feet tall and slightly built, Alexei had an olive complexion, a mass of unruly curls like Celina's and, large, expressive, dark eyes. Though her English and Spanish were proficient enough, in her native Russian which she used exclusively when speaking to her children, she spoke with poetic beauty. Before the second lullaby ended, Celina had drifted into a deep sleep.

Late that night, she woke up, groggy. Shivering, she reached down onto the floor where her blanket had fallen. Celina sighed and looked at the ceiling when she realized her pink, cotton shorts were urine soaked.

Then she heard it. Mama's voice from the bed on the other side of the curtain. As she listened, Celina's eyes filled with tears when she heard her mother's heartbreaking plea for her brother, Elian's, healing.

"Dear God, please touch his heart. Touch it with the oils of your healing. You took Giac from me, and I accepted this without question. But oh, please don't take my darling Sunbeam too. He's getting sicker, God, having more spells, and I don't know what else to do. I can't lose my boy, or any of my children again. It nearly tore my heart out last time. If it weren't for Giac, I'm not sure I would have been able to go on. *Puzhalste* dear God, punish me as I deserve for my sins but not in this way, I beg of you. Oh, not in this way—

With that, Mama's lightly muffled sobs tore at her throat, clearly inconsolable. Celina swiped at her tears. *I wish I could never cry again, I'm sick of crying. I'm sick of being so sad. Do we like have to be sad forever? 'Cuz it really seems like it sometimes.*

Pushing back her blanket, Celina tiptoed from behind the curtain and went to her mother. Standing beside the bed she touched her mother's shoulder. Alexei turned towards her daughter, tears still rolling unchecked down her cheeks. She gently caressed her cheek.

"My Linochka, did I wake you?"

Celina's cheeks flushed pink. "Naw, this did." She looked down at her shorts.

Mama patted her head reassuringly. "It's okay, *malaynkia*. Get cleaned up and put on your other shorts then come lay with me."

The Music of What Happens

When Celina returned, Mama welcomed her into bed, and she rested her head on her mother's chest. Mama's fingers played with her hair for a long time.

She finally whispered, "I'm sorry you had to hear that."

"I'm not. I-I'm scared, Mama." She glanced over her mother's shoulder at Elian, sound asleep behind her, pressed close against Little Man. "I'm scared for Eli. What if—what if the State tries to take him again? Or any of us? Mayor Ainsworth hated Papi. And he hates Tío Marcos. I know that mess last year was all his fault!"

Mama shushed her gently, motioning to the three smallest boys sleeping peacefully beside her. "We don't know that for sure, *malaynkia*. We mustn't gossip and say such things without proof."

Celina sighed and closed her eyes, sleepy again. She knew arguing was useless. *Mama's too much like Yacque. Too kind for her own good. I know Mayor Ainsworth's the one who got us all taken away last year. No one else around town is that much of a rat-faced racist!*

Mama continued to gently stroke her hair as she relaxed again in her arms. Celina closed her eyes again, her mind journeying back to the year before, not long before Papi died. Social workers had shown up at the Montoya shack with a judge's order to take the children into state custody.

It was so awful. Chaim and me fought them, but the cops said Mama and Papi were bad parents because I couldn't narc on Rat-Face Jr. and then them saying me and Javier are too mouthy. She snuggled closer to her mother as she remembered those terrible weeks. . . . *and then calling me and Chaim disturbed when we fought back. That juvy place was terrible and I was so worried about Papi and the little kids, thought I'd go crazy. At least I know how to fight.*

Tears filled her eyes just then when she remembered the visits through the glass at the juvy facility where she and Chaim had been placed. She remembered her shame at Papi's tears. *He was so sick, but he insisted on coming even though he was in a wheelchair. I wish I could have told on Cal Ainsworth. But none of those government people like would've backed me up. And then I'd have gotten myself beat up all over again. Cal was just too big and awful to fight.*

Too tired to think, Celina snuggled down and drifted off to sleep, thinking about school.

Piercing, blue eyes penetrated her soul as he shoved her hard to the ground. His terrible weight pressed her down into the hard dirt. Celina tried to twist out from under him, but he was much too heavy for the petite twelve-year-old. His fist made painful contact with her head as he whispered dire threats in her ear. Searing pain then tore through her body as though she were being ripped in half, Celina screamed in agony.

"Lina? Lina! Baby wake up! Lina wake up, it's a bad dream; wake up, Baby."

At the cool feeling of a hand on her cheek, Celina sat bolt upright, swinging and screaming. Her entire body trembled, sweat dripping down her temples. Mama's arms wrapped around her, pressing her close. "Mama's got you, Baby. Mama's got you." Clutching the front of her mother's nightdress, Celina's breath came in great gasps as she sobbed into her breast. For what felt like forever, sobs tore at her throat as she clung to her mother, her body still trembling from the inside out.

"Mama?" a soft voice called out from the other side of the curtain.

"M-Mama, is Lina okay?"

"It's okay, Yacque. You and Chaim go back to sleep now. I've got your sister," she barely heard Mama call out, softly. With Mama holding her close, Celina's muscles finally went limp, and still clinging to her mother, her trembling finally slowed, and almost before she knew what was happening, she drifted off.

"Hey, Lina. Lina?"

Celina slowly opened her eyes to Mama shaking her gently awake. "You okay? You had quite the nightmare last night. Can you help me get breakfast ready?"

Celina pushed back the warm cocoon of blankets and gently shook Evangelo's arm. "Time for breakfast," she whispered. "Don't wake Eli and Little Man."

Due to his poor health, Elian did not go to school, and Little Man attended a Spanish preschool in the same building where Mama cleaned offices.

Sitting around on the floor, the children ate their bowls of boiled rice with milk and sugar that Mama had cooked and drank their tea.

"Maybe one day it'll be Coke," Chaim declared, "Coke, Coke, and more Coke. Once I'm grown and I get rich, I'll buy us a big house with everyone's favorite sodas and even a basketball hoop and a computer like Tío's."

"Yeah," Evangelo chimed in, "Except in my house, there'll be chocolate pinwheels and marshmallows and chicken nuggets everywhere!" He grinned as he shoveled in another spoonful of rice and milk.

Mama smiled at her children's wishful conversation as she opened the morning mail. "Oh, bills, bills, bills," she mumbled, pressing her fingers to her forehead. "All Eli's medical stuff, the funeral home payment, and we still need— her voice trailed off as she sighed, deeply.

"Don't you worry none, Mama," Javier declared, "once I grow up and get rich, I'll have enough ice cream for everyone and get a PlayStation, and you'll get to live in your very own room in my house, and I'll pay all the bills and get you nice things and then tell Mayor Ainsworth and that bunch to kiss my—

"Javier Montoya!" Alexei exclaimed. "What is it with you children and your language?" Her voice softened, "That's very kind of you, son. I love you too."

While Chaim and Yacqueline packed homework in the denim bookbags Mama had sewn each of her children, Celina washed the dishes outside and put them away.

I hate my dreams. Dreaming about what Cal did. The stuff they still don't know 'cuz I just couldn't tell. It hurts my chest every time I see him.

As she stepped back inside, she furrowed her brow at the look on Mama's face as she read the letter in her hand.

"Oh, how could he?" she whispered in Russian, "how dare he!" She turned, startled, "Uhm, children, time for school."

"But Mama, how dare who what?"

"Lina, school!" Alexei replied firmly. "Oh, wait," she turned back to the table and handed her an envelope. "After you and Chaim get done at your tío's, please go to the department store, and get me the things on this list. If there's enough left, bring home quarters for laundry. Oh, and Lina, you're not working the parking lot today. It'll be too late by the time you're done with the cleaning job."

As the children started down the road to school, Celina counted the cash in the envelope and then perused her mother's list. She handed it to Chaim. "Please read that out loud for me."

Celina chewed her lip as she listened to the items on the list. She hated being in seventh grade and was barely able to read simple words. *I don't know why I'm so dumb. But Chaim's smart. I'm lucky to have him.*

"*Gracias,*" she mumbled when Chaim handed the list back. "Yacque, there's no way we'll be able to get everything on Mama's list. There's not enough money here."

Yacqueline furrowed her brow at the list of items then shook her head. "Well, we can do without the— She halted. "No, it's all stuff we need. Mama's not thinking straight this morning, is she?"

"She needs food," Celina lifted Little Man, piggy-back. "She doesn't want to eat our food. Wait a sec," she turned to Chaim, "if you and I do a really good job at Tío's and even do his lawn and weed his flower beds, maybe we can get some cash too?"

"Don't push your luck, Sis. Tío would totally give it to us, and Mama would be pissed when she found out."

"Hey, that's a lot of extra work; we're not asking for a hand-out. I know he'd agree, and what Mama doesn't know won't hurt her."

Chaim hesitated then grinned. "That's a fact. Come on, guys."

After dropping Little Man off at preschool and the others at Santa Fe Elementary, Celina, Chaim and Javier headed down the road to Santa Fe Middle School. Celina's heart thudded when she saw who stood in front of the building stairs. She sucked in air hard and pressed her feet into the ground, forcing herself not to turn and run the other way. Tears swelled in her eyes, but she blinked them back hard. Her heart was racing, but she would never let him see her fear.

CHAPTER 2

Warrior Princess

"Well, well, if it ain't the raggedy little wetback I taught a lesson to last year," Calvert Ainsworth, the mayor's son, leaned menacingly against the metal railing leading up to the school building, "Hey, Lina, long time no see."

"Yeah, you keep away from us, you—

Celina pinched Javier's arm, and his words trailed off. She turned his shoulder in the direction of the stairs and together they and Chaim hurried inside Santa Fe Middle School. Calvert's laughter followed them.

"You watch yourself, Lina! Watch yer'self real good."

Celina kept her arm tightly around Javier's shoulder until the double doors shut behind them. Her heart raced, wildly. Calvert Ainsworth was the reason she and Chaim had spent eleven weeks in a juvenile facility, and their younger siblings had been placed in foster homes. Staci Ainsworth, Calvert's sister, was just Celina's age and nearly worse than her brother. Celina's sixth-grade teacher had made a report to Social Services after Calvert had beaten her black and blue for refusing Staci's demand that Celina steal essay questions for her and the three girls she referred to as "the Three Stooges." When Staci complained to Calvert, he had followed her into the woods after school. Celina shuddered. She remembered the horrible attack as though it were yesterday.

I wish I could have told. I wish I could have told them how bad he really did me. Then Mama wouldn't have been blamed like that. But I just couldn't. He'll do me even way worse if I ever tell.

The Music of What Happens

Celina shook her head to herself as she stopped in front of her locker. Even a year later, she still felt fully responsible for what Mama and Papi went through when the children were taken. As she unloaded her book bag and small brown lunch sack into the locker and pulled out her notebook and math book, she overheard several girls discussing "Ariane's party."

"It's gonna be way cool, you know. Her parents have more money than P-Diddy and she's got a swimming pool and her own horse!"

Celina froze when she recognized the speaker as Staci Ainsworth, queen bee of Santa Fe Middle School's mini kingdom, this "kingdom" being the worst clique of rich, nasty, bottle-blond jerk-ettes in the whole history of Santa Fe Middle. They were known imperiously as *First Class.* In Celina's opinion, they were just "The Three Stooges," white trash with too much money.

Ever since last year's incident, Celina had stayed as far away from Staci as possible. *Makes a knot in my stomach just looking at her face! One day, I'll get my chance and she'll be like walking different when I'm done with her!*

Her thoughts were interrupted by Staci's imperious voice, louder this time. "Well, I lied, it'll only be way cool if Ariane doesn't have to invite that half-breed, little punk my brother kicked the crap out of last year."

The girls laughed, and Celina turned, staring Staci down. "Seriously Staci? Half-breed? The 1850s text, and they want their ignorance back." She stepped around the girls, but Staci grabbed her arm, causing her books to tumble to the floor. Celina twisted hard and pulled away, but her heart was in her throat. It took little to "offend" one of the mayor's children. Nothing good ever came of it.

"Get back here! I never said you could leave!" Staci demanded.

"Or what?"

Staci whipped out her pink, sequin cell phone and waved it in Celina's face. "One teeny tiny text is all it takes. Got it?" She now stood so close Celina could smell the Cocoa Butter lotion she wore. Staci wrinkled her upturned nose. No matter whether she was actually wrinkling her nose, Staci's face always looked like she had just smelled a fart. "You still peeing the bed? Geez! Last I did that, I was two. Get outta this hall! If I wanted to smell piss, I'd hang out in the bathroom!"

Celina knew better, she had always known better. She had the wounds and nightmares to prove she should know better. "I'll leave when I'm ready."

"What did you just say to me?" Staci's voice and eyes were filled with pure hatred.

"I *said* I'll leave when I'm ready."

"Wow," Staci's number one stooge, Jaclyn, put in, narrowing her piercing blue eyes at Celina. "Looks like someone needs another beat down."

Staci sighed, still glaring at Celina. "Yeah, well, I just got a French nail job yesterday so . . ." Before anyone knew what was happening, she turned and slapped Celina hard across the face!

Dumbstruck, Celina's hand instinctively flew to her stinging cheek, and she blinked. As much as it hurt, she would never allow Staci Ainsworth the satisfaction of seeing her shed a tear. Anger flared inside her, and she almost punched Staci. Instead, she clenched her fists at her side. Papi had said she must never strike another person. Besides, she knew well that her mouth had gotten her in enough trouble already.

At that moment, the bell rang, and the girls hurried off. Head high, Celina sauntered carelessly into class. When she passed their desks, Staci, Jade, Marcail, and Ani snickered. Despite being thirteen years old and, in Mama's words, "almost a lady," Celina turned and made a face at the four. With false confidence, she smirked across the room at her best friend, Elizaveta, who shot her a fearful glance in return. At that moment, she caught sight of her teacher, Ms. Theron eyeing her. Immediately, she dropped into her seat and stared hard at her math book.

"Celina, please come here." From the tone of Ms. Theron's voice, she knew she was not in trouble. When she reached the front desk, Ms. Theron bent down so she could look straight into her eyes. "*What* happened to your face?" she asked, concerned.

Self-conscious, Celina's hand flew to her cheek. Her mouth went dry, and she raggedly sucked in air. All she could think of was last year when her sixth grade ESL teacher had called Child Protective Services because Celina would not explain the dark bruises, black eye, and busted lip.

I begged her not to. I told her over and over it wasn't Mama's fault, but she wouldn't listen to me, and if I tell on Staci today, I know exactly what'll happen next. I can't! I can't!

Celina was hyperventilating. She stared down at the hole in her worn, canvas shoe, exposing her big toe. She knew well that had it not been for Marcos, their time in state custody could have been much longer. *And it was all my fault. I can't let Mama go through that again. And I'm sure as shootin' not going back to the juvy place!*

Ms. Theron tried again, "Lina, I'm waiting." Her tone was firm but gentle. Celina looked her teacher in the eye but still did not speak, her breath coming in huge gasps. Ms. Theron bent low and whispered in her ear. "Here, let's take a few deep breaths. It's all right, you can trust me."

Inwardly, Celina sighed in relief. Now that she knew Mama wouldn't get in trouble again, she would keep her mouth shut and think about saving her own butt. Calvert was more terrible than probably anyone in town knew.

Except me.

Ms. Theron sighed and scanned the sea of students staring back at her. She was just in time to see Staci discreetly wave her cell phone at her friends, simultaneously dropping a sly wink. Turning back to a silent Celina, Ms. Theron nodded. "I see."

She turned again to the rest of the class. "Miss Staci Ainsworth, come here immediately and bring your phone."

Staci, in pleather mini-skirt and *Juicy Couture* hoodie, flipped her golden, color-treated waves over her shoulder and came forward, practically gloating. Celina looked at the floor. Her heart was beating a mile a minute, and tears filled her eyes as her hands trembled behind her back. Staci's father, the mayor of Santa Fe, was very wealthy, not to mention an unapologetic bigot who despised anyone who was not white. His children seemed to run the town almost as much as he did. Celina knew exactly what was coming next even if Ms. Theron did not.

When Staci reached the desk, Ms. Theron took her phone and showed her the reddened handprint mark on Celina's cheek. "Young lady, you are in *big* trouble. Explain yourself!"

"It's not *my* fault! She tried to-to-she shoved me! I was just defending myself."

"Wait a second, that's not how it happened at all!"

Celina whirled around at the familiar voice across the room. She had no idea her best friend had witnessed the incident but obviously, she had.

"Like Lina kept trying to leave. Staci wouldn't let her. I wasn't close enough to hear why Staci clocked her, but Lina never touched her, I swear. Staci was cutting up for those Three Stooges of hers!"

"Ok, Elizaveta, you can sit down now. Staci— she turned back.

Staci glared hard at her. "You're crazy, Jennifer. My dad says you're just a bleeding heart who wants the wetbacks to have special treatment! You give an inch; they'll take a mile! My dad says—

"Staci Ainsworth! I'd better never hear the word *wetback* coming out of your mouth. Now your father, by law, may say what he likes, however, such ugly lies are not to be repeated in this classroom. You'll apologize to Lina and then take this note to the office. By the way, it's Ms. Theron to you, not Jennifer."

She bent over her desk, scribbling on a piece of notebook paper. "I'm waiting."

How Celina wished she could gloat and relish this moment. For the first time in school history, the seventh grade's worst bully was being brought low. This was almost too good to be true. But Celina could not laugh; she was nearly choking. Ms. Theron was new to Santa Fe, still too naïve to be afraid of the wealthy, powerful Ainsworths who seemed to hold poor people in the palms of their hands. Celina knew better. After last year, she had tread most carefully around Staci. Why she had challenged the mayor's daughter in the hall just now, Celina had no idea.

I know what Cal can do; I know what her dad can do! Me and my temper!

"Sorry," Staci muttered, without eye contact, voice hoarse with rage. Easily regaining her composure, she looked up at Ms. Theron with an expression of triumph. Her voice soft and icy, she said, "My dad'll have your job for this!" Without another word, she stalked out of the classroom, nose in the air.

Celina's knees trembled as she walked back to her desk. Staci was not fooling around. Although Ms. Theron had no way of knowing this, Celina knew there was no way she would be teaching in Santa Fe for the next school year after this "offense." Mayor Ainsworth would see to that. She felt terrible, she liked Ms. Theron and hated to think of her losing her job the first year. No one knew the extent of the mayor's power, connections, and cruel ways, like his targets did; those people who lived in poverty, particularly those with little education or limited English who were often unaware of their rights and more easily intimidated.

During the noon hour, Celina and Elizaveta, like many of their classmates, ate their lunch outside, as was allowed when the weather was nice. The two girls sat under their usual shade tree at the south corner of the playground.

Elizaveta, whose mother worked as a high school math teacher and whose father owned the largest furniture factory in the city, always had a delicious lunch to eat. Because she had never known life any different, Celina hardly knew enough to be ashamed of her faded, ill-fitting, cutoff hand-me-downs and shanty home. But food. She felt like crying. Her stomach growled, mercilessly, and she knew exactly what would be in her brown lunch sack: a peanut butter sandwich and a mason jar of water as usual. She glanced at Elizaveta's lunch. The other girl had a turkey sandwich with cheese, cherry cola, an apple, and a homemade chocolate cupcake smothered in vanilla icing and topped with colored sprinkles. What a lunch! Celina didn't even own a classy lunch box like most of the other kids she knew.

She pulled her peanut butter sandwich out of her brown paper sack. "Gag me," she muttered as she wolfed down the dry, sticky sandwich, swallowing lukewarm water with each bite. She finished hurriedly when she saw Chaim and Javier watching her from the other end of the schoolyard near the chestnut trees. Having no desire to watch her friend devour that beautiful lunch, she excused herself and hurried to her brothers.

"What's up?"

Chaim grinned as Javier beckoned their sister closer. "You know, old Man Murphy who owns the bakery across the street?"

"Yeah?"

"Well, I saw him toss out a box of doughnuts just a few minutes ago. We should go fish it out. How bad can they be if they're in a box?"

Celina hesitated. "Mama doesn't like it when we eat outta dumpsters."

"Hey, I'm still way hungry, and you always say what Mama don't know won't hurt her." Javier broke in. "Now what's it gonna be?"

"Ok."

"I'm in."

The three drew straws of brown grass to see who would cross the street and get the doughnuts. Chaim drew the shortest straw, and his siblings watched from behind trees as he crossed the quiet cross-street in front of Santa Fe Middle and sneaked into the parking lot of Murphy's Bakery. Pulling over a milk crate, he climbed up so he could see into the dumpster. In just moments, Chaim was back in the schoolyard.

"I don't think anyone saw me but look at this. A whole box of perfect doughnuts with chocolate frosting! There's like 12 of them."

"That's why it says a dozen, genius." Javier rolled his eyes as he flipped open the lid and shoved a whole doughnut into his mouth in one bite before grabbing another.

"Don't be a pig!" Chaim scolded in a whisper-yell as he also grabbed two. Celina munched hers, thoughtfully, enjoying tiny bites.

"Hey now, what about the others?" She put back her second one. "There's just enough to share with the little kids if you two stop now."

Both boys agreed and as the bell rang, the box was hidden under the school stairs and covered with grass.

Celina deliberately took the long way to history class. Though she knew it would make her late, it was better than running into the "*Prada Princess*" and her ladies-in-waiting.

"Stooges," Celina muttered, "can't even think for themselves."

Unlike Ms. Theron who was young and fun, Mrs. Chandler, the seventh-grade history was a fat, old, slave driver. What Celina hated the most about her was that she seemed to go out of her way to make her read aloud as often as possible.

She knows I can't read good, and that the others all laugh at me. What a tool!

In Celina's opinion (and if truth be told, that of her other pupils, as well), she should have retired forty years ago. Ignoring the gawking of her classmates, Celina tiptoed to her desk. Mrs. Chandler was concentrating on reading silently over the assignment while her students waited quietly. Celina tiptoed to her desk, hoping her teacher would not notice.

"Well, if it isn't our smelliest spic, late for class!" Staci whispered loudly. Celina almost halted. A good socking in the mouth would knock "Her Highness" down a peg or two. Wisely, she kept on walking. She was already in enough trouble without making it ten times worse.

Mrs. Chandler did not seem to have noticed her tardiness, but Staci made sure that she did. She raised her hand. "Carol?"

"Yes, Miss Ainsworth," she responded through clenched teeth. She didn't like Staci very much. The real thorn in Mrs. Chandler's side was the fact that the teachers at Santa Fe Middle had been "requested" to call Staci *Miss*. Staci, when she thought of it, called her teachers by their first names.

Gloating across the room at Celina, Staci spoke, her voice several octaves higher than normal and containing a syrupy-sweet tone that made Celina's skin crawl.

"My dear Carol," she began aggravatingly, "Celina Zagoradniy just came in late."

"*Comer mierda*, Staci! The name's Montoya!" Celina shouted before she could stop herself.

"Now that's enough out of both of you!" Mrs. Chandler scolded, slapping her desk with her hand. "There is no reason for this disruptive argument. Yes, Miss Ainsworth, Lina was tardy, however, it profits you nothing to gloat about it. I was well aware of the situation. Lina, you are to see me before you leave today. We do not use vulgarity in *any* language when speaking to our classmates, and for the millionth time, your *legal* last name is Zagoradniy! Now everyone pay attention: 1977-1981, the Carter Administration is especially remembered for . . ."

At three o'clock, after resource-room English, Celina walked back to Mrs. Chandler's classroom. The no-nonsense history teacher eyed her sharply, "Lina, I know you must work to help your family, so I shall not keep you, however, I expect a ten-sentence report for the school bulletin board on rudeness towards our classmates and the example you feel you should set. Turn it in in two weeks. You may go."

"*Comer mierda!*" Celina muttered under her breath as she stalked from the classroom and into the empty science lab where Elizaveta was waiting for her.

"Mrs. Chandler on your case again?"

Celina rolled her eyes. "Honestly, Lissy, the way she runs that classroom, you'd think she'd been the brigadier general in Vietnam instead of her husband. Let's get out of here. I can't be late for work. The rush'll be getting started soon. See you tomorrow."

"Wait, Lina, I'll go with you."

"No, I can— Celina halted, mid-sentence. Calvert might be waiting for her. "Sure Lissy, but you gotta be fast. I can't miss the rush."

As they hurried down Main Street, pudgy Elizaveta asked breathlessly, "So what in the heck happened with the *First-Class* witches this morning?"

Celina slowed to a fast walk to keep pace with her friend. "Well, before math, Staci and the Three Stooges were giving me crap again. You know Staci, always shootin' off her big, fat mouth, calling me a wetback and a half-breed. Then she clocked me in the face when I wouldn't play her stupid games. I swear, Lissy, I've had it up to here with her. I just gave it to her right back! Boy, she hated that!"

Elizaveta's mouth dropped open at this revelation. "No way!!*Ay mierda!* You backtalked *Staci*! After last year? Cal's gonna' beat your lights out, and then—well—you know what'll happen then. Lina, don't say you're as calm as you look or I'll say you're *mucho loca*! Are you literally *asking* to go back to that juvy place? No one stands up to the Ainsworths! No one!"

"Well, it's about time someone did! They've been pushing people around for as long as I can remember! Heck, Lissy, it's the twenty-first century now. We're just as good as any white kid; sure and my family sure don't steal anyone's money like she's always saying. We'd *never* take their charity! Kid you not, I'd rather starve to death than touch Mayor Ainsworth or any of that bunch's, filthy, greasy money." At her friend's worried expression, Celina smirked, carelessly, "Staci don't scare me none. She's nothing but white trash in a bad *Ferretti* knockoff! Oh," Celina put her hand to her mouth in mock horror, "my bad. "Her Highness," she made mocking quotation marks with her fingers, "wouldn't be caught dead in a knockoff! Guaranteed social suicide, you know."

Elizaveta laughed, albeit nervously. "My best friend's high," she muttered, more to herself than Celina. "Oh, Lina," she said, louder this time, "when will you ever learn?"

"Never, I guess. Oh, I know how much trouble I'm in, but I just couldn't help it—Oh, here we are. *Adios*, Lissy."

Each day after school and on Saturday, Celina worked in the parking lot of Barrios and Son Supermarket, the twenty-four-hour grocery store owned by Aleman Barrios, one of her father's many half-brothers. When Celina was ten, her uncle had reluctantly agreed to allow her to help customers with their groceries so long as she stayed out of the building. He had also agreed to pay her a small sum for keeping his parking lot clean and neat. Celina worked until dusk, carrying grocery bags for tips, picking up trash, and sweeping the expansive lot. She was not the only one who worked. Chaim did yard work for wealthy families in downtown Santa Fe, and Jackie and Evangelo worked with him. After preschool, Little Man stayed with Mrs. Esteban, a widowed neighbor. She had agreed to care for him during school hours in exchange for yard work and ironing. After school, Yacqueline and Soledad looked after Little Man at home, kept hous,e and did Mrs. Esteban's ironing. Mama cleaned houses and offices and, because she trusted no one else to look after the sickly Elian, she kept him with her. Javier, like Celina, worked the parking lots too, collecting newspaper, cardboa,rd and other materials to recycle. While cleaning up parking lot trash, Celina was careful to set aside all recyclables for Javier. The two loved to joke that they were getting rich while saving the environment.

Running into the supermarket, Celina grabbed the push broom and left her shoes in the employee breakroom. They were only two years old and already wearing out because, of course, Chaim had worn them first. It would not do to wear them through when Javier must have them next.

She poked her head into her uncle's office. The short, balding man with a beer belly and Napoleon complex, sat slouched in a swivel chair, smoking a Havana. Swarthy, with no resemblance to Giacamo Montoya, he wore a too-tight, blue t-shirt, bearing the name of the store. Beads of perspiration dotted his forehead.

"¡*Hola, Tío* Aleman,*"* Celina greeted him cheerfully. As usual, her uncle glared at her as he wrote down the time of her arrival. His glare only deepened when Javier appeared beside her.

"Hey, *Tío,"* Javier waved, retrieving his Hefty bags from a locker. Celina rolled her eyes as they headed outside. What did her stingy uncle have to glare about anyway? He paid her only one dollar per hour to keep his parking lot in apple-pie order though Celina figured with as much dirt, trash and carts she was continually hauling away that she was worth quite a bit more. It had been quite an ordeal three years ago for Mama to persuade him to allow her to work his parking lot though it cost him so little. It had been almost as much of an ordeal two years earlier to convince him to let Javier collect parking lot recyclables though it did not cost him a penny.

"So, what are you doing here today?" Javier inquired, "I thought you and Chaim were gonna clean *Tío* Marc's house to pay for those groceries."

"Chaim took Jackie and Evangelo instead."

"Oh. Gee, I'm hungry," Javier rubbed his stomach, his face pained. "I wish me and you could just finish off those doughnuts, but I know it's not right. Hey," he pointed across the parking lot, "wanna' see if anyone's thrown out any of the good stuff over at McDonald's?"

Celina rolled her eyes, "Not really. Besides Mama doesn't want us eating out of the dumpsters. Look what I lifted yesterday." She drew 2 cigarettes from the pocket of her denim cutoffs.

"Oh, *si, gracias,*" Javier always carried a matchbook. He lit both cigarettes and the children sat down on the sidewalk for a quick break. Javier swiped away the sweat beads on his forehead and took a long drag of his cigarette. "Look," he slipped off his sandal and pulled out some quarters. "I got this yesterday from the Marlboro Place. Just sitting there on the ground in the parking lot. Want a soda bottle?"

Celina's eyes widened as she counted the coins in her brother's hand. "Four dollars." She almost nodded. Her mouth watered at the thought of an ice-cold Pepsi. She had only had soda pop a few times before, but she had never forgotten how delicious it was. She slowly shook her head.

"I wish. But there's so much we need. The rent's due tomorrow and the copay on one of Eli's meds went up again. Also, Mama said my cot needs a new sheet. I think we need all the money."

Javier bit his lip and glanced away. He then turned and grinned mischievously at his sister, "Well, if you'd only quit pissing in bed so much, maybe your cot wouldn't need a new sheet."

Celina gasped and punched his arm. "You're no one to talk. Let's get back to work. Smoke break's over."

"Well, I'm done here. Think I'll check out back the Baptist church across the way. Kids are always littering during their youth group parties. Dumb bunnies." He slung the black trash bag over his thin shoulder, staggering slightly under the weight, as he set it into his shopping cart and started out of the parking lot and down the street.

When she had started working at Aleman's, Mama had made her promise that she would always be home by nine. However, tonight there was a rush with so many customers to help. It was after eleven by the time Celina started home. Exhausted, she was glad she had made nine dollars in wages and twenty-two dollars and sixty-seven cents in customer tips. Hopefully, with this kind of money, she wouldn't be going home to well-deserved discipline for being so late. When Celina finally arrived at the Montoya shanty, all was quiet.

"Mama?" she called out hesitantly, her voice just above a whisper.

Instantly Mama appeared from behind the hanging sheet where the older children slept. She placed a finger over her lips. "I was just checking on everybody. How was your day, *malaynkia?*" Alexei ladled some lukewarm soup from the iron pot into a small bowl.

Celina shrugged and sighed as she dropped her book bag onto the floor beside her chair. "Okay, I guess."

"Yacque made this today while I was at work. She and Little Man cleaned out Mrs. Esteban's attic this afternoon. She paid them with this sack of beans she didn't want."

Celina looked as though she had been slapped. Rolling her eyes, she shoved the bowl to the center of the table, trying to ignore her growling stomach. Her peanut butter sandwich from lunch had long since evaporated. Mama began to say something but thought better of it.

"How was school?"

Celina did not talk about the incident with Staci. The last thing her mother needed was more to worry about.

"Well, I was like barely late to history and Mrs. Chandler made a federal case of it! She's making me write stupid sentences for it. To

The Music of What Happens

hear her tell it, you'd think she'd busted me snortin' coke with the Bustamente kids!"

Mama shook her head, reproachfully. "Lina Montoya, that isn't appropriate conversation for a nice young lady, and you mustn't be disrespectful of your teacher either. How was work?"

Celina gasped, lightly, "I almost forgot!" she reached into her school bag and pulled out several handfuls of coin and a small wad of bills. "There's thirty-two dollars and sixty-five cents there, you can count it. What a day! This'll be a big help with the bills, *sí?*"

Smiling, Mama touched her daughter's cheek. "Absolutely. But Lina, listen, there are to be no more late nights. The rules around here are not going to change every time there's a late rush at the store. Your curfew is for your safety so I don't worry and so you're rested for school. Do you understand?"

Celina nodded as she yawned expansively, and Mama patted her hair. "But yes, my love, you did a wonderful job today, as always. The boys did well today too? Chaim and Jackie cleaned your *tío* Marc's house and even did his yard, and Javier brought home twelve dollars from the recycling center. Why he must have been to every parking lot in the city!"

Celina did not smile. "But it just ain't enough Mama," she sighed, "it ain't ever enough."

"Lina—" Alexei began

"Sometimes I wish we were rich like Staci's family," Celina interrupted, tears of exhaustion and frustration filling her large, dark eyes, "then we could have nice stuff like a car and a house, and we could make Eli's insurance quit screwing up with his meds all the time. And when dumb bunny people are mean, we could stick up for ourselves and our family and not have to be scared! We wouldn't have to wear garage sale clothes, and *this*— she motioned angrily to the untouched bowl of bean soup on the table. "We wouldn't be eating thrown-out *charity* beans! I can just hear that *bruja,* Mrs. Esteban, now, 'Oh, those poor, starving Montoya's will eat this pig slop and be so grateful! It makes me sick— Celina's voice trailed off as she looked at the floor. "Oh, Mama," she mumbled, cheeks flushed, "I'm sorry. I-I didn't mean that."

"You're overtired, *malaynkia,*" Mama whispered, understandingly, taking one of her daughter's roughened hands in her own. "Listen to me, Linochka, we *are* rich. We have each other, and our pride and dignity. No one can take those things from us unless we let them. If you look at it that way, it's not so bad. We're certainly far richer than the mayor's family can ever hope to be."

Celina smiled at this. She felt a little better.

"Okay, now, let's get you in bed." While Celina rested on her cot, Mama sat beside her and softly sang *Rozhinkes Mit Mandlen,* Celina's, favorite, Jewish lullaby, while stroking her hair and cheek. It was not long before she had drifted off into an exhausted sleep.

"Mama?" Celina came out from behind the curtain the next morning. Alexei looked up from her tea, her eyes shadowed and swollen. "Mama, what's wrong?"

Mama did not reply only reached for her daughter's hand. "Lina, it's gonna be okay. Don't you worry. Don't you worry about anything."

As Celina stared down into her mother's eyes, she shook her head to herself. *She's trying to tell herself not to worry. But what's she worried about? I swear, if that tonto, Mayor Ainsworth, is already trying to make more trouble . . .* She glanced at the letter spread in front of her mother.

"It's in Russian. Is that from *Tsyo-tsya* Annushka? Can you read it to me?"

Mama covered the letter lightly with her hand. "It's impolite to look at other people's mail, Lina," she reminded, gently. "Please make a slice of toast for your breakfast. I made hot tea and I want you to drink a mug of it before you go to school. You sounded as if you were coming down with a cold last night. I'm afraid of you catching something and giving it to Eli."

Behind her mother's back, Celina rolled her eyes and sct a slice of Jewish rye to toast on the hot plate. Her mother continued, "Oh, these chilly nights. I don't know what I'm going to do about you. It cannot be healthy walking all the way home night after night. It gets so cold,

The Music of What Happens

and that jacket is nearly worn through. Tonight, I'm going to check the money jar and—

Celina shook her head hard. "No, no, Mama. We gotta' hang onto the extra cash. I mean, we can't trust Eli's crap insurance. They're always jacking us around, and then he ends up without meds and stuff until they pull their heads out of their— Alexei shot her eldest a warning glance, and Celina halted. "I'm just saying, I don't need a new jacket. Not like he needs his meds. This one's only like three years old! I can make it last longer. Besides, it's nearly June. It'll get warmer."

"That doesn't matter," Mama argued, "it's always cold at night."

"It's okay," Celina insisted, "I'll be fine. I-I'm not gonna get sick. I swear."

Mama sighed and turned back to writing on a sheet of paper beside the letter. Her mouth was set in a firm line, her stroke marks hard and heavy. Celina shuddered to herself as she poured herself a mug of the strong Russian tea that she disliked with a passion. It was difficult to make Mama angry but when one did, it was watch out time. Suddenly she looked up.

"Lina, I—

She halted, and Celina turned just in time to see Chaim come around the curtain, sleepily rubbing his eyes.

"You must have your toast and tea, *Vaquero*, or you'll be late for school. Lina, please wake the others."

While the other children nibbled their toast and sipped their herbal tea, Celina and Yacqueline spread peanut butter on bread and filled mason jars with water for their lunches.

As she kissed each of her children goodbye, Mama slipped two envelopes into Celina's hand, "Please mail the one with a stamp and buy groceries this afternoon with the other. The kids can go with you. It's unlikely any of you will be working in the pouring rain today. Yacque and Sol, you two come home from school, as usual, to look after Little Man."

As the children trudged through the rain and mud, Javier stuck out his thumb at an oncoming car. As the car whipped past them, Celina and Yacqueline laughed at him.

"Really, Jav, all seven of us?" Yacqueline giggled.

"Yeah, and we look like drowned sewer rats. Save your energy. No one's picking us up. Besides Mama would have a fit!"

"Look," Celina changed the subject, "Mama hid this letter from me when I tried to see. She wrote it to someone in Russia. Chaim, can you read it for me?"

"Yacque's better at reading Russian."

Carefully peeling back the flap, Celina unfolded it and handed the letter to her ten-year-old sister.

Yacqueline read slowly, "My dear brother—

"It's from *Dyadya* Menachem!" Jackie exclaimed, "he-he never writes to us. Chaim always says he's too rich and got his nose in the air. And he never liked Papi even though—"

"Hush," Celina flipped her brother's arm.

Yacqueline continued, "I must say I was u-upset by your letter at first. My children are so dear to me. But-but after much re-reflection I realize the course our life has taken is not what Elian needs. My son gets sicker the older he gets. He's only seven and he can't even go to school. He has Medicaid, the only charity my late husband would ever take, but the treatment he gets here is simply not enough. I will accept your offer on the condition that if he is very unhappy, he must be allowed to come home.

I've broken my heart through my own selfishness. My children deserve better, all of them. If I didn't love them so much, I wouldn't have fought so hard for them last year. What happened wasn't Lina's fault, still, she blames herself. But my love for my children is flawed through selfishness. They're not children anymore. Lina's only thirteen but she's a little woman, not the girl she should be. They all work too hard. I've stolen their ch-childhoods. I must find a way to make sure they have what they need. That's something Giac and I have always struggled to do. I must somehow be willing to give them what they truly need. I wonder all the time anymore if I'm not what they need. Even in the Bible, the real mother was willing to give up her own child so that child might live. I accept your offer with a broken heart.

The Music of What Happens

Alexei

Celina's jaw went slack; her heart was pounding. Chaim's chin quivered. Tears rolled down Yacqueline's, pale, thin face as she folded the single sheet of paper and handed it back to her older sister.

Javier angrily kicked at imaginary pebbles on the ground. He muttered between clenched teeth. "Mama's right. We're *not* children, and we need to work harder. We owe it to her and each other."

Celina motioned for her siblings to follow her. They were drenched from standing on the sidewalk for so long. "That's not what Mama means. She wasn't blaming us. She's scared. She's scared we can't get by. But you're right. We need to work harder." She glanced behind her, "Mama's gonna be mad as hell when she finds out we read this."

"I'm glad we did," Soledad countered, "at least now we know we have to help Mama better."

"Does Mama want to give me away, Lina?" Evangelo asked, dark eyes worried.

Celina bent to her knees and looked straight into her little brother's eyes. "No, she doesn't," she replied, firmly. "She's just worried and very sad right now. And we've gotta' help her more, right?"

"Right, Lina."

Celina hugged the little boy then Chaim lifted him in his strong arms to ride piggy-back "Okay, let's get to school now. We're like way late."

As they hurried, Celina wadded up the letter and wrapped a rock around it. She hesitated then thought better of it and put it in her pocket. Her breath came in great gasps. *Poor Mama. She thinks she's a bad mama, and she doesn't know she's the best mother in the world.* Tears threatened and Celina brushed at them angrily. *I'll talk to Chaim. If we quit school, we can find even more work out there. I can even clean houses during the day and work at Aleman's in the evening. Mama doesn't have to know. All she'll know is we're getting better wages.*

"Hey, me too. She's my mama too!" Javier protested when Celina mentioned she and Chaim quitting school and going to work.

"No, no, *hermano*," Chaim shook his head. "You're not very big. People'll notice. I'm bigger so I can pass for older. And Lina talks older. We can get away with it. We need you to look after the younger ones and make sure they're okay and that everyone keeps workin' hard and doing their share."

All that day, Celina could hardly concentrate and did terribly in her studies.

Why? Why didn't Mama tell us it was getting too hard? When was she gonna' tell us about Eli? She can't make us live with Papi's brothers! She just can't. We can't leave her all alone. She's not thinking straight. And Dyadya Menachem, just who in the heck does he think he is? We don't even know him, and he thinks he can take Sunbeam just like that! Well, he's got another thing coming!

"Lina Zagoradniy, when I asked you a question, I expect a reply. Now for the third time what is the capital of Indonesia?"

"Huh?" Celina startled out of her reverie, "Oh, Moscow."

The other children laughed, and Staci flashed Celina a scornful look. "Get out the dunce cap."

Celina bit her tongue hard to keep from making a retort, and Mrs. Chandler was stern.

"Lina Zagoradniy, review your geography assignment and be prepared to get an A on tomorrow's pop quiz. And as for you, *Miss* Staci Ainsworth, your name has just made it to the blackboard. One more rude word out of you, and you'll find yourself helping me with classroom cleaning during recess today."

Celina and Elizaveta exchanged a knowing look and snickered. They both knew that the possibility of work was the only trick that would make Staci shut up. The Ainsworths were above manual labor; they employed Hispanic servants for such things. As soon as she heard their giggles, face flushed with anger, Staci whirled around to face them. Both girls dropped their eyes to their books.

The Music of What Happens

That afternoon, Celina headed downtown to do the grocery shopping and six of the younger children decided to come along. Yacqueline, alone, remained at home to do the cleaning and Mrs. Esteban's ironing.

The Montoya youngsters were an almost pitiful sight traipsing down the streets of Santa Fe together with worn shoes and their clothes faded and ill-fitting. Despite obvious poverty, they were always well-groomed with faces and hands clean and hair combed. Most of the good folk of Santa Fe felt sorry for the fatherless family and had offered to help in the past. Very proud, however, Mama and Papi had always steadfastly refused charity.

The younger ones especially adored visits to the grocery store. Of course, even Little Man understood that they could not afford extras; they didn't care. It was fun just looking around and dreaming. As they waited just outside the sliding glass doors for Soledad to bring a grocery cart from the middle of the parking lot, Celina lit a stolen cigarette, took a few puffs and passed it to Chaim. "Last one unless Javier jacks a few from Aleman's office. So enjoy."

When Chaim didn't take the cigarette, she turned to see him staring wistfully across the street. She handed the smoke to Jackie and turned in the direction he was looking. The red sign on the gray stone building read *Santa Fe Food Bank*. When he finally turned back to her, Celina shook her head and commented, stoutly, "Don't even think about it. That's *charity*, Chaim! You know Montoya's don't take charity. Come on now."

Inside the store, Celina re-counted the small roll of bills carefully as she made her selections. She sighed, frustrated. This week they had just thirty-five dollars for food. Somehow it seemed that there was less each week, and Celina had to make that money stretch as far as possible.

Thank goodness for those grocery bags from Tío.

As Celina placed items in the cart, Little Man patted his sister's bare leg. "What?" she muttered, preoccupied with the various bags of rice and beans on the shelves in front of her.

"Look, Lina!"

Celina glanced down to see him holding a package of marshmallow fudge cookies. "Don't these look so yummy? Have you ever ate 'em before?" His dark eyes sparkled.

Celina bent low and whispered in her brother's ear. "We've talked about this, Immanuel Montoya; we can't afford to buy garbage. Now put 'em back."

"Well, my oh my, if it isn't Celina Zagoradniy and the garbage pail kids."

Celina shut her eyes hard and moaned, inwardly. *Oh, why me?*

Turning to face Staci, she smiled, tightly. Staci waved the air in front of her nose exaggeratedly and took a step backward. "Garbage pail kids, no kidding! Do you beaners always have to smell like that? Seriously? I mean, soap's cheap and water's free!"

Before Celina could respond, Staci smirked and motioned to the cash in her hand. "Oh, that's right, I remember, it's the first of the month: ya'll's free money."

With Staci's patronizing sarcasm grating on her nerves, Celina turned her back and pretended to be interested in the canned goods while she willed Staci to leave. But Staci did not leave. Instead, she grabbed Celina's arm and spun her around to face her. Celina yanked her arm away, clenching her other fist tightly at her side.

"What the—

Staci spat at her, "Instead of stealing us working people's money, why don't you like tell your lazy mother to get off her butt and get a real job!"

Celina froze. In that moment, she no longer cared. She no longer cared that Staci was white and rich. She didn't care about going back to the juvenile center, she didn't care about what Cal or even Mayor Ainsworth could do! Staci had no right! How dare she say that about Mama who worked long hours cleaning offices and rich people's houses to take care of her family! How *dare* Staci!"

Celina turned for just a moment to Chaim who was just as enraged as she was. When their eyes met, she barely shook her head.

"I didn't hit you back at school," Celina said, through clenched teeth, barely keeping her voice low, "but you just crossed the line *big time!*" She turned and punched Staci in the face as hard as she possibly could. Chaim spun the cart around and the Montoya children calmly walked away as though nothing had happened.

Sobbing in pain and rage, Staci screamed, "You're gonna catch it, Lina! Your whole family's gonna' catch it! Nobody touches me!"

Trying to sound braver than she felt, Celina shouted back as they turned down the next aisle, "Oh, grow up! Gonna' sick your daddy on me, you coward? Get a life!"

"I'll get you, Lina! *I'll get you!*"

CHAPTER 3

Anything but Change

The siblings were unusually quiet during the walk home. Piggy-backing Little Man, Celina appeared perfectly calm, even proud of herself. Inside she was positively shaking!

Oh, why'd I go and do it? she berated herself. *Now Staci'll tell her dad, and he'll harass Mama then Cal's gonna—* she squeezed her eyes shut at that memory. *Then Mama'll get reported again and the little kids might get taken away and Chaim and Javier and me'll get our butts thrown in the juvy place again! Oh, why am I such an idiot? I am in such major trouble! Mierda!"*

Lost in thought, Celina did not even hear someone calling her name until an Escalade came to a stop beside her.

"Get in quick, all of you," Marcos motioned from the driver's seat. As the children climbed in, Celina crawled up front next to Elian who threw himself into her arms. His peaked face was tear-streaked, and he was trembling.

"*Tío*, what's wrong?" Celina implored as the vehicle sped off down the dusty road. "Why do you have Eli? Where's Mama?"

"Your mama fainted. An ambulance just took her to Santa Fe General. She and Eli dropped by my office to say hi. She stood to go and passed out on the floor."

When the group arrived at the hospital, Marcos directed the children to sit down in the waiting area while he spoke to a nearby nurse.

Celina helped Elian onto her lap. He was warm again, his breathing heavy. She held him against her, and he laid his head against her chest. Celina's arms fit easily around his thin frame. Although Elian was nearly seven, he weighed the same as Little Man who was just four. His little body shuddered as he inhaled, raggedly.

Although it seemed like a lifetime, it was just fifteen minutes before they were summoned to Mama's room. Only Celina and Chaim were old enough; Javier and Yacqueline looked after the younger ones in the waiting area.

Mama lay in a clean hospital bed, with an IV in her arm. Her face was the color of chalk, and her wild, black curls, damp with perspiration, lay tangled on the pillow, a stark contrast to the snow-white bedding.

"What happened, Mama?" Celina ran to her mother's side. Alexei tried to sit but weakly leaned back against the pillows.

"I-I'm ok, my sweet girl. It must have been the heat. That's the last time I—" She forced herself into a sitting position. "Marc, can you call a nurse? I need this thing out of my arm. We gotta get going. I've got the Jackson house still to clean and—where's Elian?"

"He's with Javier. Alex, please lay down. You can't go just yet. The doctor wants you to rest for a while and—"

"Oh, I'm sure that doctor needs more rest than I do. Please, Marc, I need to get out of here."

Celina winced at the panic on her mother's pale face.

It's true; we kids don't work hard enough. She works too hard trying to take care of all of us. Geez, Mama, please rest.

"Mama, Sol, and I can do the Jackson house. We'll go now. Yacque, Chaim, and Javier can take the little kids and go look for jobs—the rain's stopped."

Before Mama could answer, a nurse popped her head in. "Mr. Gonzalez, Mrs. Montoya, the doctor would like to speak to you two without the children."

Her heart in her throat, dark eyes wide, Celina turned to the nurse. "Please, what-what's wrong with my mama?"

Mama placed a hand on Celina's cheek. "*Dochka*, it'll be okay. Let us talk to the doctor for a minute."

Reluctantly, Celina and Chaim exited the room. As the door closed behind them, they each seemed to know what the other was thinking as they pressed their ears against the door.

Celina sighed. She could only hear a little. ". . .significant malnourishment, . . . too thin. . . exhaustion, must rest . . . eat."

Celina stepped away from the door when she could hear no more. She turned to Chaim, dark eyes wide as she whispered. "She-she's starving. Starving because of us. Oh, Mama, what the— Her voice trailed off.

She turned abruptly and headed for the waiting area with quick, firm step, Chaim right behind her. Once in the waiting area, Celina took charge: "Chaim, *por favor* take the little ones with you and try to find some weeding jobs or whatever. Except for Eli. Mama would have a fit. Javier, please stay with him until Tío comes back. Yacque, Sol, you two come with me. We've got the Jackson house over on Presidio to do, and I think Mama also cleans Morganstern's downtown on Fridays. We got a lot of work to do. Javier, when you're done, please stop by Aleman's and do my job. Ok?"

Everyone in agreement, Celina and her sisters left the hospital and rushed down the street in the direction of the bus stop.

"I don't know what to do about Mama, Tío. I mean, she's supposed to rest for like two weeks, but it's like I need to tie her to the bed. Like seriously. I mean, me and Yacque and Sol are doing all the house and office cleanings and keeping Little Man with us, and the boys are working harder than ever. All Mama needs to do is rest and look after Eli, and he's easy as pie. But she won't. She's all over the place, trying to find more houses and stuff to clean, and I'm afraid she'll get sick again. I don't-I don't know what to do."

Celina stared down at her windburned hands, folded in her lap. She sighed deeply as she repeated. "I-I don't know what to do. C-could we clean your house again in exchange for the good foods the doctor wants her to have, you know, whole milk and grains and fruit and stuff? Could we *por favor?*"

Marcos, sitting beside her, on the bench at the quiet park on Main Street just days later, nodded as he wrapped an arm around Celina's shoulder. "Of course, you can. And it'll be okay, Lina. I'm trying to figure out some things to help more as well. It's just so darn hard when—"

Celina's head snapped up, eyes flashing. She threw up her hands. "Why are grownups always trying to figure something out? Why don't you just do it? That's what me and the kids are doing! We're not trying to figure it out, we're doing it! Chaim and me heard some of what that doctor said to Mama! *Malnourishment.* I can't spell it, but I know what it means! He said she was starving, that she's too thin. It's all because of us, isn't it, Tío? Because she has all of us to take care of?"

"Lina, no, it's—

"It is! She wrote to *Dyadya* Menachem in Moscow. He wrote her a letter wanting to take Elian 'cuz he'll have better medical care and good food and stuff, and Mama's gonna let him! She might give away the rest of us too, her letter said she doesn't think she's a good mom! But she's the best mama ever! I don't *care* how poor we are! I don't *care* what anybody says! We-we've got the best mama ever— Celina's words ended in sobs as she buried her face in her hands.

As Marcos' arms wrapped around her, she clung to him, weeping into his shirt. "I don't want Mama to feel this way, but I don't want her to starve because of us! Like seriously, Tío, we-we're trying! Us girls clean four houses a day sometimes and the boys are—I-I didn't have any idea just how hard Mama works until now!"

"Oh, Lina, little Lina," Marcos murmured, softly. "You're right, *nena*. Grownups always trying to figure things out when the solutions are often staring us in the face. I wish your parents had let me help you all more. I don't want you to worry. You worry too much for a little girl. I promise I'll talk to your mama tonight. I'll come by after you're all asleep." He lifted her chin so that she looked into his eyes. "No more worrying, child."

"Marcos, good evening," Celina heard Mama open the shanty door. "It's so late; what are you doing here?"

"Could I just have a few minutes of your time?"

"O-of course. Come in and sit."

From her cot behind the curtain, Celina turned on her stomach and raised on her elbows to hear the conversation. For a few minutes, the adults did not speak. Finally, she heard Marcos speak sternly but kindly.

"Alexei, why are you back to work already? Why aren't you getting rest like the doctor said?"

Mama sighed. "Oh, Marcos, I'm all right. Besides, there's no time. I have nine children to feed and take care of. There's no time for me to be in bed. Also—"

"They're growing up too fast, Alexei. Much too fast."

"Don't you think I know that? Don't you think I know what a terrible mother I've become? I never wanted anything more than I wanted the best for my children, and I've failed them! God forgive me, but I've failed them."

Celina drew a shuddering breath as she blinked back tears at Mama's words. *Mama always said we held hands and smiles that all the money in the world couldn't buy. Oh, Mama, I know you're tired, but please don't give up. Puzhalsta don't give up!*

"Alex, I know what you're thinking, but it doesn't have to be this way. You don't have to look for better lives for the children. Elian belongs here with you, his mother; they all do."

"What are you saying? I—"

"I know about the letter."

"What letter?"

"Don't pretend. The kids saw the letter to your brother; they read it. And it broke their hearts."

"*Bozhimoi,* my children. My poor children!" Mama wept. "Marc, I never meant for them to see that. I shouldn't say this, but I was almost out of my mind with hunger. I had to stop writing twice because I was seeing double. Yes, I agreed to Menachem taking Elian. Because he can better care for him! Don't you see? And the others, don't you think I know they work too hard? They're not even children anymore. It's not fair to them; it's wrong! *I* was wrong! Giac was wrong! Our kids deserved more, better! If only we could've stopped long enough to—"

At this, Celina pressed her face into the pillow to muffle her sobs. Her mind whirled around and around but she could think of no solutions. *Oh, Tió, what can you possibly do? We're gonna lose our brother, and we're gonna lose each other!*

"Alexei, you know your brother. He's a rich man now, isn't he? Money hungry. The only reason he wants Eli is to make money from his violin talents, isn't it? And if keeping him healthy longer can make that happen, then he will. Everything you've told me about the man . . . he'll use that child up until there's nothing left. You know it, and I know it."

"*Da*, I know it! Do you think I'm blind? Of course, I know it. Marc, I'm wearing down. I shouldn't say this to you, but I'm wearing down and wearing out. You remember, even the doctor said I was killing myself. I don't know how much longer I'll be able to work as hard as I do. And my children do so much after school that—"

"Alex, they're not in school."

"What? Of course they're in school."

"No, they're not. At least the girls aren't. Lina let it slip the other day at the park that they're often cleaning four houses a day. They would need all day for that. They're not in school."

"Oh, dear Lord, what am I going to do with that girl? I—"

"I know. They're only trying to help. Lina and Chaim are so worried about you. They're all doubling their efforts." Marcos paused and exhaled hard. "Alex, I have a solution. I want you to think about it. I'm not trying to shame you; you *are* an incredible mother. You've sacrificed so much for these children; you all can't be separated like that. It would destroy each of them and you. I want you to marry me. Please?"

"What? Marry—Marcos, I-I can't. I just lost my husband, I—

"Look, you know how much I care about you and especially the children. This isn't a question of love; I'm not asking you to share my bed. It's a question of what is right. What I'm offering is a chance for the children to be children, to grow up with choices for their future, consistent good food, and quality medical care for Eli. They wouldn't have to work or worry. Neither would you. You must see the sense in this." His voice softened to a hoarse whisper. "You must."

For a long time, Mama was silent. Celina's mouth was wide open at this. *Marry Tío? No, no way. I mean, Papi just died. How can she even think such a dumb thing? She can't be! Tío's our pal, not our papa. What the—*

To Celina's shock, Mama finally said, "Okay, Marcos. But only because my children need you, and as they get older, they'll need a father more and more desperately. You're very kind, and I thank you."

"*Gracias,* Alexei. It's an honor." Without another word, the shanty door shut behind him.

As the roar of a truck engine told her Marcos had left, Celina could hear Mama weeping into her hands on the other side of the curtain. A part of her longed to go comfort her mother, but she could not. Celina shook her head to herself.

What is she doing? We just lost Papi, and now she's doing this?

Two days later, Mama and Marcos were married at the city courthouse with the children and Marcos' friend, Kym, looking on. As Celina stood directly behind Mama, she shook her head to herself. *This is disgusting. Everyone's gonna think she's like a gold digger or something, that she only married him for his money. But I guess it's true; she kinda did.*

Riding home in Marcos' Escalade, Celina sat in the very back and stared out the window. Chaim and Javier sat beside her and didn't look any happier than she felt. When they pulled into the driveway of Marcos' hacienda-style home, Javier shot both brother and sister a pointed look, meaning that they should talk in private. Celina tapped Yacqueline's shoulder from behind and was met with a nod.

The elder, four, Montoya children were the closest of siblings and, though they included the younger children in almost everything they did, they often slipped away together to plan, plot, navigate and strategize the more adult things of life. Luckily, this time, the younger children did not ask to join them. They rushed to the house ahead of Mama and Marcos, who laughed as they followed them in.

Celina barely smiled. Despite everything, she knew this move would be a good thing for the younger ones, Elian especially. The Montoya children enjoyed the occasional visit to Marcos' home. He had toys and electronics and kept a special drawer filled with snacks.

Celina giggled. *Jackie always eats way more than his share of the snacks! He's gonna get fat now that we live here!*

A whistle from Chaim broke her out of her reverie and she followed her brothers behind the house. She sighed deeply when she entered the cool shade among the grove of trees. Javier sank down to sit against the stone siding and Celina sat beside him, Yacqueline and Chaim remained standing. Celina fished her red lighter and a forgotten cigarette out of the pocket of her cutoffs. She took a drag and handed it to Javier.

"So, what do we think about all this?" she mumbled.

"I dunno," Javier shrugged, "I'm just mad Mama didn't even ask us what we thought. She just went and did it."

"Well, you know Mama doesn't owe us an explanation just 'cuz she gives us one sometimes."

"Yeah, I know. It's just that—

Yacqueline piped up, "Look I'm not much happier about it than you guys but look at it this way: wouldn't you like it better to be Tío than some guy we don't even know?"

The children sat for several moments in thoughtful silence. Celina nodded. "Yeah. I guess you got a point there. At least we know Tío, and he cares about us because of Papi. But I still wish Mama hadn't done it. Papi hasn't been dead a year yet! She should've trusted us; that we could work harder than ever, and she could rest more. She didn't even let us show her. Like at all. And that butt chewing she gave us girls when she found out we weren't going to school anymore. Geez! I mean we were just—

"Well, as I told you, Lina, Mama could've got in big trouble for that. It's a good thing that rat, Mayor Ainsworth didn't get wind of it somehow. We'd have been in a whole mess of hurt!"

"So, what do we do?"

"I guess we make the best of it," Yacqueline said, gently. "Papi wouldn't want us to cause problems or be little crappers. We don't have to be happy about it, but we have to be respectful. We all agree on that?"

Reluctantly, Celina and Chaim nodded. Javier didn't look up as he kicked at loose soil on the ground. Finally, he mumbled. "Yeah, I guess."

When she entered the house, Celina made her way upstairs to Marcos' third-floor library. Musically gifted, she had taught herself to play the piano years ago and always enjoyed the opportunity to play Marcos' glossy, black, baby grand. This time she simply wandered around, looking over the curio cabinets of antiques. As she picked up a porcelain German Hummel miniature of a couple dancing, she caught sight of a photo that had always hung in the living room until now. The gold-framed, professional photo of a beautiful, red-haired baby girl, Marcos' adopted baby daughter, caught her attention.

"Little Kitty-Cat," Celina mused, straightening the black draping ribbon that hung over the photograph. "She sure was a cute kid."

"Lina?"

Quickly Celina set the picture back down on the hutch shelf and pretended to be engrossed in a dish of sea glass.

Marcos entered the room at that moment. The smile on his face vanished when he saw the photo. "Oh. I-I meant to put that away." He grabbed it and placed it face down in the drawer below the shelf. His chin quivered, briefly. He sighed as he smiled, tightly, at Celina. "Sorry. After all these years, I just haven't let go. Silly of me. But I have you guys now." He touched her shoulder. Celina stepped back just out of reach.

"No, Tío," she contradicted, "Look, I appreciate what you're doing for Mama and for Eli too, but that doesn't change that we're Giac Montoya's kids. You were Katherine's papi; you ain't ours."

Marcos barely nodded, his voice thick as he said, softly, "Time for supper."

The next week, Mama and Marcos took the children shopping for new clothes at the Markham Mall. Mama had said it was high time they wore more than plain tee shirts and denim cutoffs that had to be passed from child to child until they wore through.

This is nice and all, but I kinda like my tee shirts and cut-offs I mean, since when have I ever worn anything else?

Though tentative, Celina joined her siblings in thanking Marcos for the shopping trip. At the mall, Mama accompanied her, Yacqueline and Soledad to the girl's areas while Marcos went with the boys. As they shopped, Celina's hesitation turned to panic. How would she ever know what to choose? Current fashion meant nothing to her. As she looked through the racks, she tried to think of the kinds of tops, pants, and skirts Elizaveta and even Staci wore when making her selections.

In the end, she was fitted with dresses for Mass, skirts and coordinating sweaters, jeans, shorts and leggings, tops of many different styles and designs, pajamas and several pairs of shoes.

While the girls and their mother picked out socks and underwear, Mama said Celina should begin wearing a training bra. Celina was genuinely excited! Elizaveta had been wearing a bra for a year now, and though Celina had been begging for almost that long, Mama had always replied that it was not yet her time.

"Why can't *I* wear a bra?" pouted Soledad, as Mama and Celina selected several.

"Because— Mama began.

"Because," Celina interrupted, haughtily, mimicking Staci, "you, my little one, have nothing to uhm—how do I say this— put in a bra."

Soledad stuck out her tongue. "Oh, like you do?"

Celina ignored the retort and continued, aggravatingly, "Bras are for *women,* Sol. Now if you take my advice—

"I'd rather take rat poison! And *you're* not a woman!" Soledad turned back to their mother. "Mama, I need a bra too, *please!"*

"Soledad Montoya, lower your voice!" Mama returned, her tone soft but equally stern, "a nice young lady doesn't talk loudly about underwear. When you and Lina will ever remember that, I'll never know." Alexei rolled her eyes and threw up her hands. "Now I'm sorry, *malaynkia,* but nine is too young. Your sister is older, and it's her time. But don't worry, your turn will come before you know it, I promise. As for you, Celina Iliana Catarina Natyscha Zagoradniy-Montoya, not another word, *ponyala?"*

Celina nodded vigorously. She knew well that when Mama used her full name, she meant business. Although she managed to keep a straight face, Celina inwardly quaked with laughter over her young sister's "need" for a bra.

"Don't be disappointed, Sol," Yacqueline consoled as they walked away. "I can't wear a bra yet and I'm older than you."

"Well, you're different. You don't *care!"*

"How do you know I don't?" Yacqueline replied, kind and rational as always. Celina rolled her eyes.

As they rounded the corner with their shopping carts, they almost immediately ran into Marcos and the boys whose carts were also full.

"You ladies finished?" Marcos asked.

"Da," Alexei replied, distractedly, inspecting her sons' selections.

Marcos turned to his stepchildren. "So how about lunch at Milagros' Buffet before we go home?"

The children were astonished. As far as they could remember, they had never eaten in a restaurant, and now they were about to dine in the most popular restaurant in town.

The trunk of the Gonzalez's suburban was loaded to overflowing with shopping bags and boxes. Chattering excitedly to each other about their purchases, the children piled into the car, and they were off.

When they entered the restaurant, Alexei was the first to speak. "Marc, please find us a table. I need to give Elian his medication." Alexei motioned for Elian to follow her, and they disappeared down a hallway. When she was out of sight, Marcos ushered the others to a large table, and Chaim and Javier added some extra chairs. Jackie tugged at Celina's sleeve as she stood, gazing up, in awe, at the sparkling, crystal chandelier, hanging directly above them.

"Lina, look over there!"

Celina's gaze moved quickly in the direction he was pointing. What she saw made her gasp. Buffet tables were laden with food. Meats and fish of different kinds, pizzas and a taco bar, mashed potatoes with gravy, salads, Jell-O, breads, muffins and desserts. Celina had never seen so much fresh food at one time. The array of delectable aromas permeating the air made her mouth water. She could scarcely wait. At that moment, the others joined her and Jackie.

"Mary, Jesus, and Joseph!" Yacqueline shook her head, in awe, her arm around Little Man's shoulder. She tried to say more but could not.

Just then Marcos joined them. "Hey, you guys," he teased. "Delicious food is meant to be eaten not admired. Come now, let's fill our plates. Remember, you may have whatever you like."

Celina went slowly. Everything looked and smelled delicious. She and the others had had such foods occasionally but usually as leftovers they had sneaked out of restaurant dumpsters.

This is a whole other ball of wax. I can hardly wait to dig in. And not a pot of beans in sight!

When the family sat down together, Mama cautioned the children against eating too quickly of foods their bodies were not used to. All did their best to pace themselves.

"G-Gee, Tío, this is-this is just great!" Javier exclaimed between bites. "It's just . . . well . . . great!"

Mama and Marcos laughed as Mama gently reminded Evangelo once again to slow down. The five-year-old was practically inhaling his shepherd's pie.

After everyone had eaten their fill, the children enthusiastically thanked Marcos. "Oh, quit being so polite," he teased them, "I'm your stepdad not the President of the United States." Grinning across the table at Mama, he whispered to them, "Now am I gonna look like a pig all by myself, or is anyone else up for dessert?"

Mama protested, gently, "Oh, Marcos, please. You mustn't spoil them."

Marcos simply smiled and the children's eyes grew wide with pure shock and delight.

"Tío," Soledad breathed, "are-are you serious?"

"Course, *nena*. When's the last time you guys had some soft ice cream or—" Marcos halted at Soledad's wide dark eyes round with anticipation.

"It-it's been an awful long time," Jackie piped up. Celina kicked him under the table, and he fell silent.

Marcos stood quickly and beckoned them, "Well, follow your old tío to the land of ice cream sundaes."

Mama declined dessert. Little Man, his tummy warm and full, was falling asleep in her arms. Small children should not eat sweets, Mama said. As Celina followed the others to the dessert area, she glanced back at Mama, cuddling Little Man close. She bit her lip.

That doctor's right; Mama's way too thin. I wish she'd have dessert. I don't want her to get sick or faint again like that.

At the self-serve dessert counter, Celina stood a moment in complete indecision staring at the buffet of delightful choices, many of which she had never tasted. Finally, she created an ice cream sundae with brownies, several sauces, whipped cream and a cherry on top. Marcos and Mama grinned at the children's exclamations of delight as they enjoyed their desserts and traded around, allowing each other to taste.

So engrossed were the Gonzalez's in their dessert that they did not immediately notice a rather intoxicated man sit down at an adjacent table. He ignored the plate of hot food in front of him but instead stared, transfixed, at Mama. She was wiping pudding from Jackie's mouth with a napkin and did not immediately notice. The moment their eyes met, however, her jaw dropped, her face drained of color. Celina turned in the direction her mother was looking.

She glared at the stranger and mouthed, *What?*

The man ignored her, and Celina nudged Marcos under the table as he stood and moved unsteadily over to their table. Leaning down, he grinned, wickedly. He was so close now that Celina could smell the repulsive odor of cheap tequila on his breath. The man wore dirty, oversized jeans, a black wifebeater and a blue cotton overshirt, unbuttoned and disheveled. Black curls fell to the base of his neck and his dark eyes were familiar somehow . . .

"Member me, Princess," he slurred at Mama, "got yer'self another man, huh, Princess? Gotcha' a bunch of snot-nosed brats too? So jes' how many *hombres* you had since me, huh?"

Angry, Celina opened her mouth, but Mama placed her hand over hers. Marcos did not speak but stood immediately and grabbed the other man by the back of his overshirt, Pulling the much shorter man onto his tiptoes, he turned him around and moved him firmly and quickly in the direction of the main door. The children watched their stepfather tentatively, not sure what to expect. Celina rolled her eyes when she saw Javier and Jackie share a wide grin. She knew her younger brothers were hoping Marcos might fight the other man in the parking lot. Instead, to their disappointment, their stepfather gave the drunken stranger a single hard shove out the restaurant door. He stood watching as the man stumbled from the parking lot and then returned to their table.

"Let's go."

As they drove home, Mama did not say a word, merely stared out the passenger side window. Celina was sure she saw a tear or two slide down her mother's cheek. Marcos, clearly uncomfortable, did not press her.

I don't get it. Mama's not scared easily at all. What's going on here?

Although she tried to shrug it off, Celina could not help but feel certain that this was not the last they would see of the stranger.

CHAPTER 4

Beneath Still Water

"Javier, I don't want to hear anymore! I can't believe you would do something so stupid and reckless! And downright illegal! Marc and I could have been in a world of trouble right now because of your actions! Go to your room! I'll deal with you later. Evangelo Montoya, what in the name of—"

Celina arrived downstairs to the sound of her mother's voice angrily scolding the two boys at the same time. She sighed and turned around to sneak back upstairs. Mama had been so testy of late. Ever since . . .

Ever since that day at the restaurant and that dumb drunk. She knew him, she had to have! But how, and why was she so afraid? That's not Mama at all.

But Mama did not mention it. Not once. As out of sorts as she had been for the last few weeks, Celina had not had the nerve to bring it up herself.

She's just gotten so angry at us kids. And Tío—well, she won't hardly talk to him either. Hmm.

Flopping onto the bed, she turned on her *Diamante Rio* playlist, put on her headphones and cranked up their latest song to drown out Mama now scolding Soledad. A tear slid down her cheek.

Why won't she talk to me? We've always been close; I'm sure I could help, but all she wants to do is yell over the most dumb bunny stuff!

She sat up and sighed, staring out the window at the downpour. Since moving to Marcos' upscale neighborhood on Destiny Boulevard, Celina had made no new friends yet. There were two nearby families with daughters her age, however they attended private school, moved in Staci's circle and were unfriendly, to say the least. However, it had been raining hard for the last two days, and there was nowhere to escape to for now.

Just then there was a knock at her door. Chaim stood there, smiling. As if he'd read her mind, he tapped the pocket of his rain-dampened jacket. Celina grinned as she followed him out the back door.

"What about Javier and Yacque?"

"Looks like Javier's grounded 'til the next century and rightly so. Mama's *so* mad! She found out about him and Gershon and Martin taking Principal Mihailov's car and joyriding down to the 7-11 during recess the day before school let out. He's in like *major* trouble, and it wouldn't shock me at all if he gets—"

Celina gasped. "Ohhhhh, I told him nothing good would come of that! I literally told him, but the three *amigos* knew best! From what I heard, he hotwired it, like Tío Pancho taught us to do. I bet he's gonna be stuck in his room all summer! And Mama—"

"Dang, do I know it," Chaim sighed heavily. "Mama's acting psycho. That's why I just had to run to the corner and grab a pack." He lit one and passed it to Celina before lighting his own.

"And if Mama or Tío catch us . . ."

"Yeah, I know, I know. After that last butt chewing—but Mama acting like she is, I'm too stressed out."

"Me too."

"Lina! Chaim! Where are you?"

Frantically, the two took a last long drag on their cigarettes and buried the butts before rushing inside.

"Yeah, Mama?"

They exchanged worried glances when Mama bade them come upstairs to the living room. Celina breathed a sigh of relief when she smiled and asked them to sit down with the others. Marcos sat nearby. Mama's eyes were red and puffy, and Celina looked down at her hands. She just knew something was seriously wrong.

"Children, I'm so sorry for how I've been acting lately. How upset and angry I've been." She sighed and looked away out the window. "I-I want you all to know that what's going on right now isn't your fault. I'm so sorry I've been so— I'm struggling with some things, but I'm working on it."

Celina glanced at Javier. His eyes were red and swollen too, and he refused to look up.

"Mama," Yacqueline broke in gently, reaching for her mother's hand, "It's okay. We're all okay. You're having a hard time. *Puzhalste* let us help you get through it like you've always helped us."

Alexei gulped, clearly holding back more tears. She squeezed the little girl's hand. "Thank you, my sweet one. But this is something Mama needs to figure out alone. But I can promise two things: one, that I'll be a much better mama from here on out, and two, that I love you all so much, and I *will* be well. I'll be myself again. It'll just take a little time." She opened her arms, and her children willingly came to her. As Mama and Celina hugged tightly, she sniffed her hair and then mouthed, "We'll talk later."

Marcos who had kept silent through the entire exchange, finally changed the subject. "So, it's been ages since I've had any decent music in this house. Lina, would you like to play a couple of songs for us? You're proficient, aren't you?"

Celina rolled her eyes as she stood. Why she had graduated from "proficient" when she was eight!

How dumb is he anyway? He's heard me play before. Her conscience pricked her. It had been at least that long since Marcos had heard her. She groaned inwardly as she headed for the stairs behind the rest of her family, Celina rolled her eyes again. She had no desire to be near Marcos right now.

He tries to act like he's our papi. He isn't, and he never will be. Can't he get that through his head? Honestly, grownups can be so thick sometimes!

The Music of What Happens

When they arrived in the spacious library where Marcos kept his late wife's, beautiful, baby grand, he motioned for Celina to come closer. Dutifully she sat down and sighed as she fingered the smooth, black and white keys. The Montoya's had never owned a piano. On the occasion she wasn't working, Celina practiced at the church. Father Domingo had given her a key two years earlier when he saw just how incredibly she played.

It's like Eli with his violin. I hardly ever got to play, but when I did it was my everything. Everything to my heart. And now, it's how I pray for Papi. I know he can hear me somehow.

Celina's mocha eyes shone as she began to play *The Mystery of Your Gift*. Despite never having music lessons, she was naturally accomplished. Even still her hands trembled at first. Mama, standing beside her, began to softly sing along, her hand on Celina's shoulder. Out of the corner of her eye, Celina saw Marcos pick up his guitar, strumming, gently, as he accompanied the piano. She smiled again. Her entire family surrounded her, and within a few seconds, they were all singing along. Even Elian, Evangelo and Little Man tried to sing along, though Evangelo could not sing on key, and Elian and Little Man did not speak English.

As the song ended, a small arm draped across her shoulder. She turned to see Elian smiling at her, his tired eyes sparkling in the light from the piano lamp. He whispered, in Russian, "*Puzhalste* play Papi's song, sis?"

Celina could have cried as she gently squeezed his hand. Brother and sister shared a look of complete understanding, and Celina nodded to herself. *I was wrong. I thought the little ones were all forgetting Papi, and Tío was all they needed any more. But I was wrong. He hasn't forgotten. Elian still remembers who our father is.*

"I will, help me sing?"

Elian's smile was heart-melting. As Celina began to sing *Si Volvieres a Mi*, she felt a warmth wash over her like a peaceful river, and she blinked back tears of joy as she started into the second verse with mounting enthusiasm. She found the beautiful, familiar song so uplifting it carried her from the depths of her sadness and made her want to . . .

I want to never stop playing. I want to make up for lost time. Like a prayer. I haven't prayed in so long ever since. . . Papi, can you hear me? Can you hear my music? If you can see me and the kids from heaven, I hope you're proud. I miss you, but the Holy Virgin and Her Son know best. Tío's good to us and good to Mama. But don't you worry, you're the only father I'll ever have. I promise.

"This is not just gonna go away," Javier declared to Celina as they sat behind the house, "even though Mama said I'm not grounded for the *whole* summer anymore. But geez, weeks of her acting weird, and then she says sorry, and we all get back to normal? I don't think so. Something's not right. Mama never acted off her rocker like that even when she was starving so bad."

Celina was silent but glanced at Yacqueline, quietly sketching in her drawing book beside them on the picnic table bench. When she caught her older sister's eye, she shook her head. "I'm pretty sure he's right, Lina. But I think I know what's going on: Mama's in love."

Celina's dark eyes widened. "She w-what—

"I saw them kiss last night on the stairs. They didn't see me. She kissed him with her mouth open like she used to kiss Papi."

Heart pounding, her hand over her mouth, Celina glanced up the second story window that was Mama's bedroom. "She-she wouldn't— was all she could manage.

Javier leaned forward, gripping his temples. "Wow. Just wow," he whispered. "It's been three months, only three months. And—

"Kids? Lina, Yacque! Come inside."

When the girls and Javier arrived in the foyer, Mama and Marcos were putting on jackets, and Mama's purse was over her shoulder. "We're going down the street to meet the Gomez family for board games and dinner. Who wants to come?"

Celina alone requested to stay home. The Gomez family had four children, but none were around her age. After her family had departed, she flopped down on the couch with a copy of *Seventeen* magazine.

I wish I were as pretty as some of these girls.

Later that evening, Celina found herself in the library playing *Moonlight Sonata*. When she was done, she wandered down the hall and into Mama's bedroom, even though she knew she shouldn't. She stood and stared at the king-sized bed for a long time then dismissed the nagging thought in her mind. At that moment, she noticed a drawer barely open in the bottom of Mama's dresser. As she reached down to close it, she first opened it just an inch further. She furrowed her brow at the small wooden box inside. Mama's name was carved on the top in Cyrillic. The box was locked with a tiny padlock.

Where's the friggin' key?

Celina began to rummage through the other drawers and finally found it tucked into a sock. Sitting down on the bed, she opened the box. Her eyes widened and she smiled at the treasures hidden there. A kerchief, the lace edges now yellowed with age was the first thing she took out and set beside her. Mama's initials, in Cyrillic, were stitched in pale blue in one corner. A *mezuzah* came next then a wooden pin, hand painted with tiny flowers and greenery, three pale blue flowers pressed and still retaining their color beautifully. Lastly, Celina lifted out a thick, black journal. She cocked her head at what was under the journal. Mama's wedding ring from Papi. Tears filled Celina's eyes as she slipped it onto her finger. Her chin quivered. She angrily swiped at her eyes and put it back. She then removed a thick envelope, resealed with tape. Celina could not read the big words of the return address, although she could see it was from an address in Texas. On the back of the envelope was some Russian writing in Mama's familiar hand. Celina shrugged as she put it back unopened. Lastly, she took out a single document, folded in half. She was surprised when she unfolded it: *her* birth certificate. Celina's mouth fell open as she read:

Celina Iliana Catarina Natyscha Zagoradniy
DOB: 5/15/1990
Birthplace: Galveston, TX
Mother: Alexei Zagoradniy
Father: Martinez Pancorro

Speechless for once, her heart thudding wildly in her chest, Celina sat forward, eyes wide, pressing her fingers against her temples. "What the— she halted then reread the words on the birth certificate. "Wait a sec—what's this? Papi's my father! This has gotta be a mistake! This isn't right."

In shock, Celina picked up the black journal. Her heart sank when she saw it was written in Russian in Mama's smooth script. "Oh boy, this is *really* gonna take some time."

Glancing at the clock on the nightstand, she figured she would have at least an hour or two before the family returned. As she opened the journal, a small wallet-sized photo fell from between the pages and fluttered to the floor. Celina furrowed her brow when she saw the unfamiliar face. It was a young, Mexican man, no older than twenty. She gasped when she realized she was nearly his spitting image. Though handsome with dark, swarthy features and curly, midnight black hair, his partial grin was self-satisfied and arrogant, his penetrating black eyes cold. On the back of the picture was scrawled in unfamiliar hand: Martie Pancorro.

"No, no, no, no!" Celina kept repeating to herself. "I-I— She turned the pages in the black journal. She read only a little here and there because it was quite a chore deciphering the Cyrillic cursive. Finally, she arrived at a page dated 4/28.

Dearest Tatiana,
Praise God! I am finally going to marry my darling Martie, the love of my life. We will be wed tomorrow . . . It saddens me not to be wed under a chuppah, but as long as I can marry in a holy place . . . I'm so happy,

dearest friend . . . I shall write no more tonight. Until tomorrow when we meet again.
    Alexei

For over an hour, unable to stop, Celina struggled and fumbled her way through the haze of Russian writing. The pages that followed the happy entry contained mostly rushed, cryptic messages until Celina arrived at a shocking entry:

Dearest Tatiana,
    So sorry I am to have neglected you for so long. Martie comes home drunk and angry at night. When he's drunk, he beats me and for days after I can barely stand. He's so strong! I have bruises all over . . . I hurt so badly. I can tell only you, Tatiana. Even my dear friend, Shalib, I can't tell. I hide everything with makeup . . . so frightened of Martie now. He hits me so hard I'm afraid he will kill me . . . I was such a fool, Tatiana. I barely knew him, but he made me feel so loved and special. Not like my father who cared little for me. Now he hates me . . . I don't know why. I've nowhere to turn and no one to turn to.

Stunned, anger mounting, Celina forced herself to read on. Entry after entry detailed Martie Pancorro's horrifying cruelty.
    "*Hijo de—* her voice trailed off, "how could anyone hurt Mama like that?" She then turned several pages to an entry dated 10/12:

Dear Tatiana,
    Martie left yesterday for El Paso with his drinking buddies. They'll be gone as long as they have money. All he does anymore is drink and rage. . . today I saw a doctor because I've been so sick. Oh, dear God have mercy, I'm pregnant! I've been pregnant for about eight weeks. I can hardly believe Martie's beatings haven't killed it, but when he returns, I know he'll end up killing it. I want my baby, but if my child is to survive, I must leave. My papa often said that a good Jewish girl does not leave her husband. Maybe I'm

no longer a good Jewish girl, but I'll soon be a mother, a state that transcends religion and teaches one what is truly important . . . I will not let him kill my child. I care for this baby more than religion, more than duty, perhaps more than God. If this makes me bad, so be it.

Yours,

Alexei

By now, Celina's head ached, but she was riveted. Mama ran away the next day and traveled for many weeks to Galveston. Here she found work and waited out her pregnancy.

May 16:

My daughter was born yesterday. She's more beautiful than I ever dreamed possible, but she looks so much like Martie. My little girl is my forever reminder of what I had hoped to one day forget. I named her Celina, Celina Iliana Catarina Natyscha Zagoradniy. I couldn't give her Martie's name. . . too painful for me at present and for her later on. I've decided to keep her and try to love her . . . but I hardly know how I shall bear it. I'll be looking into Martie's eyes through my daughter every day for the rest of my life.

Celina could scarcely force herself to read further but she was glad she did. A beautiful entry detailed Mama's meeting and befriending a poor young truck driver from Mexico. He was slowly dying of a degenerative heart condition, and his name was Giacamo Montoya. Celina hardly realized she was holding her breath as she read on. Papi's declarations of love for both Mama and Celina, his proposal, their marriage. "Little Celina deserves the most loving family. You and I can give her that . . . you and I together," he had told Alexei when he proposed.

As she read these words, Celina had to blink back tears. "Papi loved me. He didn't care that I wasn't his for real. He just wanted to love me, he called me his warrior princess. He loved me for real. Why didn't Mama ever tell me? Was she ever gonna tell me? I didn't think Mama ever lied, but she's been lying for thirteen years." Tears filled her eyes as a realization flooded her mind. "I-I never should have been born. Am I still just a reminder of this guy who kept beating her up until she ran away? What does she think of me now? She didn't want me then. Why did she lie?"

Unable to read any further, Celina sat in shocked silence for a long time. For some reason, Milagros's restaurant kept pushing its way back into her thoughts. Again, she rummaged through the box and finally picked up the picture of her biological father. She studied it quizzically for a moment and then snapped her fingers. "The drunk!" she exclaimed, *"That* was my *father!* No wonder Mama was so scared; she was scared Tío was going to find out! Or I would!"

Her mind reeling, Celina tucked her birth father's picture into the pocket of her shorts and carefully rearranged the other items in the box. Lastly, she placed the diary on top and returned the little box to its hiding place. Mama's awful secret.

Her thoughts troubled and Martie Pancorro's picture burning a hole in her pocket, Celina left the room and made her way slowly downstairs. Suddenly, she heard Chaim calling her from the foyer. "Lina, we're home, and Tío's taking us kids to the pool! Hurry and get your stuff and we'll meet you in the car!"

For a moment, Celina pushed aside all thoughts of Martie Pancorro as she rushed excitedly upstairs to get her suit and towel for an evening at the Santa Fe YMCA pool.

Despite her efforts to keep it hidden even from herself, Celina looked at Martie Pancorro's picture almost daily. The more she studied him, the more real her startling resemblance to him became. Their eyes were nearly identical, and she had, without a doubt, inherited his mouth and wild, black hair. Now that Celina knew the man in the restaurant was not simply an obnoxious drunk, she felt terribly se. *What if he finds out about me? Even worse, what if he already knows?* Celina hated these intrusive thoughts, but she could not brush them aside. Ever since reading

Mama's horrible diary entries, she had not been able to shake the awful feelings of fear and dread that hung over her heart like storm clouds.

Life as the stepdaughter of a wealthy attorney was so much easier than their previous lives, Celina had to admit, and it was so nice to no longer have to work for the cranky, stingy Tío Aleman, but Celina missed Papi terribly.

Sure, we were poor, but were still so happy, the eleven of us. Mama always said that we didn't need money to be happy. We held hands and smiles that all the money in the world couldn't buy. Why couldn't God make Papi better? I know Marc's good to us, but Papi loved us."

Besides these thoughts, Celina worried that Marcos might find out about the diary and the secrets of the past. Had Mama or Papi ever told Marcos? How much, if anything, did he know about what had happened all those years ago?

As time passed, Celina was dismayed when she realized Yacqueline was right. Mama was in love. Although she tried not to notice, she could not ignore the looks and kisses they tried to hide from the children.

But I saw them, and Yacque's seen them. They're in love. I've never seen Mama kiss anyone like that except Papi. Why? He's barely been gone a year. And this wasn't supposed to happen; this wasn't about love. Marc said so. They lied. I could—

"Lina?"

Celina started and looked up fearfully. She relaxed when she saw Mama standing in Celina's bedroom doorway. "Y-yeah, Mama?"

"The others just left to go play at the ball diamond down the street, and Elian and Little Man are napping. Would you come to my room for a chat? It's been a while since we've had time to talk alone."

Heart thudding, Celina reluctantly followed her mother down the plush hallway carpet to her bedroom. *Does she know that I know?*

But Mama only smiled as she patted the bed beside her, and Celina sat down. Alexei spoke, gently, "Something's bothering you, Lina."

Celina's breath came in heavy gasps. *She knows.*

"Mama, I-I'm sorry I—"

"Don't be sorry, *dochka*. You've done nothing wrong. Oh, my sweet," She gathered Celina close against her breast, "I think I know. It's Marc, isn't it?"

Celina closed her eyes hard as relief flooded over her. Mama did not know her secret.

"You wonder how I know? *Dochka*, you've been so quiet these last weeks, and you're barely eating. What is it?"

Celina shrugged, "*Ne'at chevo*. It's nothing."

"Oh, Lina, talk to me. Let out your worries and feelings, even if they are anger. It's ok. It really is ok. So much happened so quickly, and we barely took the time to talk to you children. I should've."

"It's okay," Celina shrugged again, "I get it."

"Do you? Do you realize how much we needed Marcos? I had to. I had to put aside my pride somehow or we, me and you children, I'd lose you all, we'd lose each other. I never wanted to tell you this, but I was starving myself. I hated so much the thought of my children going hungry. I went without. Maybe too much, too often. And it wore down my body. I'm not strong enough to work like that anymore; I never will be, Dr. Gabrielle says. And both Jackie and Little Man's births were way too complicated— her voice trailed off. "We needed Marcos, my Lina. You children especially."

"You too."

"Yes, me too. But what do you mean by that?"

"Don't pretend, Mama. I've seen you two together when you think no one's looking. You've kissed him the same way you used to kiss Papi. You're in love, aren't you? You're in love with Tío."

For a long moment, Alexei stared down at her hands before nodding her curly head as she looked up. "*Da*, I am. *We* are."

"Mama why? It wasn't supposed to be this way. I knew you were starving, Chaim did too. We heard what the doctor said. That's why we went looking for more work, Chaim and me and Javier and the girls, we wanted to prove to you we could take care of our family, and you wouldn't have to work hard anymore. Why didn't you just tell us? Isn't that what families for? To look after each other? You always told us that. But you don't really believe it, do you? I wish you would have trusted us. Me and Chaim and Javier and Yacque, we could have taken care of you and the little ones, and we could've done it without anyone's charity! Heck, Mama, I can pass for 16 if I try; it's all in the way you talk. And there's Chaim, he's big and strong and really smart too. We could have done it together, all of it, but you didn't give us the chance!"

Tears sparkled in Alexei's dark eyes as she tenderly touched her daughter's cheek. "My little woman," she whispered, brokenly. "Oh, Lina, I'm *so* proud of you, all of you. You've always been such hard workers. Something you inherited from both your Papi and me."

Celina's stomach dropped. *I didn't inherit a dang thing from Papi. I wish I had. He was the best father ever.*

Mama did not appear to notice her daughter's discomfort as she continued, softly, "But that was my problem too. You're still children, yet you and the girls had already quit school to work full-time."

Celina's eyes grew wide. "You were upset about that, I know, but how *did* you find out? Did someone from school rat us out? We didn't even have a phone."

Mama's smile was gentle yet knowing. "You accidentally let that slip when you were talking to Marc, and he told me. That's when I knew, when I knew for sure. That's when I knew I was losing my children. I-I couldn't let that happen, my Lina. Your father didn't finish third grade. Your abuela Auria had too many children and no father for any of them. Your papi was the eldest and she needed his help with the little ones so she could work. You also know I was taken out of school by your *dedyushka* when I was just eleven. In that sense, your papi and I never had a chance, but I promised him before he died that each one of our children would graduate high school. You all were just growing up too fast, and that was my fault. My pride, mine and your father's. Lina, as much as I dearly loved and still love

The Music of What Happens

your papi, he was wrong about some things. He was too proud, and I became the same way. And our pride turned to selfishness. Also, you know that we could not afford to properly care for Elian. He needed so much more than I could give him no matter how hard I worked. *Da*, we needed Marcos."

For a long time, Celina was silent. *It wasn't supposed to be this way. It wasn't. What next, are we going to be expected to call him papa? No friggin' way!*

"And you're in love with him?" Celina shook her head, knowing the answer.

"Lina, I'm pregnant."

Celina gasped and Alexei halted as if realizing she had just disclosed a forbidden secret.

"Mama, no!" Celina cried, in horror. "You-you can't be." Tears sprang to her eyes. "It wasn't supposed to be like this!"

"Lina, *puzhalste* hear me—

But she was not given a chance to finish. Celina rushed from the room and down the hall, slamming her bedroom door behind her. Flinging herself onto her bed, she began to sob, bitterly. "Why? Oh, why? Marcos' baby? No, I hate this baby, and I hate Marcos!"

Finally, she cried herself to sleep.

"So, looks like we're going to have an addition to the family next year," Marcos smiled as he reached for Mama's hand at dinner the next evening. Celina's stomach dropped. She looked down at her plate, concentrating on the tiny trickle of gravy beside a brown flower stem on her plate. She could feel Chaim's eyes on her, though she stubbornly refused to look up.

"Your mama and I are expecting a little surprise middle of next year."

Celina finally glanced up, surprised to find Mama watching her intently. Celina ignored her and turned in the direction of the other children who all appeared as shocked as she had been yesterday.

Mama still has her own room. I didn't even know they were together.

The little ones were excited. A new baby in the home had always been a joyous occasion to be celebrated. "What's it gonna be, a boy or girl?" Little Man squealed, "I wanna baby sister so I'm not the baby anymore."

Mama and Marcos laughed. "Well, whatever it is, son, we'll all love it very much, won't we?"

Although the older children, Celina included, politely congratulated Mama and Marcos, Celina had no idea what her siblings were thinking. Besides the initial shock on their faces, none reflected anything more.

Marcos also had some news specifically for Elian. He and Mama had engaged a semi-retired, Jewish violin teacher to come to their house weekly to tutor Elian.

"G-gee, Tío," Elian's gaunt face broke into a huge grin, "*muchas gracias!* I-I can't wait!"

Celina grinned to herself. *Yeah, right! That tutor better be dang good, or Eli'll be teaching him before long!*

While she and Yacqueline did the supper dishes and cleaned the kitchen, as usual, Yacqueline's small hand, wet with soapy water, lightly touched hers. Celina looked up as she passed a pot to her sister to be rinsed. Yacqueline, her eyebrow lifted, tilted her head in the direction of the stairs. Celina knew her sister was requesting a chat. She nodded as they finished the dishes.

After dinner cleanup, Celina met Yacqueline in her room. The younger girl stared down at her hands for a long time.

"What is it, sis? I never seen you look like this?" Celina sucked in air sharply when Yacqueline looked up at her, tears standing in her dark eyes.

She never cries. She never ever cries. Oh, what's wrong?

Yacqueline impulsively leaned her head on her sister's shoulder. "Lina," she wept, "I think Mama's gonna die! Remember what the doctor said before? After Little Man? She's not supposed to have any more babies."

Celina's eyes widened at this. She had forgotten, but Yacqueline had not. She swallowed hard. *So, why'd they do it? That's about as dumb as me getting pregnant. And I didn't even know that—*

Yacqueline cried to her sister, "I don't want Mama to die! Why didn't she listen to the doctor? Lina, we already lost Papi; we *can't* lose Mama too! I mean, what-what—

Heart pounding, Celina wrapped an arm around her distraught sister's shoulder, "I know. *Yo sé.*"

"But what do we do? She can't die. We'd have to go to California or something and live with Papi's, other brothers! If they'd even let us! We'd all be split up! Lina, I-I—

"Breathe, sis, breathe. You're totally getting ahead of yourself," Celina turned to fully face her sister. She gripped her shoulders, not roughly. "Don't freak out on me, you can do this! Just breathe. Mama's gonna be okay; *we're* gonna be okay . . ."

She released Yacqueline's shoulders as she gradually calmed down and her breathing returned to normal. "Sis, I'll talk to Mama. I don't know what to say but I'll figure it out. You're right. I'd forgotten. But we got this, right? We'll take good care of Mama and each other, right? We always have."

Eyes still filled with tears, Yacqueline nodded.

"We got this?" Celina repeated, looking deep into her sister's dark eyes.

It's not fair she has to worry like this. Yacque's always done the taking-care, and she's only ten. If only Mama—

"We got this," Yacqueline murmured in assent, pushing her long black braid over her shoulder. She gulped and nodded, determinedly, "We got this."

Later that evening, Celina sat alone in her room. Marcos had taken most of the children to the mall arcade, but Mama had asked Celina to remain behind and help with Elian and Little Man.

Like I'd want to go anyway. All she could think of was what Yacqueline had reminded her of just an hour ago. She could not get out of her mind the ominous words Dr. Gabrielle had told Mama four years ago: *"Alexei, don't ever get pregnant again. It'll kill you."*

CHAPTER 5

Back to School

After supper, Celina ran Elian's evening bath while Yacqueline vacuumed the living room and minded Little Man.

When her seven-year-old brother finished bathing, Celina gave his thick mop of curls a final rinse and then waited outside for him to put on his pajamas and brush his teeth. Lost in thought, her eyes widened when she heard a soft sob from behind the door. Heart in her throat, she opened the door to find her sickly brother sitting cross-legged on the floor, his head in his hands. When the door opened, he looked up, tired, dark eyes startled.

"Eli, what—

Elian slowly got to his feet, and Celina caught him close in her arms. The little boy wept into her shoulder as though his little heart would break.

Ay Dios mío, he never cries. He's always been so strong inside; he's like Yacque-he never cries!

Although Elian was small for his age, so was Celina, and he was almost too heavy for her to lift. She struggled to her feet, her brother clinging to her neck, crying. She carried him down the hall to the bedroom he shared with Evangelo and Little Man. Setting him on the bed, Celina cradled his face in her hands as she sat on her heels in front of him.

"Eli, what's wrong?" she choked hard, desperate not to cry herself, "what's wrong? Does your chest hurt? Does—

"Lina," Elian gulped, between more tears, "am-am I gonna d-die?"

"What the— no way, Sunbeam! What dumb bunny told you that?"

"L-last year in J-Javier's math class, remember that bad boy, Carlos? H-he died!"

"But you-you're *not* a bad boy!"

"Then-then why am I always sick?" Elian wept into his hands, "why ain't I like you all? Lina, I'm so tired of it all. I want to run too. I want to play and go to places like you all. If I'm not a bad boy, then why am I sick all the time? Doesn't God love me at all? I-I try so hard to always be a g-good boy. I— oh, Lina, I don't wanna die! I don't wanna go down in the d-dark in a big wood box like Papi did; I ain't so brave like Papi was."

By this time, Elian, who preferred to speak primarily Russian, was switching back and forth between Russian and Spanish so rapidly that Celina could scarcely keep up with him. She pressed him close in her arms. His slight frame trembled. She blinked back tears over his shoulder.

"Oh, Eli, you're not a bad boy and you're *not* gonna die. I don't know why you're sick, but I know that if you *did* die, you'd go right to heaven to be with Papi and you'd play the violin for God and the blessed Virgin. You'd make people smile there, the way you do here."

Elian wiped his eyes with the back of his hand as he surveyed his sister thoughtfully. "You-you always know how to make b-bad stuff feel better, Lina. *Spiseeba.*" He hugged her again, resting his curly head on her shoulder. Celina closed her eyes as she held him.

God, please don't make a liar out of me. We all know how sick Eli is, please don't take him away like Papi. We need him, and he needs us.

Now that her brother was calmer, Celina set up his breathing treatment and laid out his array of medications. As he dutifully gulped his pills, washing them down with drinkable yogurt, she readied his heart monitor, a small device he wore through the night, and his C-Pap that would alert the family in case he stopped breathing. She shook her head to herself. No seven-year-old should be relying on so much medication and devices to keep him alive.

Alive sure, but not even healthy. And he's too smart for his own good; he knows he's gonna die sooner than the rest of us. I just hope that . . .

"Lina?"

Celina blinked, startled out of her reverie. She forced a smile as she tucked the warm quilt around her brother. He sighed, wheezing, slightly. "C-could you sing *Holy Water puzhalste?*"

Celina ran her fingers through her brother's curls as, soft and low, she sang Elian's favorite hymn. Before the song was over, he had drifted into a peaceful sleep. Celina startled at the sound of her name behind her. She turned to see Mama beckoning her from the doorway.

Following her mother out of the bedroom, she turned once more to her brother's bed. She shook her head sadly then followed her mother down the hall to her bedroom.

Mama sat on the bed, cross-legged, as she folded laundry, fresh from the dryer, and Celina joined her. When they were finished, Mama leaned forward and stroked back a long curl that had fallen forward into Celina's eyes.

"Lina, I know what I said yesterday came as quite a shock. I should have come up with a better time, a better way to say it. I'm sorry for that. But you're my big girl now, and I'm going to need your help."

Celina furrowed her brow at this. "Mama, I thought you weren't supposed to—

"I know. I know I wasn't supposed to get pregnant again after all the complications from delivering Jackie and Little Man. I know, and I know you're worried. But this child was meant to be, not planned at all but meant to be. You know," Alexei sat back against the headboard, "after Little Man, it didn't matter that I shouldn't have children anymore. It didn't matter at all. But now it matters. Besides adopting little Katherine, Marc's never had a child of his own. I want to give him that. I love him that much even after being married only a few months. I don't know exactly how it happened that I've fallen so hard for him, it just did. We have no control over who we love, only what we choose to do with it. Sometimes I think it's because I came to realize that it wasn't just a sense of duty that made him propose marriage to a woman he didn't love and take on nine children that were not his own. It was selfless, genuine caring and partly because of this, I've grown to love him deeply. Almost as much as I loved your father. In some ways, as much. But I'll be needing help. I don't want to worry you even more, but I'm gonna need you all so I don't end up in the hospital for a long time. Will you help me, *malaynkia?*"

Celina stared down at her hands for a long time.

It wasn't supposed to be this way, but I totally won't let Mama down.

She nodded. "We've always taken care of each other. You know you can count on it, Mama."

Alexei sighed as she smiled her thanks. "I know, Lina. And I know you're angry that things turned out this way. Sometimes life doesn't turn out as we planned or expected. I did not expect to love Marc; I didn't expect him to love me, and I certainly didn't plan— she shrugged—but it was God's will. Not planned but truly loved. This child will have all the love in the world. I know I'm not healthy enough to be pregnant, but this baby was meant to be."

"Sure Mama." Celina exhaled heavily.

"And Marc," Alexei continued, "please give him a chance; he loves you all. I understand why you and Chaim and Javier hold back. Yacque's trying but she holds back too. I understand, my sweet one. This is all so new. It's okay to give it time. But please don't close your heart in anger. Don't be afraid to love; a heart as big as yours always has room for one more. Believe me, he's not trying to take your papi's place in your heart; he's looking for his own. Rest in that, my little one, rest in that. It'll take time but it's gonna be okay."

Celina nodded thoughtfully but did not reply.

"Now there's one more thing we need to discuss, and that's my pregnancy. I saw Dr. Gabrielle yesterday. She told me that if I'm to safely carry the baby to term, I must be on bed rest for most of my pregnancy. Marc says we can hire some help until after the baby's born if I think we need it. However, I don't believe we need to waste money when I have far superior help here already. Lina, I know you, Chaim, Javier, your sisters, and even Jackie are all capable enough to be a tremendous help to Marc and me. Can I depend on you, Linochka?"

Celina's heart swelled with pride at Mama's compliment. She too knew that there was no need to bring a stranger in to keep house and care for Mama. She and her siblings would be more than able to manage the household with some help from Marcos until Mama was well again after the baby.

I'm not just mad, I'm totally pissed! Why did this have to happen?

Despite her feelings, Celina was determined not to let her mother down. "Sure thing, Mama. Don't you worry. I'll talk to the others. We'll take care of everything."

In response, Mama opened her arms and Celina moved close. In her haunting contralto, Alexei sang the Russian lullaby she had sung so many times since her children were babies. Sleepy, Celina rested her head on Mama's breast, and she rocked her daughter gently as she sang.

Yeah, I'm mad at Tío. I'm just plain mad. But I won't let Mama down. Family's still family. Of course, I'll take care of her the best I can. And-and this baby too.

Wrapped in Mama's arms, Celina drifted off to sleep amid the haunting strains of the lullaby and began dreaming, dreaming about a little boy with Marcos' mocha eyes and wavy black hair. The next thing she knew, she was lifted into strong arms and carried down the hall. She tried to open her eyes, but they were too heavy. A warm quilt was drawn over her and from a distance, a deep resonant voice whispered. "Sleep well, Lina. I love you."

Although it was not easy to accept that Mama was having a baby, Celina was determined to keep her promise. School began again in September. Marcos and Mama consulted with Dr. Grosvenor about the possibility of Elian beginning school that fall. Despite some improvements in his condition, the doctor still ruled public school as a negative, so Elian, once again, stood on the front porch with Mama and watched longingly as his other siblings merrily started off for their first day of a new school year. He would be tutored by their mother and stepfather so that he would be ready to attend school at grade level whenever his health permitted it.

This year, for the first time, the Montoya children wore brand new school clothes and carried real lunchboxes and backpacks. When they arrived at Santa Fe Elementary, the building was abuzz with the general excitement and mayhem that always accompanied the start of a new year.

As the older children separated to seek out their new classrooms, Celina remained just long enough to escort Little Man to the kindergarten classroom. Little Man clutched his sister's hand tightly, bouncing up and down as he walked along beside her. Celina smiled down at the excited child.

When they arrived at his classroom, Little Man wandered about investigating the learning centers in the bright, cheery classroom. Celina could see that it took effort on his part not to touch things. She glanced at the teacher who was watching the little boy from the other side of the room. The older woman in a pinstripe suit and string of pearls finally called him to her.

A dry clean suit and pearls? In kindergarten? Good luck being covered in peanut butter and finger paint. Especially from Little Man!

Celina barely held back a snicker as she stood protectively behind her brother.

"I like to test my ESL students' English proficiency before the start of class. Not sure where this little guy was last week during that meeting."

As the teacher, who introduced herself as Mrs. Wilmar, looked down at Little Man, Celina rolled her eyes. Mrs. Wilmar did not smile back at the five-year-old, bobbing up and down, as he grinned at her. "What's your full name?" she asked, almost sharply.

Celina bit her lip when Little Man hesitated. If only she had taken a few minutes to quiz her brother once more in the English words Marcos

The Music of What Happens

had been teaching him all summer in preparation for kindergarten. The Gonzalez family did not speak English at home, and Little Man had attended a Spanish-speaking preschool program last year; he knew no English beyond the survival words Marcos had taught him recently. Celina felt like kicking herself. She could have easily given her brother a quick quiz on his English, but no, she had left poor Little Man to do the best he could on his own.

The child stared at the floor for a moment and then looked his teacher in the eye as he replied slowly but in perfect English. "My name is Immanuel Giacamo Jesus Raoul Guiellermo Montoya."

Mrs. Wilmar blinked but did not comment. "How old are you?" she asked.

Little Man did not reply but confidently held up five fingers.

"What's your dad's name?"

"Papi. But he go away to God now."

Celina glanced away, blinking back a sudden rush of tears. She then bent down to look into her brother's big, sleepy eyes. "You got this, *hermano*. I'll see you after school. Be kind to my brother please," she turned to Mrs. Wilmar as she hurried from the room and down the hall. Chaim and Javier were already at school and Celina glanced at her iPod. She had just ten minutes to be down the road to Santa Fe Middle. As she hurried down the sidewalk, Celina smiled down at her brand-new outfit: stonewash, flare leg jeans, a red, spaghetti strap top, edged in lace, and a black, velvet bolero. White, platform sneakers completed the ensemble. Mama had helped her tame her wild curls, and she wore a pair of rhinestone stud earrings. Celina grinned at her reflection in a small puddle beside the sidewalk.

Staci's gonna be so shocked, and she'll never be able to say I smell from wetting the bed again. Hah!

Heading down the 7th-grade hall on her way to 8th-grade hall, Celina felt suddenly overwhelmed and longed to be back in seventh grade with books, classrooms, teachers and a schedule she was familiar with. Stopping before the rows of lockers, she searched the name cards until she found one marked: ZAGORADNIY, C.

Celina fumed, inwardly, *Dumb bunnies! Won't they ever get my name right?* Pulling a black sharpie from the backpack, she flipped over the white note card and carefully wrote in block letters: MONTOYA, L.

Inside her locker, she found her schedule taped to the door. She then searched out room A3 where she would begin the day with accelerated arithmetic. When she found it, Celina stood, timidly, just inside the door. No one else was there yet, and her new teacher sat at her desk reviewing the student roll. She was probably not past thirty years old and pretty with green eyes and long blond hair pulled back in a ponytail. She smiled at her first student as Celina approached her desk.

"Good morning. It looks like you missed first-day assembly but that's okay. I'll check you in now." She picked up her pen and ran her finger down the list. "What's your name?"

"It's Lina Montoya. People try to make me say Celina Zagoradniy. No disrespect, but I don't answer to that."

Celina waited for her teacher to argue, as others had done in the past, but the teacher, who introduced herself as Mrs. Reeves, only smiled and wrote something on the roll. "Lina Montoya, I'm pleased to meet you. Please have a seat at desk ten."

Within the next few minutes, twenty-five boys and girls, most somewhat dressed up for the first day of school, swarmed into the classroom and hurried to their desks. To Celina's dismay, Staci Ainsworth's desk was right beside hers. She swallowed back an astonished snicker.

Staci in advanced math? That sure must be her daddy's doing.

The mayor's daughter wrinkled her nose. "Well, my, my, fancy little beaner, now, aren't we?"

Celina did not speak, staring straight ahead at the front of the room. Staci continued, sarcastically, "What happened to the piss-smelling rags?" When Celina still did not reply, Staci added, "So, is it true your mom was sucking up to that rich spic lawyer last spring? My daddy said Gonzalez got so drunk he married her!"

Anger boiling inside her, it was all Celina could do not to rearrange Staci's nasty face again. She knew it wouldn't do to get suspended for fighting fifteen minutes into the school year. It was also well-known throughout the city that Mayor Ainsworth had been after Marcos for years, trying to mar his professional reputation.

I don't think much of Tío right now, but I'm not getting involved in that mess, for sure!

At just that moment, Celina realized what had just happened because of her mother's remarriage. Since Mama had married Marcos, they were no longer poor. They were probably richer even than the Ainsworths. They didn't have to be afraid anymore. The relief that thought gave Celina was the best feeling she had had in years. No longer would she have to tread carefully around Staci and watch everything she said and did. She could stand up for her family without worrying about damaging consequences.

We're not trash! Celina nearly cried to herself. *We're just as good as any of them, and we got money to prove it!* The thought brought a broad grin to her face. It felt so good to be equal. Marcos was highly respected throughout the Southwest. The town trash wouldn't *dare* make trouble for his children. Until now, Celina had not realized just how much she had to thank her stepfather for.

At that moment, Staci's mean voice broke into her thoughts. "So, what are we trying to prove this year, Celina Zagoradniy? Just so you know, the rags suited you much better. At least they were real!"

Celina rolled her eyes as she spoke for the first time, with a real confidence she had never felt before. "Geez, Staci, jealous much? Just grow up. Grow up and get over yourself!"

Staci's eyes widened at the retort. "What did you say to me, you dirty wetback?"

"You heard me, Staci. Oh, and before I forget, two things." Celina added, her tone low yet icy. "You are nothing but ugly racist trash like you're fool daddy. I'm not a wetback or any of the rest of that crap you're always running your mouth about, I'm Mexican Israeli and proud of it. Second, *Miss,*" Celina made sarcastic air quotes, "Ainsworth, if you wanna keep your pretty, little face pretty, you best not stick your nose in the air at me again. Just like last spring, you stick your nose in the air with me, it's gonna get punched! We clear?"

The astonishment that covered Staci's face was reward enough for Celina. She turned away, her heart overflowing. She was truly proud of herself. Staci started to speak but fell silent as she could not find the words.

Celina smiled sweetly at the front of the room as the teacher stood.

"Eighth graders of Santa Fe Middle, welcome to a new year. I hope you're all ready to dive into your arithmetic studies with determination. Allow me to introduce myself. I am Mrs. Reeves from Philadelphia. Now let's get to work . . . Eyeing Staci and Celina especially, she added, sternly, "with no nonsense. Please open your arithmetic books to page three and complete the four corresponding pages." As the students worked, Mrs. Reeves wrote the word SILENCE at the top of the blackboard in block letters.

After math, Celina paused in the hall to consult her schedule. *Next stop: C9, Reading Support with Mr. Gallagher. Oh, joy, they put me in the reject class again!*

Celina easily found the classroom and desk five and organized her things, including her sketchbook for when things got especially boring. The other six students were already there, readying for class. Moments later, a tall, thin man of about Marcos' age entered and stood behind the desk. He had a receding hairline and a pair of tiny, thin glasses that perched on the end of his rat-like nose. Bulging, beady eyes reminded Celina of a Chihuahua. The teacher addressed the class in the highest, whiniest voice she had ever heard in a man. She and her friend, Lincoln, exchanged a wide-eyed glance and barely stifled laughter.

Lincoln, the braver of the two, waited until the teacher turned his back to call out, in an obnoxious, nasal voice, "*Yo quiero* Taco Bell!"

Celina nearly choked. Mr. Gallagher shot Lincoln a warning glance but did not speak. Lincoln leaned down to Celina and whispered. "Offer to donate to Chihuahua rescue. I dare you!"

By this time, Celina was barely holding back gale-force laughter, tears rolling down her cheeks. "Lincoln, shut up! Your big mouth is gonna get us busted!"

She turned away and pretended to be deeply attentive to her new teacher's introduction; instead, she was sketching a perfectly horrible picture of the teacher in her sketchbook. She winked at Lincoln so he would know he would be called on at recess to show off his rhyming talent by matching the sketch with a disrespectful poem. The two were famous for their line drawings with accompanying verses directed at stuffy authority figures at Santa Fe Middle. These "anonymous" drawings always ended up pinned to the bulletin board in the main hall for their classmates' amusement.

At the end of his speech, the teacher began writing simple words on the blackboard. While the teacher's back was turned, Lincoln sneaked a wrist rocket from his desk and placed a hard, little bean in it. With a wink at a fascinated Celina, he let the little bean fly! Lincoln was skillful with his slingshot, and the bean struck Mr. Gallagher squarely on his backside.

The teacher yelped and whirled angrily to face the class. "Who did that?" he demanded; his high, feminine voice filled with what Marcos liked to call "righteous indignation." The children fell silent. Celina barely suppressed the urge to burst out laughing at the sight of Lincoln's impish grin and Mr. Gallagher's furious countenance.

"Lincoln Rothmore, come here right now and bring me that slingshot!"

Lincoln paled as he stood and, carrying his beloved slingshot, made his way to the front of the room. Mr. Gallagher glared down at him. He snatched the slingshot from the boy's hand and stuffed it into a drawer in his desk. He then grabbed a notepad and scribbled on it for a moment. Lincoln glanced back at his classmates and pulled a fake sad face as he rubbed his bottom mockingly. Celina was gagging and choking into her hands trying not to laugh. Mr. Gallagher cut his eyes at her.

"Something funny, Miss Zagoradniy?"

She gulped. "N-no, sir."

Mr. Gallagher turned back to Lincoln and handed him the note. "Go to the office."

Lincoln winked at Celina as he made his way out the door. Mimicking Mr. Gallagher, he rubbed his behind as he went, causing the other children to erupt into peals of laughter. The situation only worsened when, instead of going to the office, Lincoln kept peeking back into the classroom door or turning so that only his bottom poked into the open doorway. He reached back and rubbed it again and again then peeked back in, making faces. Lincoln was a genius at making hilarious faces and the entire class was unable to stop laughing and barely able to stay in their seats.

"Lincoln, get to the office immediately!" Mr. Gallagher hollered more than once, his high-pitched voice practically squealing.

"*Yo quiero* Taco Bell!" Lincoln replied from just outside the door.

Celina buried her face in her sketchbook, keeping her head down to avoid laughing out loud and risking being sent to the office, as well. Poor Mr. Gallagher was unable to maintain order, and everyone was relieved when he finally dismissed.

"Hey, Lina!"

On her way to Biology, Celina turned to see Lincoln coming down the hall. She punched his shoulder, playfully. "You dumb bunny! You broke up the whole class!"

Lincoln grinned, brown eyes dancing with merriment. "But what a way to go! Wasn't it epic, Lina, to see that sissy jump? He just about went through the ceiling!"

Celina giggled, although she knew she shouldn't. If Mama learned of what happened, she would be in trouble. Alexei Gonzalez considered encouraging a troublemaker in his misbehavior as bad as having committed the crime yourself.

Biology was followed by lunch. Eager to see how her brothers had enjoyed their new classes, she grabbed her lunchbox and hurried to the cafeteria. Celina scanned the room and finally spotted Chaim and Javier sitting at a table near the back.

As they ate, the eldest Montoya children told each other about their morning. "I got the worst, dumb-bunny brats in two of my classes!" Javier informed them. At this, he received his older siblings' undivided attention. "Our cousins, Dulcinea and Deniz, were sent to the office this morning!"

"Oh, those two," Chaim bemoaned, between bites of his salami sandwich. "I don't think they'll ever grow up and quit acting the *tonto*! What did they do this time?"

Javier nodded and continued, "We were all reading our social studies lesson quiet as mice when Mrs. Eddy, my teacher, sat down and screamed! Literally screamed! Turns out she had sat her butt straight down on pushpins. Like the *big* kind not little tacks!"

Celina's jaw dropped. "And to think we just *have to* be related."

Chaim nodded, "Couple of major dumb bunnies, both of 'em."

Javier nodded vigorously as he continued. "Well, everyone starts laughing, right? And Mrs. Eddy's face turned tomato red, her eyes burst into flames, smoke came out of her nose—"

"And then she barfed up pea soup," Celina rolled her eyes, "what is this, the *Exorcist*? Quit dramatizing everything!"

"Good grief, zip it, Lina," Javier growled, in frustration, "can't I get through here?"

"Whatever. Just quit dragging it out. Tell us already!"

"Well, Mrs. Eddy was so mad she just about sent the whole class down the hall to purgatory. Luckily, she decided to search our desks instead. She found the pushpins in Dulcinea's desk; and that ain't all, she found a whole carton of smokes in Deniz's desk. Heck, they were just normal cigs like we all used to smoke 'til Marc read us the riot act, not weed or anything crazy."

"Turns out," Javier leaned forward so as not to have to speak loudly, and his siblings did likewise. "Dulcinea was planning to market 'em at recess for a profit, and Deniz was her patsy, of course. Mrs. Eddy grilled him about it for about five minutes, scared the crap out of him too. Yeah, that's about all it took and let's just say he was singing a *very* incriminating tune by the time she got through with him. Dulcinea though, she wouldn't confess to nothing! She just wanted that pantywaist brother of hers to get blamed for it all, even though she was the brains behind the whole thing, as usual. Total Judas! But no matter, the proof was there, and Deniz squealed like a piglet, spilled her whole plan! Mrs. Eddy was like *way* ticked off! Oh, you should have heard her talking to Principal Mihailov, acting like she'd headed some big drug bust or something over a simple carton of Marlboro's."

"Geez, what a drama queen!" Chaim put in, biting into his apple, "I never liked her last year for sure."

"Yeah, I didn't either. Total tool," Celina added.

"Well, looks like the twins got themselves suspended for like two weeks. Poor Tía Marisa!"

Celina and Chaim chuckled at this, but Javier wasn't finished. "Oh, and then in math, there was Antonio, that sneaky rat who just moved here from Tucson. You'll never guess what that dumb bunny did."

"Wait a sec," Celina broke in, "isn't he the one who made Evangelo cry at the park last week when he called him a fake Mexican?"

"That's him all right, the *pendejo*. And he's still got the black eye you gave him for that!"

With a laugh, Celina motioned for her brother to continue.

"Well," Javier returned to the topic at hand. "Antonio rubbed a huge wade of bubble gum in Cynthia Villa's hair. My math teacher, Ms. Harmon, tried to send him to the principal, but he crawled under his desk and spit at her when she tried to make him come out; he cussed her out in front of the whole class! He called her a word so bad even *I* don't dare say it out loud! He got suspended and has to have visits with the school shrink when he gets back."

"How awful!" Chaim gasped, horrified.

"Yeah, total loser," Celina agreed.

After lunch, it was time for recess. Celina and Elizaveta sat under the oak tree at the far corner of the playground and talked. They had not seen each other in nearly three months because Elizaveta had spent the summer in Tombstone visiting her grandmother.

"Wait a sec . . . it was *you* that punched Staci last spring?"

"What, you heard about it?" Celina picked at a loose thread at the bottom of her tank top.

"Well, sorta. Staci's little sister, Cyrene, is in my brother, Ramos' science class over at the elementary school. She told her friend, Mariane, who told her friend, Jassia who told Ramos' friend, Vince Cyrus-Morgan who then told Ramos that Staci had a big run-in with a Mexican girl from school. You know I'd just left for Tombstone right before school let out. I never dreamed it might be you! Well, Cyrene said Staci had this humungous black eye for weeks. She whined to her daddy, but lucky for you and your mama, Mayor Ainsworth's running for State Senate this fall, and he was having enough problems kissing up to the governor and all to worry about his kids' crap. She also whined to Cal but his creepy girlfriend, Mia, you know, the Barbie doll cheerleader with the shotgun mouth, had just dumped his stupid butt that morning. Our poor Calvie was heartbroken!"

Elizaveta pulled an exaggeratedly sad face, and Celina burst out laughing. "So, as you might have guessed," she continued, "he was locked away in his room, moping over Mia, so he wasn't any use to Staci either. Wouldn't get too wound up though, Lina," she warned in conclusion, "not sure who he's dating now, but Cal's like totally back to his old self, maybe worse. I'd watch it if I were you."

Celina simply shrugged as she stared off in the distance, absently watching a group of boys kicking around a soccer ball. She would stand up to Staci Ainsworth if it killed her.

I won't go back to groveling like a worm—I won't! I'm just as good as she is, she reminded herself, proudly, *and I'm not backing down!*

Recess was followed by English. Celina and Elizaveta were both in ESL English, so they grabbed their workbooks and hurried to room G8 together. During class, Lincoln placed a huge, mud pie he had made at recess on Ms. Keenan's chair. Ms. Keenan was none too happy to sit down in her dry-clean-only, silk skirt into a big pile of gooey mud and responded by instantly escorting the perpetual troublemaker to the office. Celina could not help but feel sorry for Principal Mihailov who appeared to be working overtime the very first day. At three o'clock, the bell sounded, signaling the end of classes.

Upon the Montoya children's arrival home, they found Mama waiting in the kitchen with warm chocolate chip cookies and cool milk, ready to hear about their day. Though just nine weeks pregnant, Alexei's beautiful olive complexion was pale and ashen, and her wide, dark eyes were cloudy with exhaustion. Celina pretended not to notice, doing her best to hide her worry.

If she looks this bad already, how's she gonna' make seven more months of this?

"... and then the twins got suspended for like ..." Javier's retelling of their cousins' antics interrupted Celina's reverie. She forced a smile as she bit into a soft, warm cookie. She chewed it slowly, her stomach feeling as though it were in knots. She glanced at Elian through the kitchen doorway. He was fast asleep on the living room sofa, an afghan drawn over his thin frame. Celina shook her head to herself.

After her siblings had eaten their fill and hurried off in their individual directions, Celina offered to clean up so her mother could rest. Little Man was already napping upstairs, and she glanced again in Elian's direction.

Reading her daughter's mind, Alexei touched her shoulder, "He's just tired. Don't worry."

"But I *am* worried, Mama. I'm worried about both of you," Celina's words ended in a tired sigh.

Before she could finish, Mama drew her into her arms, "Oh, *dochka moya*, whatever would I do without my little Lina?" When she finally broke the embrace, Alexei held Celina from her and looked into her daughter's eyes. "I promise you, Lina, it's going to be okay. I'll be okay. It's going to be harder until the baby's born, but I promise I will be well again. And in the meantime, Tío's here to help you all. You're not alone; none of you are alone. We're family. We're in this together, right?"

Celina nodded, vigorously, "Of course, Mama."

Marc's not much for family when this crap's all his fault! He should've known better!

But Celina did not voice her thoughts aloud as Mama headed upstairs for a nap before dinner. By the time the kitchen was spotless, the clock in the living room read four-thirty pm. Elian's violin tutor always arrived promptly at five. She tiptoed into the family room and gently roused her brother. Shortly thereafter, Herr Seligman arrived, and he and Elian headed to the library for their lesson.

Meanwhile, Celina dusted the living room furniture and vacuumed. As she worked, she prayed silently. *God, take care of Mama please, but especially take care of Elian.*

CHAPTER 6

Legacy

Celina brushed a stray curl out of her eyes as she scrubbed the spaghetti sauce pot with a sponge. She paused, sighing deeply.

"Something wrong, sis?"

Celina turned to see Yacqueline coming in from the dining room, arms filled with dirty dishes. Celina shook her head as she turned back to the sink. Her younger sister's hand on her shoulder stopped her.

"You're tired?" Yacqueline observed. "Want me to finish up here?"

Yeah, I wish. I am tired. And I still got homework and stuff, but Yacque already does more than her share.

"Naw, it's okay, I'll finish up these dishes. Could you fix something light that Mama can eat and some Russian tea? No sugar."

Mama was now six months pregnant, and those months had taken a toll on her. As her health deteriorated, Dr. Gabrielle had given the orders to go on bed rest or be admitted to the hospital. Celina had insisted that they could take care of Mama just fine and that it had been settled already. As she carried the tray with a small bowl of vanilla pudding and a mug of hot tea upstairs to Mama's room, she swiped at the beads of perspiration on her forehead.

"Man, that kitchen gets hot," she whispered to herself. "Hey, Mama," she said, softly, as she appeared in Alexei's bedroom doorway.

The Music of What Happens

Alexei's dark eyes brightened as her daughter came to sit on the bed beside her. She set aside her book. Her smile vanished however when Celina offered the tray.

"I brought your supper. Vanilla pudding that Yacque made and Russian tea. How's that?"

"Thank you, *malaynkia,*" she sighed, "I'll have a bit of tea for now."

Celina's eyes widened at this. Mama had said this too many times in the last few days to suit her.

"Mama, what—no—y-you gotta' eat! Dr. Gabrielle said you lost weight again at your last appointment. That can't be good for that kid."

"I can't, Lina. It's pointless." Alexei sighed again, "I'll just bring it right back up again." She closed her eyes and leaned back against her pillows.

Celina sucked in air sharply and placed a hand on her arm. When Mama looked up, she spoke sternly, the way Alexei spoke to her when she meant business. "Now, look here, Mama, you *have to* eat. It's not good for you to lose more weight, that's what the doctor said. You're just gonna get worse and then they'll put you in the hospital, and me and Yacque can't take care of you right if you're in the hospital. Now try—Celina dipped the spoon into the bowl and held it out, "*puzhalste?*"

After a long silence, Mama nodded, "I'll try." When she had finished a portion of the bowl, Celina helped her sip some tea.

It's not much, Celina told herself, *but a little food for that kid's better than nothing.*

Picking up the tray, she stood to leave, but Mama reached for her hand. "Tell me what's been happening lately."

At her mother's invitation, Celina lay down beside her. "We're all doing pretty good, I guess. Chaim's new glasses weren't working so well for him, so Tío Marc took him back to the eye doctor for better ones. Was he ever happy? He can finally see the board clear as day from the back of the room. Javier got an A on both his math test and, can you believe it, his *spelling* test last Friday. He's *still* bragging about it!" As she warmed to her subject, Celina's demeanor lost some of its gloom. "You know Yacque's as good as gold. She looks after Little Man by herself and does more of the cooking and cleaning than I do. I don't have to tell that girl anything!"

Mama smiled, and Celina continued. She told how Soledad had become the world's worst brat since their mother had been forced to take to her bed. Celina and Mama laughed together at a funny story of Jackie and his first "girlfriend." She mentioned Evangelo's exceptional performance in T-Ball, shared that Elian's health seemed to be holding its own for now, and that, the other day, Herr Seligman had related to Marcos that, in his professional opinion, the boy was a definite violin prodigy. Upon hearing this, Alexei's eyes filled with tears of joy, pride, and love.

"Oh, and Little Man's doing great in kindergarten. He's super smart. He's even started correcting *my* English when we do his spelling homework. He can say so many words and he's only been in school for five months. He can already spell his first and last name and count almost to 100 in English with no mistakes."

Alexei smiled and wrapped an arm around her daughter. "I'm so pleased you're all doing so well. I can hardly wait until I can be back downstairs with you all."

Celina sighed, inwardly. The last thing she wanted to talk about was her stepfather, but she was sure her mother would ask. "You see Marc at night, but he might not have told you he misses your cooking. He won't eat my cooking—he's on a strict diet."

Alexei's dark eyes widened, concerned. "A diet? Uhm, do you know what kind of diet?"

"Simple. No toxic waste."

Mama laughed as she rumpled her daughter's curls. "My goofy girl."

Before her mother could ask more questions, Celina stood quickly, "I'd better have Eli get in the tub, it's nearly his bedtime."

Without a backward glance, she strode abruptly from the room and downstairs. After Elian, whose bedtime was earlier than the two youngest boys due to his illness, was in the bathtub, Celina called Jackie and Soledad to the table to do their homework. She rolled her eyes as her youngest sister complained that she wanted to finish her puzzle upstairs before bed.

"Sol, *por favor* stop whining! Homework happens every night. You're nine years old! Get used to it! You wouldn't dare act like this if Mama or Tío was here."

"Well, they're not here, and I'm tired of you always acting like a grownup lately and being so bossy!"

Celina threw up her hands as she stalked from the kitchen. "Fine! Get an F on your history! See if I care!" Out of the corner of her eye, she watched her sister and was relieved when she sat down at the table and slammed open her textbook, nose wrinkled in disgust.

As she vacuumed the living room, Celina fumed, *If it weren't for Tío, Mama wouldn't be pregnant and sicker n' a dog! The stupid jerk didn't give a crap if he got her pregnant when he knew how bad it could be. Estúpido pendejo!*

Even as she thought these things, Celina knew she should be ashamed. *I get that they had to get married, I do. I get it. But it doesn't mean he and Mama had to fall in love, did it? And it sure doesn't mean they had to have a baby!*

As Celina came down the stairs from putting Elian to bed and Evangelo and Little Man in the tub, Marcos arrived home. As usual, he hurried upstairs to see his wife and then came into the kitchen where Celina and Yacqueline were packing lunchboxes for the next day.

"Hey girls," he said, softly.

"Hey, Tío," Yacqueline smiled, returning the fist bump he offered.

"Your supper's on the stove," Celina motioned to a covered plate of spaghetti. She glanced at Marcos out of the corner of her eye. He uncovered his plate and she noted how he sighed ever so slightly.

Tío and the kids must be sick of spaghetti by now. I know I am. But what could she do? Besides beans and Spanish rice, it was the only meal Celina could prepare without a catastrophe. Yacqueline was a better cook than her older sister but as the Montoya's always had limited food to work with, even she wasn't terribly experienced.

Celina turned to leave the kitchen when Marcos stopped her. "I have something for you."

"Well, I should make sure Evangelo and Little Man are in bed," Yacqueline countered as she slipped out of the kitchen.

Curious, Celina then followed Marcos into the dining room and sat down at the table across from him. Marcos pulled a small white box tied with an old red ribbon from the pocket of his suit jacket. As he passed it to her, Celina's heart pounded, and her eyes went wide as she recognized the shaky handwriting on top as Papi's. It simply read LINA. With trembling fingers, she untied the ribbon and gingerly lifted the lid. On a piece of cotton fluff lay a small, bronze cross with the figure of Christ strung on a tarnished, bronze chain.

In awe, Celina gazed down at it for a long moment before looking up into her stepfather's face. "P-Papi's crucifix," she breathed, "I remember the story. Papi only ever met his father once. He was eleven like Javier. Abuelita Gutierrez got a letter from Abuelo Montoya. He was dying in prison in Juarez and wanted to meet his son. Papi traveled to Juarez with a priest. Abuelo gave this to him before he died. It's all he ever had of his father's." She looked up quickly. "I-I thought it went in the coffin with him. W-where'd you get it?"

"He-he gave it to me before he died. He wanted you to have it when . . . when you proved yourself."

"But I haven't done anything."

"You've done more than you realize, Lina," Marcos replied, seriously, "you've kept our home running while your mama's been sick, and you've taken good care of her and the little ones. On top of that, Ms. Moreno and Mr. Gallagher told me last night at the PT conference how hard you've been working on your reading and spelling. Lina, you've earned this. Your father would be so proud of you; he *is* proud of you."

Celina smiled as she fingered the dangling cross. Marcos reached across the table and touched her shoulder. Celina smiled awkwardly as she moved back just out of reach.

"I understand, Lina. I know. I lost my wife and my daughter. I know what you're feeling."

Celina stared down at her lap, her fingers wrapped around the cross. *I want to love Tío again. I want us to be close like we used to be. But it-it wasn't supposed to be like this. He wasn't supposed to take Papi's place like this. And what'll happen when he finds out about Martie Pancorro? It's not worth it—*

Marcos' voice then broke into her reverie. "Do you know what, *nena?*" He waited until Celina looked up and then continued, purposefully, "Freedom was waiting for me. I couldn't see it."

When Celina saw the tears glistening in Marcos' eyes, she immediately looked down. *Why does it make me so uncomfortable to see him cry when I wish I could cry right now? I know what he feels, but he doesn't know my secret, and I don't know what he'd do if he did know.*

Marcos gulped as he continued. "I-I couldn't see past their graves. I couldn't stop long enough to say goodbye and— his husky voice trailed off. "I drank myself into oblivion and worked myself sick, and the only person I hurt was me. Elessa and Katherine are happy with God. They wouldn't have wanted that for me. Elessa would've wanted me to be happy again. Like we were every time I sat in the concert halls in New York and Spain and Boston and listened to her play those grand pianos in front of crowds of hundreds. She played like you do and like Elian does, with her *whole* heart. But Lina, before I could claim freedom, I had to say goodbye. I had to let her and Katherine go. I had to give love another chance."

"I know that my marrying your mama changed everything. I know it's hurt our relationship. Oh, but Lina, she's taught me to love again something I thought would never happen; she's taught me not to be so afraid. Just her being, her gentle words, her touch, her love. She's bringing my heart back to life when I thought it was dead and buried with my dead wife and child. She even hung their pictures for me along the stairway walls with you children's pictures."

Celina nodded, briefly. She had noticed.

"Look, a part of me will always love and remember them, just as you should always love and remember your papi. But life still moves on, and so must you."

When Celina looked away, Marcos caught her hand across the table, causing her to startle. "Lina," he said, hoarsely, "your father's not coming back, no matter how much you and the others want him to."

Anger seething inside her, Celina spat through clenched teeth, "I don't have time for this!"

Marcos swallowed hard but did not let go of her hand. Drawing a ragged breath, Celina sat back down. "I'm not trying to seem uncaring. I loved Giac too. Dear God, I loved my best friend, but Lina, he's gone. I'm alive, and I'm here for you. No, I'm not your real father but I would like to think of you as my daughter. Lina, answer me this: what's wrong with having two fathers who both love you and who you are free to love? What've you to lose?"

Celina was silent for a long time, her head spinning. *I've got three!* She felt like screaming, *my real father doesn't even know I exist! I can't take any more of this. I hate the secrets! I'm sick of all the lying!*

"I gotta check on the kids, Tío."

Abruptly she left the dining room and stomped up the stairs. Angry and miserable, she was relieved to see everyone in bed asleep except for Chaim who was finishing his homework. He was so engrossed in his history textbook that he did not notice Celina standing in his doorway for a minute, desperately wanting to talk but at the same time, what was the point? Papi was still gone. Elian was still sick. Mama and Marcos were still in love. A baby was still on the way and the secrets of the past were still just three doors down the hall.

Before long, Mama increased in her pregnancy. The continuous vomiting ceased, and she was even gaining a little weight. When she was in her eighth month, Dr. Gabrielle gave the okay for her to leave her bed at times as long as she was careful not to exert herself in any way. The children were delighted to have their mother back downstairs again.

The Music of What Happens

Although most of the household responsibilities still rested on Celina and Yacqueline's collective shoulders, Mama did what she could, seeing to it that homework and chores were completed before play or screen time and of course, homeschooling Elian while the others were in school.

Just having his wife out of bed seemed to erase the worried, weary look Celina had seen in Marcos' eyes for months now and he came home from the office, often whistling. As for Celina, she avoided him entirely.

"Children, please come to the living room, all of you!" Celina heard her mother call over the banister one afternoon. Leaving her dust rag, she hurried downstairs. As she sat down on the sofa, her stomach tensed. Marcos was holding Mama's hand, and her lips were set in a firm line.

Something's wrong.

Once everyone was seated, Marcos began, "Your mother and I have something to discuss with you children. I know I never discuss cases with you all, but I must ask a huge favor of you: I've been requested to take on a big murder trial in Seattle. I have no idea how long I'll be away. They're confident that a month will be long enough, but there's no way to tell for sure."

As Marcos reached for his wife's hand again, Celina looked away and inhaled so sharply she nearly choked. She loathed the shows of affection between her mother and stepfather that became more commonplace as time passed.

After a moment's hesitation, Marcos continued, "The reason I'm telling you all this is because I must know that I can count on you children. You know your mama must be very careful not to do much. You've all been such a huge help these last months, but if I take this case, I won't be here for a while, and you'll all have to do more than your share. Soledad Marisa Alexei Catalina," Marcos added, sternly, "I've heard quite enough about you giving your sisters a hard time about chores and schoolwork. I hope I won't hear any more about it. Will I?"

"No, Tío," Soledad mumbled, staring down at her hands folded in her lap.

"*Gracias.* Lastly, Lina, please don't let your mother do anything she's not supposed to do. You and Yacqueline please make sure of this."

When Marcos glanced sideways at his wife, she rolled her eyes at him in a half-frustrated, half-playful manner. He did not respond to her reaction but merely smiled at his stepdaughters, and Celina nodded, determinedly.

Alexei sighed. "*Bozhimoi,* you three! How many times must I tell you that I feel just fine?"

Marcos, Celina, and Yacqueline ignored the remark and exchanged knowing grins. For a long moment, all was quiet.

Chaim broke the silence. "Go on your trip, Tío. We'll miss you, so please come home soon, but don't worry about us or Mama. We'll take good care of her and each other. We-we always have, you know."

Earnest nods from his siblings accompanied Chaim's statement.

Marcos opened his arms and Chaim hesitated for just a moment before giving him a brief hug. "*Gracias,* Chaim," he whispered into his thick hair.

Marcos caught a plane to Seattle three days later. Celina missed him more than she had expected to, however, with the baby's arrival drawing near, she had little time to think about Marcos, Martie Pancorro, or much else for that matter. Two weeks before her due date, Alexei lost consciousness while setting the table for supper. Although she recovered quickly, it happened again two hours later. A worried Celina telephoned Señora Ulices, a retired nurse and their next-door neighbor, and asked her to drive Mama to Dr. Gabrielle's office. The obstetrician, following an examination, gave strict orders that again limited her to bedrest until the baby's birth. Mama fumed about this most of the way home, taking out her frustration on Celina and Chaim for calling the doctor without her permission.

". . . And here, you've also wasted Señora Ulices' valuable time when I have never felt better in my life," Alexei insisted vehemently. Celina and Chaim did not reply but glanced at each other, unconvinced. Their mother's all-seeing eye took in their expressions, and she guessed immediately what they were thinking. "And don't look at me like that. Most pregnant women have some dizziness. It's the way of things."

"Twice in one day, Mama?" Celina reminded, dubiously, "Yeah, sure, maybe you're fine now, but next time you might hurt yourself or Tío's kid real bad. Tío made me promise to take good care of you, and I'm not taking chances."

Alexei snorted in disgust, something she never did and would not tolerate from her daughters. "First of all, Celina Iliana Catarina Natyscha," she snapped, "there's nothing unusual about a woman as pregnant as I am fainting, and I can't believe you would waste the doctor's time on silliness. Secondly, I will thank you not to refer to the baby as "Tío's kid." That sounds completely vulgar! This child happens to be your new brother or sister."

Celina shrugged and looked away.

"Teenagers," Alexei muttered. "And now," she continued, louder this time, "because of this unreasonable fear Marcos has planted in your mind that I'm somehow going to wake up dead one morning, you had to run and call the doctor at the first sign of nothing!"

In her excitement, Mama, who never spoke anything but Russian to the children, was switching back and forth between Russian, Spanish and even English so fast that Celina and Chaim could barely keep up with her.

Darn, Mama, chill already! Celina wished she could say, but she did not dare.

"And look who suffers the consequences. I'm the one who must lie idly in bed again for goodness knows how many more weeks. This is sheer foolishness, Lina and Chaim, and I will not stand for any more of it! *Ponyala?*"

The siblings looked at each other, sighed, heavily, and rolled their eyes as they chorused, softly, in long-suffering tones. "*Da*, Mama."

Taking note of their condescension, Alexei turned from where she sat in the passenger seat and leveled them with a warning gaze. "Don't be fresh! I mean every word I said!"

When they arrived home, Mama graciously thanked Señora Ulices for her trouble and again apologized for wasting her time. She then strode quickly into the house. When she shut the front door behind her, Celina and Chaim looked at each other and moaned.

"Give me a cigarette," Celina motioned to her brother.

"Don't got any. Remember, Tío confiscated them last week? Said he'd pull the plug on my allowance if he finds out I've bought more."

When they finally went inside, Mama was nowhere in sight. Celina plopped down on the couch and exhaled dramatically. "*Spiseeba* for cleaning, Yacque," she looked gratefully around the spotless kitchen and living room. "Anyone got any spare cash?"

"I have ten bucks that's not in savings," Soledad put in. "Yacque's got about eighteen, right? And I know Chaim has nine now. I borrowed three dollars out of his wallet earlier today for the ice cream truck."

At this revelation, Chaim sucked in his breath angrily. Soledad rolled her eyes at him as she continued. "Javier's got only five left 'cuz he sneaked down to the 7-11 with his allowance and bought candy and a couple magazines Mama and Tío wouldn't like—

"Tattletale!" Javier growled.

"I think Jackie and the little boys each have about—

Celina crossed her eyes at her sister. "What the heck are you, a banker, a spy? How do you know all that?"

"People talk." Soledad shrugged, a mischievous smile playing across her lips.

"Tell us more, smart-mouth." Javier challenged from his perch on the arm of the couch. "I betcha' know Tío's net worth too? Any more juice to be spilled?"

"What if there is? You're the last one I'd tell, blabbermouth. But yup, I do know that Marc's sitting on a nest egg, that's for sure." Soledad grinned, leaning cozily against the back of the couch.

"*Ay Dios mío,*" Chaim exclaimed, indignantly, "why you little devil, first you steal outta' my wallet when you know I'm saving for a motor scooter and now—

"You'll live. So, Jackie and Kaitlin just broke up," Soledad interrupted and changed the subject, "and he's having lunch with Sinead now. Third grade, I swear—

"Oh, please," Celina rolled her eyes, *"you're* only in fourth grade!"

"Well, I *also* know that you and Javier both still wear pull-ups at night—

Celina reddened but said nothing.

"Why, you little—

"Javier, stop!" Chaim caught his arm before he could swing on Soledad. "Sol, you too. You went too far!"

Javier gritted his teeth as he sullenly stomped away upstairs.

"Lina, what do you need money for?" Yacqueline broke in to forestall any further teasing.

Celina leaned forward. She cut her eyes at a now-silent Soledad then smiled at her other siblings. "Pizza. Unless you all want pop tarts again, we're gonna order pizza. I'm not cooking tonight, and neither are you, *muchacha,*" she patted Yacqueline's shoulder, "you've done enough for one day."

"All right!" Jackie jumped up and high-fived his sister. "It's been like ages since we've had any pizza."

Celina grinned at the thought of decent food for nearly the first time in months. "Well then, somebody get Javier back down here to do the calling, and the rest of us will round up the cash. If there's not enough, ask Mama."

Just an hour later, the Montoya children were gathered around the table biting into jumbo slices from Jacinto's Pizza Joint.

Leaving Yacqueline and Soledad to do the dishes, Celina put Elian to bed and then checked on Mama. Her mother was sleeping peacefully, but Celina could tell that she was losing weight again.

One tear then another rolled down her cheek. *Oh, Mama,* she barely refrained from sobbing. *Please don't leave us. Don't die like Papi. Don't leave us all alone! Chaim and I can't take care of these kids all by ourselves. Puzhalste don't leave!*

Celina turned away but turned back when Mama stirred. Alexei opened her eyes and raised up on one elbow, smiling at her daughter. She held out an arm, and Celina went to her. Climbing into bed beside her mother, she clung to her, the silent flow of her tears wetting Mama's chest as Alexei covered them both with her quilt. For a long time, Mama stroked her curls and softly sang *Cossack Lullaby.* The gentle song and the mournful howl of the desert wind outside soon lulled her into a deep sleep.

CHAPTER 7

Precious Little One

One morning, a week later, Celina awoke to the heavy pitter-patter of rain against the window. A glance at her watch told her it was nearly seven o'clock. Time to start breakfast.

"Aw geez," Celina mumbled as she slowly pushed back the quilts and crawled from the warmth of the master bed, doing her best not to wake Mama. Gently shutting the door behind her, she tiptoed down the hall to the bathroom. After a shower, she dressed in lavender sweater, matching skirt, and dark tights. She then roused her sisters.

"Soledad, I swear, if you sneak back into bed . . ." She left the threat hanging as she hurried downstairs. The siblings were just leaving for the bus stop when they heard a desperate cry from upstairs.

"Stay here!" Celina ordered. She rushed up the stairs two at a time and burst into Mama's bedroom. Alexei Gonzalez was sitting on the edge of the bed, clutching her swollen belly. She chewed her lip, though Celina could tell she wanted to scream in pain. Celina nearly gasped at the blood and water staining the sheets.

Mama reached out and grabbed her hand. Her eyes were wide with fear as she bit back another scream. "Lina, c-call an ambulance now. Something's wrong."

"Chaim, call an ambulance now! Somethings wrong! Javier, go get Señora Ulices! Yacque, wake up Eli and get him dressed, we're going to the hospital!"

For what felt like hours though was just a matter of minutes, Celina held Mama's hand as Alexei gasped her way through her pain.

"What's wrong, Mama? What's wrong? Are you hurting very much?"

Alexei tried to stand. She fell back, weakly but not quickly enough for Celina to miss the puddle of blood she was sitting in.

"Mama, are you okay? Is the baby okay? It's like with Jackie, isn't it?"

Alexei shut her eyes as tears escaped and she squeezed her daughter's hand. She barely nodded.

She almost died having Jackie, and he almost died because she couldn't stop bleeding. Dammit, Tío, she directed her silent ire towards her absent stepfather, *why can't you be here? You'd know what to do better than me, and Mama needs you! This is your kid!*

Another tight squeeze on her hand brought Celina out of her silent reverie. There was no way she wanted her mother to relive that ordeal.

Though she had been just five years old when Giacamo Jr. was born, Celina remembered that terrifying day as though it were yesterday. She remembered her mother's pasty white skin, hours of agony, so much blood, a baby born too small, not breathing.

"God was with us that day," Papi had said when it was over, "it's a miracle." To this day Mama thought of Jackie as her miracle baby.

"Lina, child, what's happening? I can't understand what he's saying," Señora Ulices entered the room, motioning at a pale, frightened Javier beside her. In his panic, the boy had been switching back and forth at rapid-fire speed between Spanish and Russian.

Without waiting for a response, she assessed the situation immediately and hurried to Mama's side. She checked her pulse. Alexei lay back against the pillows, gasping, clutching her stomach painfully. She moaned as more blood streaked down her legs.

"This is bad. Is an ambulance on the way?"

As if they had heard her, two EMTs entered the room with a stretcher. Celina stood back, her arm around Javier's shoulder as they quickly strapped Mama onto the stretcher and hurried downstairs.

Javier turned to her; dark eyes wide with fear. "Mama's so white, and she's all covered in blood—is she going to die?"

"No. Don't ask stupid questions. She's gonna be fine, and so's that kid. You know Mama's been through stuff being pregnant with all of us, but she's not gonna die. Let's go. Señora Ulices will take us to the hospital."

For a long time, they sat quietly in the hospital waiting area. Elian on her lap, resting his head on her chest, Celina alone sat in a chair, while her siblings made themselves comfortable on the floor, carefully out of the way of other patients. Mama had never allowed her children to take up all the seats in a public place. It had long ago become a habit for the children to stand against the wall or sit on the floor.

Mama had always told them. 'Never shame me by letting me hear that an elder couldn't have a seat because one of my children was sitting.'

Yacqueline and Soledad played cat's cradle and took romance IQ quizzes from a copy of *Tiger Beat* magazine. In hushed tones, Chaim and Javier plotted revenge against Antonio, the "sneaky rat from Tucson," as the bully was now well-known at the local middle school.

Try as she might, Celina could not get comfortable and chat with her siblings or look at magazines. She sat in silence while Elian rested against her. With her arms wrapped around him, she could feel her brother's ribs through his pajamas and her heart cried. Despite careful nutrition and proper medical treatments, Elian seemed to be steadily growing worse.

I know Dr. Grosvenor says he's too weak for surgery, and they have to wait until he's stronger, Celina reminded herself, *but he's not getting stronger! He can't die; he just can't! We can't lose our Sunbeam.*

She tightened her arms around her brother protectively. Softly she began to sing *Holy Water*. It was not long before Elian fell asleep again.

Although it felt like years it was just a few hours before a short, rotund nurse entered the waiting room. "Celina Zagoradniy?" She scanned the room.

Shifting Elian's, limp, sleeping body in her arms, Celina struggled to her feet, stumbling under his dead weight.

"The name's Lina Montoya, and that's me," she said, just in time remembering to speak respectfully.

The nurse smiled. "Please follow me," she said, kindly, "all of you. Your mother's asking for you."

When they arrived at a room near the end of a long hall, the nurse pushed open a heavy door and beckoned the children to follow her. "Señora Gonzalez, your children are here."

Hesitant and shy, the Montoya children made their way to their mother's bedside. Mama's coal-black curls lay in a sweaty, tangled mess, a stark contrast to the snow-white bedding. Her face was gray, and her eyes were closed. Beside her bed was a small crib and inside lay a tiny bundle wrapped in powder blue. By the blankets, Celina knew the baby was a boy, yet she could see nothing else amidst the wrappings. The others stood, in silence, afraid to touch either their mother or the newborn child.

Evangelo looked up at her and whispered, worriedly, "Is she dead?"

"Mama's *not* dead!" Little Man cried out, tears filling his huge, dark eyes as he gave his older brother an angry shove. Before Evangelo could shove back, Yacqueline instinctively stepped between the two. Alexei started and opened her eyes. She smiled, tiredly.

"Mama!" Evangelo and Little Man cried almost simultaneously. They would have run to her had Yacqueline not been holding their hands.

"Come," she said, softly, "meet your baby brother."

Celina remained in the shadows while her siblings gathered around her bed. She watched as her mother tenderly lifted the baby from its tiny crib. Although Yacqueline kept reminding everyone to keep their voices low, squeals of excitement and delight kept escaping. Celina turned away.

I know what I'm doing. I can see myself. But I can't help it. I'm supposed to get used to all this and accept it. But what if Tío can't accept things when he finds out— he loves us because we're his best friend's kids. But what'll he say if he ever finds out I'm not? He'll hate me; he'll want me gone. Then what?

The opening of the door interrupted her thoughts. Celina turned, expecting to see a nurse but was surprised to see Marcos,' tall frame appear in the doorway. As he stepped into the light, Alexei gasped, her wide eyes filled with tears of joy.

"My darling," he mouthed.

Mama nodded and replied, softly, "I love you."

For a long moment, the room was completely silent until Marcos barely managed, without taking his eyes from his wife's, ashen face. "The-the . . . child?"

Celina's stomach clenched. She understood her stepfather's apprehension. Because of the children's silence and the crib almost completely hidden from view, Marcos feared he may have lost another baby. Mama lifted the infant, swathed in blankets, and held him out to his father. Marcos' eyes widened; his mouth formed words he did not voice aloud. In two quick steps, he was beside the bed, gingerly gathering his new son into his arms.

Curiosity won out, and Celina moved close enough to get a glimpse of the baby. What she saw made her heart leap in her chest. The word beautiful did not do the child justice. His newborn skin was already beginning to show its dark cast. A tuft of thick, black hair covered the tiny head and his eyes, milk chocolate in color, were as wide and innocent as those of a bunny. At a glance, she saw that Marcos and his new son had identical eyes. He was, without a doubt, his father's son. Celina intently watched her stepfather's face.

"He-he's perfect; I-I've never seen a more perfect child," Marcos marveled.

Alexei smiled tenderly as she too looked down at her newest baby and then into her husband's eyes. "My darling, what else did you expect? He's you."

Marcos smiled back as, amid their tears, he kissed his wife, a kiss so soft, tender, and full of love.

Celina desperately wanted to leave the room, she didn't want to be there, but her feet felt stuck to the floor. Before she could move,

Marcos turned. "Lina," he whispered, smiling as he beckoned her, "come here, *nena*."

Obediently, Celina sat down on the bed beside her mother, and Marcos placed the baby into her arms.

"I want you to be first. You've been the main one who has taken such good care of your mother all these months and kept our home running smoothly so I could take the Ortega case. This is your moment with your new brother."

The other children watched with bated breath as Celina gently hugged the baby close. She forced a smile and tried not to look at him. He looked so much like Marcos. Gently she touched one of his soft cheeks with her fingertip and a gasp of delight escaped her lips. The baby's skin felt as though she were caressing pure silk. Next, she ran her fingers through the infant's raven black waves, as fine as the down of a baby chick. Gingerly, Celina opened the blankets. She caressed the baby's, tiny, bare feet and hands. She held a finger in front of him. Dark eyes so innocent, so trusting, locked with her own, he grabbed her finger with a surprisingly strong grip. Celina's heart melted.

Looking up at Mama and Marcos, she asked, "What's his name?"

Marcos looked at his wife, regretfully. One thing they had completely failed to discuss was names for their expected baby. Nonetheless, Mama was not stymied. She smiled broadly as she replied, "His father's name." Nodding, as if to herself, she stroked her son's downy curls, Alexei smiled again. "His name is Marcos Diego Jesus Romano Gonzalez Jr."

Celina grinned, as well, and was surprised to find that she meant every word when she looked back down at the infant in her arms and said, "I think we've found ourselves a keeper."

Mama and Marcos beamed, and Marcos wrapped an arm around his stepdaughter's shoulder. She did not respond but neither did she pull away as she had up until now.

Suddenly Mama gasped lightly and smiled, "Anyone know what today is?"

The Music of What Happens

Javier glanced at his watch. "Uhm, May 15th, Mama. So?"

"It's Lina's birthday, you sillies."

Celina's mouth fell open. She had completely forgotten her birthday.

"That's right!" Marcos enthused, smiling down at Celina, "I even have a present for you at home. We must have a party of sorts once your mother and *mi hijo* here come home."

At that, Mama broke in, "Marc, how did you come back home so fast, and how did you know where we were?"

Marcos grinned at his eldest stepson, "It was Chaim," he rumpled the boy's hair. "He text me."

Alexei's hand flew to her mouth. "Chaim Jesus Ravi de Armando Montoya!" She exclaimed, "I believe your sister told you to call an *ambulance!*"

"I did, Mama, and then I used your cell to text Tío. I knew it was taking a chance he wouldn't be in court, but he wasn't, and I told him."

"Perfect timing too," Marcos finished. "Yesterday, I closed the Ortega case. I was planning to sleep all day and fly home tomorrow, but after I got Chaim's text, I caught the Metro home. I stopped at the house just in case, but everyone was gone. I left my bags and came here."

"Just in time too," Alexei smiled at her husband and then at their tiny son who was growing fussy. Within a moment, the baby was howling and flailing his tiny fists.

Marcos looked startled for a moment and then patted the infant's head. "Such a big noise for such a little one." He lifted the baby into his arms and onto his shoulder. Celina was surprised to see the tears that wet her stepfather's eyes as he gently kissed him. "*Te quiero, mi hijo. Adios.*"

As he placed the crying baby back in his wife's arms, he turned to the older children and motioned them to follow him from the room.

When they arrived home, Celina went right to the library and sat down at the piano. All she could think about was the baby.

His little hands and feet. He was tinier even than Elian was when he was born. I don't want to, but I do love him. I can't wait to hold him again.

At that moment, an idea came to her, and she worked her fingers across the keys, trying to come up with the perfect melody. "A flat, C— Before long, a smile stretched across her face as she played a brand-new lullaby she had written for the baby.

Jumping up, she rushed from the room. "Eli? Eli!" she called.

"Yeah, sis?" Elian appeared at the bottom of the stairs, his tired dark eyes smiling as usual.

"Come here *por favor*. I think you can help me with something."

When Elian arrived in the library, Celina motioned to his violin case on the table. "See if you can accompany me. I've written a song for Baby Marcos."

"Play." Elian gently moved his bow back and forth as he listened, carefully. It was just moments before brother and sister were playing together.

"Oh, wow."

Both Celina and Elian turned, startled, to see Marcos standing in the doorway, a soft smile on his lips. "What was that?"

"A lullaby," Elian could barely conceal his excitement. "Lina wrote it. For Baby Marcos. It's called *Vaquero Pequeño*. Isn't it nice?"

"*Por favor* play it again."

Little Marcos Jr. came home from the hospital three days later. He was a contented baby who happily soaked up every ounce of attention showered upon him by his parents and older siblings. At birth, "Diego" as the family decided to call him, weighed just six pounds yet quickly gained weight. His two eldest sisters especially delighted in helping their mother care for him.

Celina's fourteenth birthday party was held two weeks later. Mama and Yacqueline baked chocolate-cherry cake and Marcos made homemade peppermint ice cream, Celina's all-time favorite. The birthday girl was not allowed to help with anything, so she invited Elizaveta over to spend the day.

"It's been so long," Elizaveta hugged her best friend when she arrived, "but I get it. Your mom needed you."

Celina led the way upstairs to her bedroom. Sitting cross-legged on the bed, Elizaveta wasted no time in spilling the juice. Celina plopped down on the floor, leaning back against her purple, plush beanbag.

"So, you've missed out on a lot while your mom's been sick. Did you hear the juice about Cal?"

Celina's eyes widened, her heart now in her throat, as she shoved a small pile of dirty clothes under her bed. She gulped and forced an excited grin. "No, do spill."

"Looks like he got someone pregnant."

"Are you serious?"

"That's the juice around school. And Staci's been keeping a low profile for sure."

"Who is it? Were they t-together?"

"They had a few dates, but they weren't ever serious. When has Cal *ever* like been serious about anyone? So, Staci told Marcail and begged her to keep it a secret. Well, we both know what an awesome secret keeper Marcail is. The news was everywhere before school even let out that day. I got the text from Lisa. *Chica,* you really gotta' talk your mom into letting you have a phone. Like seriously. Well, Staci says it was Jade, you know, her number-one toad?"

"Jade's pregnant?" Celina clapped a hand over her mouth. "She-she's only our age."

As Elizaveta continued, Celina only heard bits and pieces. She stared up at her bedroom ceiling, lost in thought. *I love babies, but I can't imagine having to take care of Diego all by myself all the time.*

"Lina? Lina? Celina Zagoradniy!" Elizaveta, lying on her stomach, leaned over the edge of the bed and smacked her friend's foot.

Celina started and cut her eyes at her friend. "Don't call me that."

Elizaveta laughed. "Yeah, I thought that would get your attention. Geez, you were off in la-la land!"

Celina blinked hard and changed the subject abruptly. "Sorry. Hey, wanna see that new romance IQ quiz in *Seventeen*? It's pretty awesome."

"Come and get it, birthday girl!" Mama called over the banister.

Celina grinned at the sight that met her eyes when she and Elizaveta entered the dining room. Her favorite supper, chicken-cheese enchiladas and strawberry milk was laid out. Next, cake and ice cream were served by Yacqueline.

As Celina folded her napkin and reached over to wipe ice cream off Little Man's mouth, he grabbed her hand, excitedly. "There is presents too, Lina. You gotta see."

"I guess that's our cue," Marcos laughed. He offered to take the baby, but Celina declined, leaning down to kiss the blissfully sleeping Diego in her arms as she followed her family into the living room. She was in awe when she saw her gifts. She had never received a birthday gift that was not either handmade or practical, like socks. The family had been too poor to afford extras when Papi was alive. As she gazed wide-eyed at the pile of brightly wrapped birthday gifts in Marcos' recliner. Evangelo took his sister's hand and led her to the sofa. Little Man was then asked to bring her the first gift. Everyone gathered close and watched as Celina tore aside the pretty paper to reveal a gorgeous, hand-knit, black sweater with hot pink trim around the neck and wrists.

"Oh, Mama, it's beautiful," Celina leaned over to hug her mother. She was then handed a small square package from Elian. Inside, in the small white box, was a heart-shaped silver locket. Exclamations of delight greeted the appearance of the lovely gift. Celina carefully unfastened the tiny clasp. On the left side was a picture of Papi.

Speaking English for the benefit of Marcos and Elizaveta, Mama explained, "Eli and I bought the locket for him to give you, but the picture was all his idea."

A smile of complete understanding passed between brother and sister as Celina bent to examine the photo. Taken not long before his death, Giacamo Montoya's tired face was gaunt and bony, glistening faintly with perspiration. Black wavy hair fell just below his shoulders, a striking contrast with his clean, white T-shirt. Papi's smile was exhausted but held the same love and tenderness that had always radiated from his very soul. Elian draped an arm about Celina's shoulders as he too gazed down at their father's picture. He grinned at his sister, but his angelic smile disappeared in a fit of spasmodic coughing that violently shook his fragile body. Celina's heart skipped as she patted his back firmly. Mama started toward them, but Elian inhaled deeply and was able to stop coughing.

Peaked face damp from exertion and his eyes watery, he smiled again and asked, "D-do you like it, Lina?"

Celina wrapped her arms around him. "I love it, Eli. *Bolshoye spiseeba.*" She did a double take when she noticed something amiss. "Mama," she asked, confused, "the other side's empty."

Mama smiled but said nothing. After thanking Elian again, Celina opened her remaining presents and lastly, she tore open a pink envelope from Baby Diego. She giggled at the thought of a birthday card from her three-week-old brother. Her laughter stopped short, however, when she saw the card. "Happy birthday to a very special sister." Inside, Mama had written a birthday message from the baby.

Dearest Lina,
Thank you for all the wonderful care you gave our mama while she was carrying me. She couldn't have done it without you. I'm so happy to be here and get to meet you. You are a terrific big sister, and I love you so much. I am eternally grateful for all your love and care, and I look forward to next year when we will celebrate our birthdays together. Happy birthday to my very special, big sister!
Love,
Your brother,
M. Diego Gonzalez

Celina's eyes teared up as Marcos read her the card. "Thanks, Mama," she gulped back tears.

"*Nyet*, Linochka," Alexei replied, "It's I who must thank you. My condition was serious, and you took such good care of me and Diego.

You helped to give your brother a chance. I couldn't have done it without you. Thank *you*, my Lina, for everything."

Everyone except Mama, still recovering from Diego's birth, joined in rowdy rounds of Musical Chairs and there was even a Pinata. During Pinata, a dizzy Javier accidentally swung his bat the wrong way, nearly whacking Little Man in the face which frightened Mama to no end, and, short as he was, Evangelo couldn't even reach the pinata. However, Elizaveta finally split it open, and everyone scrambled excitedly for the treats that came spilling out.

All too soon the party was over. While Mama and the younger girls cleaned the kitchen, Celina wandered back into the living room where her presents were piled in Marcos' favorite chair. She picked up her locket and opened it. Papi's tired dark eyes smiled up at her. How wonderful to have this beautiful reminder of her beloved father to look at whenever she wished. Her eyes then traveled to the empty side of her locket.

Whose picture should go here? Celina immediately thought of Mama, but, for some reason, even that did not seem quite right. Confused, she fastened the locket about her neck, near the crucifix, gathered up her other presents and started for her room.

As she started up the stairs, Marcos appeared and beckoned her. Celina sighed but followed him down the hall to the library. When she entered, her stepfather was alone, sitting on the piano bench. Celina forced a laugh.

"No, Tío, please don't play. I've heard you; it's painful."

Marcos chuckled then asked, "What do you think of Elessa's piano?"

Celina furrowed her brow and cocked her head to one side. "Uhmmm . . . I love it. It plays way better even than the one at church, and it's so beautiful and— she halted. "Why?"

Marcos's smile was tender as he said, "Because it's all yours, *nena*. Happy Birthday."

For a moment, Celina felt weak. "A-am I on glue, or did you just like say the piano is *mine?*"

Marcos chuckled as he reached for her hand. "Don't you like it?"

"Like it?" Celina exhaled, a bit raggedly, blinking back a sudden rush of tears. "Tío, it's the most amazing present anyone's ever given me. I *love* it. But you-you don't have to—"

"I *want* to, Lina," he corrected, gently, "and Elessa would've wanted me to. She wouldn't have wanted her treasure sitting around collecting dust. As I said before, I had to say goodbye, had to let her go." Marcos' eyes teared up momentarily as he continued. "I-I can't keep this piano a shrine to her. Elessa would've been heartbroken if she could see how it was silent for so long. But now," Marcos smiled tenderly down at his stepdaughter and brushed a stray curl from her face, "it makes music again, such beautiful music."

"*Muchas gracias,* Tío. I love it!" Their hug was awkward, but Celina realized at that moment that her heart was melting. That night, in bed, her happiness was complete. It had truly been the best birthday ever.

CHAPTER 8

No Second Chances

"Who in the heck can be calling at this hour just before dinner?" Marcos wondered, aloud, his voice tinged with irritation at the obnoxious banging that sounded suddenly at the front door. He made his way to the foyer. Celina did not even look up from her homework, but Chaim and Javier wandered after their stepfather, as did Soledad.

Suddenly Marcos called out, "Alexei, can you come In here please?"

At this, curiosity won over and Celina left her textbook on the dining room table and followed Mama out of the room. Mama halted at the sight of a slightly built, Mexican man, not much taller than herself, standing there beside Marcos. Large, dark eyes, glassy with intoxication, his faded, ripped jeans were ill-fitting and his threadbare, plaid overshirt was missing too many buttons. Rain dripped from black curls plastered against his head. He leaned easily against the doorway, grinning, idiotically, oblivious to the rain pouring behind him. The acrid odor of tequila mixed with BO caused Celina to wrinkle her nose.

He looks familiar somehow . . . ay Dios mío, he's— Celina's heart dropped into her stomach. She tried to turn away. She wanted to run and hide, but her feet would not move. Her legs felt like noodles, and her heart roared in her ears as she ducked behind Mama. She was finally going to meet her birth father face-to-face, and Marcos was going to discover the awful truth.

"Martie," Mama's soft voice was filled with shock.

The Music of What Happens

"Alex, who-what-you know this *hombre?*" Marcos cocked his head.

Before Mama could reply, the smaller man grinned dumbly through a haze of intoxication. "Hey, 'Lexei. S-sure been a hella' long time since ya' hightailed it and left me high and dry."

"Alexei, what's he talking about? Who *is* this?"

Celina could hear her mother's rapid breathing as Mama swallowed hard, "Marcos," she said, her voice surprisingly strong, "this is Martie Pancorro, my first husband. And-and Celina's biological father."

"That's right," Martie Pancorro slurred, "your ex-ole' man, that's all I am. I just figure ole' Gonzalez here oughta' know just who he got his'self shacked up with. Wait a sec? Yer' saying I got me a kid? Heck no, Princess! Martie Pancorro ain't got no little curtain climbers! Don't got 'em and don't want 'em."

"Celina's *father?* What the— Marcos's voice trailed off. "Are you serious?" Though from the expression on his face, he already knew the answer.

"Yes," Alexei barely whispered, "he is."

"How on earth did all this happen? Where—"

"Sheesh, *amigo*, at your age? Ya' oughta know just how all that happens. It's like this—"

"Stop your imbecilic rambling this minute!" Marcos all but shouted. "Children go upstairs to your rooms. Doors shut. Celina, please stay here."

Celina stepped out from behind Mama. Her heart was racing. *This is exactly what I've been worried about all this time. I always knew there was no point in fixing my relationship with Tío. I knew it! What's gonna happen now?*

Marcos turned again to his wife, eyes wide and face pale. "She-she's not Giac's daughter? You were-were married to *him*— he motioned to the man beside him, now silent.

"I married Martie when I was seventeen. He is her father. I didn't marry Giac until she was eight months old."

Celina looked at her mother out of the corner of her eye. *She's so strong. She's not afraid of either of them. Wow.*

"No!" Martie broke in, "I ain't papa to some brat! No way, Princess, ain't no way! Yer' a *liar*, 'Lexei!" his words ended in a scream. "I ain't got no dang kids, and you ain't getting a *peso* outta me with yer' lies!"

Mama's eyes darkened with rage. Her gaze scornfully swept her former husband's face. "How can you be so stupid?" she shouted at him, "how can you be so blind?" She grabbed Celina's shoulder, causing her to start, and pushed her forward not roughly. "You think I want your *money?* You drunken fool! Look at her! She's *your* daughter, Martie! Look at those eyes, that hair, that mouth! Tell me again she isn't yours!"

Alexei broke down just then, sobbing bitterly into her hands.

Celina could not speak. *I think I'm gonna puke!*

Martie was now staring hard at Celina. "Hmmm . . . maybe yer' right, Princess."

As she wiped her eyes, Mama turned to her and nodded toward the man in the doorway. "Lina, this is your birth father, Martinez Pancorro."

Nearly choking, Celina acknowledged the introduction courteously, as she had been taught, "¡Hola, Señor Pancorro."

Marcos turned in the direction of the door, and for a long moment, all was quiet as Martie stared at his newfound daughter. "What was yer' name again, Kid?"

"Lina. Celina Montoya."

"And yer' how old?"

"Fourteen."

Martie glared at his former wife. "I see ya' didn't give her my name. All this time, I had me a beautiful kid, and I never even knew. Why? Why'd ya' never tell me, 'Lexei?"

Mama shook her head hard, eyes filled with disgust. "Really, Martie? Really? So that you'd kill her before she was even born?" Eyes flashing angry fire, Alexei's next words poured forth in a torrent. "So that you could kill us both with your beatings! What, in God's name, are you thinking? No! When I found out I was pregnant, I left! I gave birth to *my* daughter in Galveston. Alone. Without her father. You should have been there, Martie. You should have been there with me to see our miracle arrive! You *never* were her father! When she was a baby, I married a man named Giacamo Montoya. He took your place, and I have *no* regrets!"

Martie glared hard at her as he shouted back, "Yer' a liar, 'Lexei! I never hit ya' all that hard! Ya' knew I always wanted a kid. A little girl to call Charaea like my mother! Ya' *knew* that, Lexei!"

Mama's eyes went wide in disbelief, "Oh, don't you even— no, Martie, *no!* You'd have killed our child and me too before she was even born if I had stayed! Believe me, I'd had enough of you! Your beatings, your drunk raging! Never having enough food because you would never keep a job and then drink up all the money I earned. I would never put my child through this from her father! No!"

During the entire exchange, Marcos had remained silent. All Celina had to do was look at him to realize he was angry; *very* angry. His dark eyes seemed to smolder with the fury of a man betrayed, and they frightened her.

He's so mad. What's he gonna do now? Is he gonna' tell us all to leave? Is he gonna' keep Diego, and we'll never see him again? What's he gonna do?

Just then, Marcos turned to her. "Did you know about all this?" His voice was flat and cold, and Celina cringed at the sound.

Suddenly breathless, Celina nodded, "*Si,*" she barely squeaked, "I knew."

This time it was Mama's turn to show astonishment. "You-you *knew*? How?"

Celina looked at the floor, chewing her bottom lip. There wasn't much Mama hated as much she did snooping. The only thing she hated worse was a lie.

"I-I found your box last year with my birth certificate and his picture, and I-uhm-uh-I read some of your old diaries."

"Well, I guess that's that," Martie sneered, "now that ya' know all about 'Lexei's dirty laundry, Gonzalez, I'll hit the road." He glared at his ex-wife as he added, "But the kid's coming with me!"

At the unexpected declaration, Alexei gasped, and Celina shrank back against her mother. "No!" she whimpered, uncharacteristically.

Alexei wrapped an arm around her daughter's shoulder and eyed Martie evenly. "Are you crazy? My daughter's not going anywhere with you!"

"You heard me, woman!" Martie shouted, enraged, "ya' said that's my kid, and that means I got my rights! Here, I'll even pay ya'! How much ya' want?"

Marcos had heard enough. He grabbed the smaller man's shoulders and practically threw him out the door into the rain. "No! Get off my property! Children aren't for sale, *estúpido tonto!*"

Martie Pancorro staggered to his feet and shook his fist at Marcos. "Jes' ya' wait, Gonzalez! Ya' ain't heard the last of me! That's *my* kid! Ain't no way I'm lettin' ya'll keep my little baby girl! No friggin' way!"

Marcos slammed the door, cutting off Martie's words. He stood, staring silently out into the rain until he had disappeared from the yard. Very suddenly, he turned back to them.

Celina glanced at her mother. Mama's face betrayed nothing as she sat down on the sofa and motioned for Celina to sit beside her.

How can she be so calm? And tío, I can't read his face either, but I know he's mad as all get out.

Marcos sat in his recliner across from Mama and Celina and stared silently out at the rain for a long time. Finally, he turned back to them. He swallowed hard.

"Alex, what happened?" His gentle tone surprised Celina. "Why did you and Giac never tell me?"

Mama sighed deeply and for a moment, leaned forward and held her temples in her hands. "We agreed," she said, softly, but firmly, "to keep our daughter safe; safe from this angry town, so many people just looking for gossip, looking to destroy others, even the children. Our kids' lives were hard enough. We agreed to tell no one. I know-I *know* I should've told you before we married. It was so selfish of me. There's no excuse, but it was complicated and—

As if he had not even heard her, Marcos shook his head, incredulously, "All these years, all these years, I never doubted she was Giac's.

Their bond was so strong," he mused half to himself. "He loved her so much, called her his warrior princess. He seemed to love her almost more than he did the others."

"He did." Alexei fought tears. "Until the day he died. Never doubt that, *malaynkia*," Mama turned to Celina and patted her cheek, "never ever doubt that."

Celina nodded but could not bring herself to speak. *But why didn't they tell me? I get it why they didn't tell the whole town, but what about me? Mama was ashamed, she must have been.*

"Tell me, Alexei, tell *us*," He motioned to Celina, "what happened."

Mama sighed again. Finally, she began, "I was just sixteen when I left Leningrad with my aunt. We settled in Texas with a couple of friends of hers. Almost immediately, our host began abusing me. I tried to make him stop but one night, he-he—" Alexei shook her head and pressed on, "Let's just say, we had to leave. I got work at a motel; housekeeper, groundskeeper. I took care of my aunt and myself. And that's where I met Martie. He was young, just nineteen. He seemed to hold all the answers I sought; the escape I'd dreamed of for so long. I was heedless, foolish in my belief in him." She teared up as she continued, thickly, "I allowed a teenager's crush to sweep away clear thought. I married him. At just seventeen, I married the boy with booze on his breath, no job and a horrible temper. He drank way too much. I forgave him. He began beating me. I hid the evidence, the bruises and blood, and again and again I forgave him. His pretty lies turned into broken dreams. In him, I thought I found the love and acceptance I'd craved all my life, especially from my father. My father, the man who could not be touched, who could not be reached. A brilliant scholar as you both know, but the simple definition of love Ravi Zagoradniy could not understand." Alexei shook her head wistfully, her eyes far away. At that moment, Celina felt as though she had caught a brief glimpse, in her mother's eyes, of the sad, lonely, little girl who still yearned for the love and acceptance her father had never been able to give her.

As angry as she felt inside, Celina's eyes teared up at this. She looked away, chewing her bottom lip, willing herself not to cry. *I know it was a long time ago, but poor Mama.*

"And then I-I found out I was pregnant. That night, after the worst beating of my life, I packed him lunch for his trip to Dallas with his drinking buddies, and I left. I left my wedding band and a note on the table. I didn't tell him about you, my girl. I was afraid, afraid he'd find us, afraid he'd hurt you. I walked, and I hitched rides. I slept on park benches and once in someone's unlocked car in front of a motel. I cleaned public bathrooms in exchange for food. And finally, I made it to Galveston, halfway across Texas. I found work there, unloading trucks that brought boxes to a warehouse—

"*Pregnant?*" Marcos broke in, horrified, "they hired a pregnant woman to do such work?"

Alexei shrugged. "I'm grateful they do. No one else would hire me because of my English. I was homeless. I slept in a different place almost every night—

Celina turned to look at Marcos. He was hanging on his wife's every word almost as if she was reading an adventure story.

"Lina, I gave birth to you in a gas station bathroom in the middle of the night. I washed you in a floor sink used for cleaning mop buckets. As I said, I worked a hard job in a loading yard just to earn enough money to afford a small shack to live in. And that's where I met your papi. We married when you were eight months old. He wanted to adopt you, but without Martie's consent—" she shrugged. "So, he adopted you in love. That's why your last name is legally my maiden name. I'm so sorry, Linochka. I never expected it to come out like this. I should have told you, but the time never seemed right. You were so devoted to your papi and he to you. The time j-just never seemed right."

Celina finally spoke, softly, "And Papi really loved me?"

"Oh, he did. *Da,* so much. He was very sick, even then. But Marc," Alexei turned to her husband, "Giac and I, we needed each other. Even if it meant only a short life together. I'd never known a man like him, a man that stole my heart and made me forget everything terrible I'd ever lived. And yet now, I've found another." She smiled, slightly. "So similar, yet so different. And I'm so sorry, my love. Can you ever forgive me?"

As Mama began to weep, Marcos nodded at Celina and dipped his head in the direction of the stairs. Celina squeezed her mother's hand before heading upstairs.

Shutting her bedroom door behind her, she sat down in the glider rocker beside the window and stared down into the rainy darkness. She barely smiled when she caught sight of Javier, standing under the eaves in Chaim's black hoodie, smoking.

Do I even belong anymore? This changes everything. They're only my half-brothers and sisters now. Papi isn't even who I thought he was. And he was my hero. What would he say to me if he were here now? I don't even know what to think anymore. The world's upside down. Oh, Papi, why didn't you tell me? You always said you loved me, but you-you couldn't love me enough to tell?

Celina reached under her pillow and pulled out the wallet-sized photo of Martie Pancorro. She sucked in her cheeks as she studied the face that so uncannily resembled her own. Celina looked up as the picture fell from her hand onto the floor. *I'm not dumb. This has changed everything.*

It was just an hour later before Marcos and Alexei called the children downstairs. Mama's eyes were swollen from crying, but both were smiling. Celina furrowed her brow.

What can they possibly have to smile about right now?

Marcos motioned for everyone to sit. "Now, listen, kids. I know that little meeting in the foyer was a bit confusing and even scary. But that man isn't taking Lina. He isn't taking anyone. We're a family. A stepfamily yes, but a *family*. And we belong together. He was drunk, he was ranting, and he said some stupid things. But don't worry, if anything *does* happen, your mother and I will deal with it. We don't want you children worrying about any of this. You especially," he turned to Celina, "it's gonna be okay. Secondly, I'm not mad at your mother. We had to work some things out and chat like grownups do, but I'm not mad. I love your mama so much, and she loves me. Now, how about popcorn and a movie?"

"So, you don't want me to go to school and stuff?"

"No, school's fine, but we'd prefer you stay close with Elizaveta or your brothers and not go off on your own for a while. I just—" Marcos hesitated. "Well, I'm just going to say I don't trust the guy, and I'm a bit concerned about his mental state. So, let's just put a few safeguards in place for a while. *Si?*"

Reluctantly, Celina nodded and sighed deeply. She turned again to her homework as her stepfather patted her head and then disappeared into the kitchen. She changed her mind and pushed her textbook toward the center of the table. Leaning forward, her elbows on the table, she pressed her fingers into her temples.

I sorta thought something like this might happen. He was way messed up. As long as I never have to see that psycho again. . . Poor Mama, he like didn't even care how awful he was to her!

Standing quickly, Celina hurried from the table, grabbing her iPod and a light jacket on her way out the door. Just then, Yacqueline rounded the corner of the house, a thick cookbook under her arm. Celina halted.

"Come with me? I need a breather, and Marc and Mama don't want me out of the yard alone for a while. I-I'm going nuts, Sis."

An understanding smile on her lips, Yacqueline touched her shoulder and without a word, they started down the driveway.

"Lina, Yacque? Wait *puzhalste?*"

Celina turned to see Elian sitting on the porch swing. The seven-year-old wore a woolen jacket, scarf, and tennis shoes and an afghan was placed over his legs. He didn't move from the swing but asked, "Can I go with you?"

Celina hesitated, knowing she should ask but wanting him with her, she pushed aside the thought and motioned him to come. Elian's smile was worth it. Celina squatted down so her brother could climb on and ride piggy-back. The walk she was planning would absolutely be too much for him.

For a long time, the children strolled, in silence down the quiet street. Elian rested his head on Celina's shoulder. Although this made him almost too heavy for her, Celina said nothing. Something made her press on.

I don't know—I don't know what to feel. I'm relieved. I'm upset. I'm—

"Yacque, have you ever wondered who you are?"

"What do you mean, Sis?"

"Well, I thought I knew who I was. I never questioned it; I never thought to. And then I find out I'm not— that I'm someone else. And it makes me wonder who I was meant to be. Don't you think I would've been way different if—

Yacqueline replied, honestly, "I guess I've never thought about it. But sis, don't. You'll go crazy with so many questions. Maybe Mama can tell you more."

"Mama didn't even tell me that much. To be honest, I'm pissed. I'm pissed at Mama and even at Papi a little bit. I guess now I understand my last name finally, but why did she never tell the truth when I asked before?" She paused on the sidewalk and shook her head. Yacqueline stared up at her, her wide, dark eyes sympathetic. "And Tío, I dunno. I just don't know. Nothing feels right anymore."

Yacqueline touched her sister's arm. "But Lina, we're all still here. And we all still love you. You're still my sister, all of our sister. Nothing changes that. Mama and Tío are still Mama and Tío. And I think Tío still loves you like he loves all of us—

"Bull! Tío loves us because we're his best friend's kids. No other reason. He wouldn't have any other reason to take on nine kids out of nowhere. His older kid died, and it feels good to pretend he likes being papa to a bunch of kids that aren't his. *Por favor*! He's in love with Mama, but he puts up with all of us. He doesn't *love* us! We're not even his!"

"Lina, that's unkind," Yacqueline broke in firmly. "Why would— he-he doesn't feel that way."

Celina's eyes filled with tears as she added. "You guys are fine. You're Giac Montoya's kids. What am I? Mama was even too ashamed to tell him about me. I've no idea what he thinks about me, but it's not love. Not after he met that guy. No way."

As they turned around to head home, Yacqueline wordlessly linked her arm with her sister's.

"Lina, please bring Eli inside and come to the kitchen," Mama called from the front door as the girls and Elian came up the driveway. Celina looked up fearfully, but Mama had already gone back into the house.

"We're busted for taking him without asking," Celina moaned.

"It's okay, Lina. I wanted to go."

"Yeah, well, that's not the point . . . Celina's voice trailed off as she squatted to set Elian back down on the porch.

"Hey, I'm sorry, Mama, I—

Mama caught her daughter's hand and led her to the dining room table where Marcos sat. Celina glanced around. Yacqueline was heading upstairs, and her other siblings were nowhere to be seen. Marcos had a manila envelope and a small stack of papers on the table in front of him. Though she wasn't sure why, Celina's stomach tensed.

When all were seated, Marcos reached over and touched her hand. She moved her hand back.

"What's up, Tío?"

Marcos sighed and motioned to the papers in front of him. "Martie Pancorro's petitioned for custody of you."

"W-what?" Celina's eyes went wide, her heart began to race. She sat on her hands as they began to shake. "But he can't, right?"

The one thing I never saw coming.

She turned so suddenly to Mama that her shoulder-length hair swung forward over her shoulder. "You won't let him, will you? I mean, you have custody of me so—"

Mama looked down for a moment and then back up as she shook her head, her red, swollen eyes betraying her fear. "No, Lina," she replied, in English, for Marcos' benefit. "On paper, no one does. Martie never knew about you, so we never worried about it, living two states away. I should have handled this differently, I'm so sorry, Lina. But no, there's no legal custody order in place. And Martie has the right to— he has the right to try, and a judge will have to decide on the matter."

Celina swallowed hard as she stared down at her hands folded before her on the table. She blinked hard at the threatening tears. "You-you won't let him, will you, Tío?" Her voice was so soft it was nearly a whisper. "*Por favor* don't."

As she spoke, she wished she could see his face and know what he was thinking, but she knew if she looked up, she would cry.

Now he knows. He knows it would be easier if I didn't live here all the time anymore. Oh, Papi, why'd you have to go? This wouldn't be happening if you were still here. It wouldn't. I know you loved me. I know that for sure.

Determined that he would not see her cry, Celina stood abruptly to flee the room. Marcos caught her hand. "Hey, hey, hey, now," his gentle voice surprised her, "sit down. It's okay, we just need to talk."

From where she sat on the other side of the table, Mama moved around to sit beside her. She held Celina's hand tightly. "I love you, *malaynkia*," she whispered, kissing her head hard. "I love you."

Marcos reached for her hand again but thought better of it and leaned back in his chair. "Lina, we must appear in family court in a hearing downtown on Monday. My partner, Kon Dugan, will represent us. He's more familiar with family law than I am. Whatever questions the judge or Pancorro's lawyer asks you, just tell the truth even if you have to say you don't know, just tell the truth. It'll be okay. All we can do is our best."

Celina gripped Mama's hand as she forced out words, "Will I have to live with him?"

"I doubt it. With the marks against him, most likely not. But you gotta know that judges don't always make the right decisions. You just have to know that. But we're gonna fight if we have to. This will not go the other way without a fight."

"And Lina," Mama added, "we'll be right there with you. Tío's right, just tell the truth, and we grownups will handle the rest. I don't want you to be afraid. There's a lot in our favor. Please come talk to me if you feel afraid or sad or anything at all." Drawing her close against her breast, Alexei kissed her daughter's hair, then again, her own eyes swelling with tears as she did.

Although Celina prayed time would pass slowly, it was not to be, and Monday was upon them well before she was ready. After the other children had left for school, Elian and Baby Diego were taken to Senora Ulices's home for the day. Marcos, Mama and Celina then drove downtown to the city courthouse. When they arrived at room 221, a receptionist, sitting behind a small desk, looked over a clipboard of notes and pursed her lips.

"So, it looks like Celina will be waiting here with me for—"

"Where's that old judge anyway? He told me to have my ass here at 10. Well, I'm here. He's the one who's late!"

Celina started and shut her eyes on Martie Pancorro's impatient voice behind them. Marcos glanced back at the other man, disapprovingly.

"Mr. Pancorro, Judge Freeman will be here in a few minutes. Please sign in and have a seat."

"Yeah, right," Martie muttered as he elbowed Marcos to the side and signed the roster.

"*Pendejo*," Celina muttered.

Mama squeezed her hand once and barely whispered, "Mind your manners now."

As the family took their seats, Judge Freeman, in black robes, stepped from a side room and motioned Kon Dugan, Mama, Marcos and Martie into the room. He motioned for Celina to remain seated. Reluctantly, she leaned back in the leather chair.

The receptionist eyed her sternly over the top of thin glasses. "Now I have things to do. I don't have time to babysit. Mind yourself and don't bother anyone."

Celina glared back at her and then put in her earbuds but not before the receptionist, nose wrinkled, muttered, "Spoiled, disrespectful teenagers."

What IS your problem? Celina wanted to demand, but she wisely remained silent and stared hard ahead at the closed door where Mama and Marcos had disappeared. She gulped, suddenly realizing she had been holding her breath.

Why the heck did they make me stay out here? This whole mess is all about me!

After what seemed like forever, Celina started when she felt a hand on her wrist. She opened her eyes and pulled out an earbud, relaxing when she saw Mama. Alexei's mouth was set in a firm line, but she forced a smile.

"Lina, Judge Freeman wants to talk to you alone."

Her knees trembling, Celina followed Judge Freeman into the conference room. She sat down in a huge, leather, swivel chair adjacent to the judge at the long table.

Breathe, just breathe.

"So, Lina, am I right?" The balding man in black robes smiled at her.

"Yes, sir."

"So, I've just talked with your mother and biological father and stepfather. I think we've come to a decision, but you're fourteen, so I want to know what you think. You don't know your biological father, do you?"

"No, sir."

"Do you want to know him?"

"Not particularly."

"Why?"

"Because-uhm-I read some of my mama's journals. He used to beat her."

"People change. He's a bit rough around the edges, but he seems nice. No criminal record either."

"Maybe. But I had a father already. A good one. The best."

"Ah, yes, Giacamo Montoya. Your stepfather told me about him. I'm sorry for your loss. He sounded like a wonderful person. I appreciate you telling me how you feel. However—he sighed, and his voice trailed off as he wrote on a pad of paper.

Celina's stomach tensed, sickly. "However, what?"

"However, as much as your mother has a right to you, so does your father. He's a parent just as she is. He has a right to see you and know you and be in your life. I understand that there was a time when she felt she couldn't stay with him, and maybe that's all true. But that was then, and this is now. It's been over fourteen years. People change, grow, mature. And it looks like your biological father has done some of that. No, he's not perfect. He has issues, but I'm sure none of which—

"Did you know he's a drunk?" Celina blurted out.

"He assured me that that was a one-time thing, that he was upset and drank too much that day. Even still, it's a valid concern. Lina, my idea is to—

"Your Honor, please don't give him custody of me. I have a family already. I don't want to live with him."

"Custody? Oh, no, child, not custody; at least not at this time. My idea is to give you two a little time. School lets out next week, and what I want is for you to spend the summer with him in Los Alamos to get to know each other. Just the summer. We have a court-appointed, family advocate that will check on you two weekly as a safeguard. You won't be alone that way. Before school starts, we'll meet again to determine custody and visitation arrangements. What do you think?"

"Do I have a choice?"

The judge sighed and shook his head. "Not really, honey. You'll have more say in the custody/visitation agreement at the end of the summer. What I want now is for you and your biological father to have sufficient time together before we make any big decisions."

The Music of What Happens

As Celina left the room, her eyes swelled with tears. Angrily, she blinked hard. *I don't even know him. Besides that, I'm not a little kid anymore. I should like have a say in this. And what about the end of the summer? What happens then?*

Celina looked up to see Mama standing in front of her. Uncharacteristically, she grabbed her mother close, clinging to her as she cried into her shoulder. Mama held her for a long time, stroking her hair, and murmuring words of comfort. When Celina finally broke their embrace, she caught sight of Marcos sitting a few feet away, staring down at his hands.

He won't fight for me. And I know why.

Before heading home, Celina stopped by the bathroom to wash her face and refix her hair. For a moment, she stared at her reflection. *I'm not even yours anymore, Papi. And I know I'm not coming back, at least not for good. I've been a real brat, and I know Tío's gonna be glad to get rid of me. And I can't blame him.*

Despite having just washed her face, Celina broke down again, collapsing to her knees on the stone tiles. She ignored the grime digging painfully into her bare knees as she wept into her hands.

As Marcos backed the car out of the courthouse driveway, Celina stared, almost unseeing, from the backseat at Martie Pancorro as he walked to his beat-up jeep. Although he was too far away to see them, he grinned broadly in the direction of the Gonzalez's Escalade. She looked away.

CHAPTER 9

Custody

"Lina?"

Celina glanced up reluctantly.

"Did you hear my question?" Ms. Leighford asked, "Can you solve the equation on the board, and please take off the hood on your sweater."

Celina sighed and stood. She stared unseeing at the blackboard. She barely shook her head and sat back down.

"Lina, I know you're having a hard time right now, but I do need you to take your hood off."

Just leave me alone.

"Yeah, you look homeless. Whose ginormous hoodie is that? I bet your new daddy—"

"Staci Ainsworth, that's enough!"

Staci leaned back and whipped her compact out of her desk and focused on fixing her lip gloss. When Celina glanced in her direction, she smirked. "Are you back in the crap shack yet? I bet you will be soon. Gonzalez has gotta' be way pissed that—oh, speaking of pissed, you totally smell like piss again and—

"*Staci!* I said *enough*!"

Abruptly, Celina fled the room. She stormed down the hall to the restroom and locked herself in a stall. Sitting on the back of the toilet, tennis shoes on either side of the toilet seat, she sat there, shaking. Finally, she pushed back her hood, her greasy stringy curls hanging, plastered against her head. Bleary-eyed, she leaned her head back against the wall and closed her eyes as she chewed her nails. Staci was right. Chaim's black *Marlboro* hoodie hung almost to her knees.

"Lina? Lina, are you in here?"

Celina rolled her eyes to herself. *Why do these dumb bunny grownups think they get it? I don't even get why I have to leave like this. I hate this guy! I hate him!*

"Lina?" A soft knock sounded on the stall door, "please come out, honey. It's gonna be okay, let's talk."

Sighing deeply, Celina yanked her hood back up on her head and unlocked the stall door to see Mrs. Vriloczek, the school psychologist, standing there, smiling, sympathetically. She patted Celina's shoulder. "Ms. Leighford said I'd probably find you here. Let's go talk."

"I told you before, I don't need to talk," Celina mumbled, "thanks anyway."

As she stepped around the counselor, the woman caught her hand. "I spoke to your mother this morning; she wants you to have a few sessions with me. It's okay, let's go to my office."

Celina gently removed her hand from the woman's and stared at her through hooded eyes. "Ok," she mumbled.

"So, your mama brought me up to speed on what's happening with your family. She's really worried about you."

"I don't see why." Celina picked up a paperweight from the coffee table separating the couch from the counselor's chair. She turned the wooden cube around and around in her hand several times before setting it back down. Mrs. Vriloczek waited quietly for her to look up.

"Maybe because you don't even look like yourself anymore. I've never known you to come to school looking like— well— not like yourself, honey. Is that your brother's sweater?"

"What if it is? We used to wear each other's clothes all the time when we were poor."

"Lina, look up at me please."

Celina tucked her legs under her and looked up, reluctantly.

"Honey, let's sort this out. Are you afraid or sad or angry?"

What do you think I am, you twit? I'm pissed! And I'm scared. I'm not scared of that drunk moron, I'm scared of Tío. I'm scared of what's going to happen when this is over. I wouldn't blame him one bit if he told Señor Pancorro to—

"I'm pissed," she mumbled, wishing she could bring herself to tell the truth. "He's messed up everything. I've got a family! I don't want him in my life. I *had* a father! I'm not looking for another one."

As Celina trudged back to class, she ran into Elizaveta on her way to the restroom. Her friend linked arms with her.

"I'm sorry, Lina. I know Mrs. Vriloczek's a pain. She thinks she knows everything."

Celina shrugged. "Naw, she's okay. She means well. I just don't want to talk right now. Have you seen Chaim or Javier?"

"No, but I did see Jade. She's already showing, and yeah, it's totally Cal's baby," she whispered, gossipy.

"Yeah, okay, Lis," Celina stepped around her friend and meandered down the hall toward the 7th-grade hallway, leaving Elizaveta staring after her.

Celina started as the bell sounded and the halls became bedlam. Tucking her hands under her armpits, she moved almost unseeing through the crowd of students heading to their next classes.

Suddenly, she was shoved hard into a row of lockers. She twisted instinctively and swung around. Staci stepped back, and Marcail let go of her other arm. Jade blocked her in with her arm.

Staci yanked off Celina's hood and feigned disgust at her flat, greasy curls. "Uhm, gross! Not trying to upstage me anymore, are you now?" She poked Celina hard in the chest and then again. "Back to smelling like piss again, are you?" She poked Celina yet again in the chest.

Without warning, Celina, who had felt like she was walked in a fog for the last two weeks, grabbed Staci's wrist and twisted it hard as she spun her around and shoved her face into the locker! Her fingers tangled in Staci's golden waves; she slammed her head twice against the metal door. Still holding her wrist in an iron grip, Celina turned partially to see Marcail and Jade both coming at her. "Try it both of you and I'll snap her arm. Don't think I won't!" To emphasize her point, she squeezed Staci's arm harder and pushed it further up her back.

"*No!*" Staci bawled, in pain, "don't break my arm! Please don't break my arm!"

"Lina!"

Celina recognized Mrs. Vriloczek's horrified voice behind her. She shoved Staci hard away from her, so hard that she stumbled backward and fell flat on her bottom. When Mrs. Vriloczek's hand touched her, Celina flipped the woman's hand off her shoulder. The counselor began to speak, but Celina didn't hear her as she rushed away toward the seventh-grade hallway. Arriving at the door in front of Chaim's math class, she waited outside the door until the seventh graders were released.

"Sis!" Chaim's voice broke into her thoughts, "It's warm out. How come you're wearing my sweater?"

"Just a little cold is all," Celina mumbled, "got a cigarette? I'm desperate."

Chaim glanced around, then pressed close to his sister and slipped one into her hand. "Last one," he whispered. His dark eyes were sympathetic as he gave her hand a quick squeeze, "Take it easy, Sis."

"I'm ditching. Wanna come?"

"Well, I've got an earth science quiz in thirty minutes—aw, what the heck. Let's go." Chaim caught Celina's arm and turned her in the direction of the back exit.

"So you won't talk to Mama or Marc or Ms. Vriloczek. Will you talk to me?" Chaim took a huge swallow of a Big Gulp then offered Celina some. She distractedly declined but grabbed a handful of buttered popcorn as the movie previews flashed before them on the big screen.

"We're at a movie, bro. Not really the place for a long chat."

"We're the only ones here."

Celina sighed and nodded. "I don't know what to say, *hermano*. I get that I can't do anything about spending the summer with Señor Pancorro but—

"Wish I could go with you, Sis," Chaim patted her arm as he shoveled another handful of popcorn into his mouth. "But you'll be back before school starts."

Celina leaned back in her seat and sighed, tiredly. *Would he understand? Would he get it that Marc won't want me back? He's Papi's, he's got nothing to worry about, even if he wasn't the golden boy he is.*

"I guess."

"Of course, you will. I've been doing some reading. Family law. Tío's partner gave me this one book. It's about custody and child support and such. Once that guy finds out that he'll have to pay child support, he'll split. Like a drunk would ever–

"Would you shut it for like five minutes?" Celina swallowed hard, "I don't want to talk about this. Can we just watch the movie?"

Dark brown eyes understanding, Chaim nodded, and the two were silent for the duration of the film.

"So where have you two been?" Marcos asked from the dining room table when Celina and Chaim entered the house at four o'clock.

"Uhm— Chaim began to speak then fell silent. Celina glanced at her brother. Marcos looked stern. Clearly, he had gotten a phone call from the school.

"So, Lina gets into a fight, and then you both ditch? What's up? Lina, please don't look at the floor when I'm talking to you and take your hood off."

Celina gulped back threatening tears and looked up. Her stomach growled but as of late, she had little appetite. Obediently, she pushed back the hood, revealing greasy, stringy, black curls plastered against the base of her neck.

"Oh, honey, you're looking like hell lately. Alexei?" he called out, "can you meet me and Lina in our bedroom? Yacque, can you finish dinner? Sol, set the table for your sister please. Chaim," he turned to his stepson, "homework. We'll talk later."

"Lina," Mama said, gently, as she sat down on the bed beside her, "we gotta' get this depression handled. Mrs. Vriloczek said you would hardly talk. I want you to talk to *someone*. You're hardly eating or showering anymore, and I'm worried. I know where this is coming from. It's only two weeks away now, isn't it?"

Celina sighed. *I wish I could ask. I wish I knew how Tío feels. He's been nothing but kind since this happened, but this is like his way out of having a brat like me around. And he has no reason to love me anymore anyway. I've lost papi and now I've lost Tío too. I wish I could tell him I'm sorry but it's too late for all that now.*

"Marc—" She halted and shook her head as she choked, "I'm sorry."

"Sorry for what, Lina? None of this is your fault. Why would you be sorry?"

Explain yourself! Her mind screamed at her. But she couldn't. *I know the answer. Tío has no reason to love me anymore.*

The day after school let out dawned bright. When Celina awoke, she stood in front of her bedroom window, staring down into the yard for a long time. The rich, green grass practically glistened in the brilliant sun.

I just want to be here. I don't even know him. What about my brothers and sisters? What about Eli? What if I never see him again?

Celina swallowed hard around the lump in her throat then trudged down the hall to the bathroom. She was just getting out of the shower when Mama tapped lightly on the door.

"Lina, breakfast," she whispered. Celina didn't respond as she dressed carefully in a blue, crop top over a white tank, denim shorts and white platform sneakers. She stared at her reflection in the mirror. Wide, almost frightened, dark brown eyes stared back at her, her lips curved up just so and her olive skin was a bit darker than Mama's. As dark as . . .

"His." She whispered. "And Mama always said my eyes were the color of Turkish coffee, but she never told me that his were too."

The other children had been allowed to sleep late as this was the first day of summer, and Mama did not want the youngest ones crying when their sister left. Alone at the table, Celina stared down at her plate of *blini* with jam and bowl of kasha. Usually her favorite breakfast, she could barely swallow even a bite as she pushed the food around her plate. A footfall startled her as Marcos entered the room with his newspaper and sat down across from her, just as Mama left the room to get Diego, crying hungrily in his crib upstairs. Celina sighed. The last person she wanted to talk to was Marcos.

Almost as if reading her thoughts, Marcos reached over and touched her hand, sighing when she pulled back. "Lina, I—

"Marc, it's okay. I get it. I've been—

"Lina, I'll fight for you."

"Why? I'm not who you always thought I was. I might as well like be a stranger. Tío, I may be young, but I'm not dumb. If I were you, I'd want to get rid of me too."

"Now that's not true, it's just that—

"Just what? Just what's best? It's best that I be with someone I don't even know? That I get used to it 'cuz that's what it's going to be like from here on out? If you wanted to fight for me, you'd have done it already. It took all of two days for you all to decide to send me off with that drunk. What's wrong with you all? And then to tell me you care, that you love me, that you'll fight for me. Don't bother, Tío! I know the truth. Just because Mama couldn't be bothered to tell the truth all these years doesn't mean I won't!"

"Lina, please don't say such things about your mother. You don't know what you're saying. What she did was to put you first. She put you first from the moment she found out she was pregnant. She loves you."

"Loves me? People who love people don't lie to them for fourteen years. People who love people don't say things like 'I hope I can love my child but how can I look at her through his eyes every day for the rest of my life?' Yeah, she totally said that in that stupid diary of hers. And you, yeah, you'll fight for me all right. As much as you'd fight for Diego if you had to? I don't friggin' think so!"

Tears filling her eyes, Celina stormed from the dining room. Grabbing her duffel from the foyer, she slammed the door behind her and sat down on the porch swing. Martie would be arriving any minute. She put in her earbuds and turned up her favorite *Diamante Rio* song. Her eyes widened at the lyrics. She had never thought of them as she did now.

I was a fool. I turned my back. The love he offered crushed on the ground. I was a fool.

Celina swiped at her eyes. "I gotta tell him I'm sorry," she whispered, desperately. "Maybe I can make him understand. I don't wanna leave my family!"

Just as she stood to go back inside, the roar of a jeep without a muffler, disturbing the peaceful neighborhood street, startled her. At that exact moment, Mama came onto the porch and grabbed Celina tightly in a bear hug. Celina clung to her, wishing she could beg her mother to let her stay, wishing she dared run from him.

I wish I could stop the world and rewind it back to when Papi was alive. No matter what, he loved me. He showed it every day. I know he'd have fought for me. I was his. He decided I was his, and I was!

"Well, 'Lexei, I'm here for my kid," Martie's irritating bravado was evident in his voice as he swaggered up the stone path to the porch. "Come on, Kid. Let's hit the road."

"I'm saying goodbye to my *mother*, Señor Pancorro, do you friggin' mind?"

As Celina hugged Mama once more, she whispered, "Please hug Eli for me, and tell the others I love them. Mama, I don't want to leave. I know that—

Mama leaned forward, pressing her forehead against her daughter's and whispered back, "Remember, you're Giac Montoya's daughter. Be kind and respectful, as he would have you to be. Make him proud; make me proud. And don't you worry, you'll be home before you know it."

Celina winced inwardly. After the way she had spoken to Marcos just now, after the way she had acted for a year now . . . *I'll be lucky if ever see any of them again.*

Without a word, she turned and started down the porch steps, Martie reached forward and grabbed her duffel.

"Uhm— she rolled her eyes when he ignored her and threw it into the back of the jeep.

As the jeep peeled out of the driveway, Celina's eyes were glued on the third floor, sliding glass door where Marcos stood, staring after them as they disappeared in a cloud of tan dust.

For the first hour, Celina and Martie drove in silence. Celina kept her earbuds in and pretended to ignore him. She covertly studied his profile.

He looks so much like me, she marveled, *people always said I had Papi's colors and Mama's face. They didn't know anything, that's for sure.*

Finally, Martie broke the silence. Celina sighed as she took out an earbud. "What?"

"Jes' wanting to get to know ya' a bit, Kid. Can we talk? Thanks to 'Lexei, I dunno crap about ya'."

For a moment, Celina was silent as she stared hard at him. *The last person I want to talk to is him.*

She sighed, dramatically, "I suppose. Nothing else to do."

"So, I'm from Cuelican, but I lived most o' my life in Texas. Moved to Los Alamos about three years ago, and that's where I met Jen."

"Who's Jen?"

"Jenita Marquez. She's my girlfriend, sorta." Martie grinned, wickedly, and Celina rolled her eyes. "Now as far as 'Lexei goes—"

Celina whirled around in her seat. "Señor Pancorro, what say we like leave my mama outta' this? I know what you're like, I know what you used to do to her! You got nothing to say that I wanna' hear so don't even *think* about talking smack!"

Before she could react, Martie swerved hard against the shoulder of the highway. He grabbed her arm. "Or what?" he shouted in her face, "*or what?* Now, listen here, you little brat—"

Celina wrenched her arm from his grasp and sat back against the passenger door. "No, *you* listen here! Either leave my family alone or you'll have a summer from hell, I can promise you that. You don't have any right talkin' smack about my mama! She never talked smack about you to me! Though she sure as heck could've!"

Martie stared hard at her from the other side of the console. "Ya' sure got a mouth on ya', Kid. Now listen, I don't wanna lay down the law first day but you either do as I say or—"

"Or what?" Celina challenged, "you'll hit me? You'll beat me up like you did my mama? Why don't you just go ahead and try it. I'm *not* my mama! I'll have your sorry butt thrown in jail faster than—"

"Now, come on, Kid," Martie broke in, trying to make peace. "I wouldn't hit ya', and I'm not wantin' to fight. Just want to figure ya' out a bit. Never knew I was a papa all these years."

Celina sighed. "Okay. Talk."

"So nuthin' 'bout 'Lexei, so what grade ya' in in school?"

"Going into ninth."

"Well, that's really good. Me, I didn't have much chance for school. My mama died when I was just a little kid and then . . ."

Though she tried to listen politely, she eventually found herself growing sleepy as Martie droned on, seldom expecting a reply.

When Celina awoke suddenly, it was dark, and she sat alone in the jeep. Blinking hard as her eyes adjusted to the darkness, she finally made out the silhouette of a tall building directly ahead of her. A small flashing sign in the window read VACANCIES.

We're at a motel?

As she stepped out of the car, she grimaced at the litter and bottles around the yard. Gingerly stepping over them, she made her way to the motel door. The smell of marijuana, stale alcohol and BO was overwhelming as she stepped inside. Glancing about, she shook her head to herself. The rust-colored carpet was badly stained, and the walls were covered in smudges and peeling paint.

Seriously? Gross!

"Can I help you, Kid?"

Startled, Celina turned to see who she figured was the manager sitting behind a badly scarred, wooden desk in the corner. As she made her way over to him, the scent of BO and alcohol became stronger. The manager wore a white, wife beater, stained with ketchup and mustard, and his long stringy hair needed washing. Gap-toothed, he grinned, and it took effort for Celina not to wince at his yellow teeth and the smell of his breath. She forced a half-smile.

"Is Señor Pancorro here somewhere?"

"Oh, him? The Mexican guy?"

"Yeah, him, the Mexican guy," Celina rolled her eyes.

"Oh, he's somewhere, but not here. He got a room though; he told me to show you when you came in. Down the hall, second door on the right. Room 7."

"Grass-iass," Celina sarcastically mispronounced as she slung her duffel over her shoulder and made her way down the hall.

When she arrived at Martie's room, she sat down carefully on the unmade bed, taking care to avoid the stained sheets. Through the dusty, flickering light on the ceiling, she looked around. Old pizza boxes, acrid-smelling Chinese take-out boxes and empty tequila bottles littered the dirty floor, and a rat nibbled at a slice of half-eaten pizza. The room reeked of BO and rotting food. Celina sighed deeply.

"So, this is how it starts. I should have figured. Drunks sure aren't good for much." Pulling her duffel onto her lap, she unzipped it and rummaged through it for a piece of grape bubble gum. She smiled, half-heartedly. Mama had made sure to pack her favorites of everything: clothes, bubble gum, photos, comic books and extra batteries for her iPod. A tear and then another trickled down Celina's cheek.

"I miss them already," she mumbled, "even Tío. I just want to go home. Maybe if I apologize and promise to act better . . . she sighed. "Tío's plain old fed up with my dumb bunny self by now." Celina blinked back more tears. "What if something happens, and I never see Eli again?" This thought was enough to bring on sobs, and she wept into her hands for a long time.

Hours later, the door swung open, and Martie Pancorro stumbled in, drunk. Celina stared hard at him but said nothing. She moved from the bed and pulled up the old rickety chair in the corner of the room. Martie did not acknowledge his daughter's presence, only fell onto the bed, instantly passed out. Celina put in her earbuds and pulled up Mama's lullabies on YouTube. She closed her eyes and leaned back in the chair as she listened to *Rozhinkes Mit Mandlen*.

It's not near as wonderful as when Mama sings it to us, but it's all I've got.

The next morning, her stomach growling, Celina stepped out of the room, leaving Martie snoring in bed. A stocky woman in a leather, biker's jacket had taken over for the night manager and she smiled when Celina appeared.

"You're Martie's kid, right?"

"Unfortunately."

The middle-aged woman laughed and nodded. "Yeah, he's something, that's for sure. My goodness, I expected a little girl, but you're pretty grown up, pretty as a picture too. Where'd you come from? I never even knew that boy had kids."

"That makes two of us, lady."

The biker woman cocked her head and studied Celina closely. "My name's Tina. I ride motorcycle with Martie when he comes around. You hungry, Kid?"

"My name's Lina, and yeah, I'm pretty hungry."

"Vending machines aren't working, as usual, but Mcdonald's is right around the corner. You got money?"

Celina nodded as she disappeared out the door. For a long time, she sat on the bench against the motel's, cracked siding as she ate her egg McMuffin and sipped her Coke. "Geez, Mama would like totally lay an egg if she knew I was eating McDonald's." She giggled, halfheartedly. "I used to think that rule sucked, but now— she shook her head sadly.

"Hey, Kid," Martie finally popped his head out the door. He squinted, painfully, despite the overcast skies. "Got me a splitting headache, so don't mind me. Let's hit the road."

"Señor Pancorro, like where *are* we going? We're way out of Santa Fe." Celina took out an earbud after a couple hours on the road.

"I live in Los Alamos, Kid. We'll be there in about an hour and a half."

Almost before Celina knew it, they were pulling up in front of a small, brown frame house with a tiny porch facing the road. She shook her head out the passenger side window, scrutinizing the trash-littered yard. Martie appeared not to notice as he put the jeep in park. When he threw open the front door, Celina right behind him, he startled her when he yelled, "Jen!"

A woman appeared from behind a partition, separating the small living area from an even smaller kitchen. She stared at the floor for a long minute. "What, Martie?" she mumbled.

"Here's the kid. What was your name again?" he turned to Celina.

Are you flipping serious?

"Lina Montoya."

Martie shook his head sucking in his cheeks as he glared hard at the floor. "Yeah, well, if I'd had any say about naming you, I'd—well, when the judge says you're living with me for good, I'll—

"You'll what, Señor Pancorro? And no judge is gonna' make me live with *you*! I'll just spill the juice about you passing out drunk last night. You're disgusting, and I'm *not* living with you!"

She stepped out from behind Martie and nodded, politely at the woman in the kitchen entrance. "*¡Hola,* I'm Lina."

"Jenita. I'll show you your room. It's at the end of the hall."

Casting a withering glance in Martie's direction, Celina slung her duffel over her thin shoulder and followed Jenita to a room at the end of a small hallway. The room had a twin bed, a small dresser and a peeling, yellowish, tile floor with dirty grout. Celina couldn't help but smile at the scads of photos pinned all over the walls. When she turned back towards the door, she saw that Jenita had already left.

Setting the duffel on the hastily made bed, she moved from wall to wall, examining pictures of Martie, Jenita and friends. She paused at one; her eyes went wide. A small picture at the far end of the room was Mama.

She barely looks older than me.

Celina unpinned the photo and studied it. Mama wore a green and black corduroy dress, faded and stained. Her dark eyes were almost more tired than Celina had ever seen, but happy, as she looked up at Martie. A teenager himself, he stood beside her, arm wrapped around her shoulder. His white and red striped shirt was oversized and slouchy, and his grin was awkward, bordering on idiotic. For a long time, Celina stared down at the photo in her hand. Setting it beside her, on the bed, she rummaged through her duffel and pulled out a picture of Mama, Papi, propped up with pillows on the bed beside her, and all nine of the children either sitting on the bed or the floor in front of the bed. Marcos had taken the photo six months before Papi passed away. She swallowed hard as she pinned it to the wall at the head of her bed.

After washing up in the bathroom, Celina wandered back down the hall to the kitchen. She halted at the sight that met her eyes. Martie and Jenita, sitting on the counter before him, were kissing passionately as Martie feverishly slipped her sweater up over her head, exposing her pink bra.

Celina's jaw dropped, and she turned quickly to leave. At just that second, Jenita who had just seen her out of the corner of her eye, pulled forcefully from Martie's grasp and, flushing bright red, clutched her sweater in front of her as she hurried past Celina and disappeared down the hall. Martie stared first at the floor and then at Celina.

"Awkward," he mumbled, chuckling.

Celina eyed him scornfully as she turned her back, "Get a room, sex machine!" she threw over her shoulder as she stalked down the hall slamming her bedroom door behind her. A while later, she started at a knock on the door.

"C-come in."

The door opened, and Martie Pancorro stood in the doorway and stared at her for a long, tense moment.

"What?" Celina asked, not disrespectfully.

"I-I'm sorry, Kid."

"O-okay, Señor Pancorro," Celina replied, uncertainly, not sure what he wanted her to say. Her heart raced. She had not been expecting an apology.

"Okay, Kid," Martie Pancorro nodded. "and . . . the name's Martie. No one calls me señor, and it makes me nervous."

"Martie then."

"Do-do you want some-some supper?"

"No. Thanks anyway, Señ-I mean, Martie."

Celina shut her eyes as the door closed behind him. She drew a shuddering breath, clasping her sweaty palms together.

Around ten, another knock sounded at her door. At Celina's invitation, Martie appeared again. "I just came to say g'night."

"Oh. *Buenos noches,* Martie."

He nodded and turned to leave then turned slowly back. For a long time, he and Celina stared at each other from across the room.

Celina's heart pounded, and Martie's eyes looked almost frightened. "What?" she finally asked, softly.

Martie hesitated. "I-I don't know you, Kid," he finally said, hoarsely.

Celina bit her lip as she looked down her hands folded in her lap. *What would it have been like to have known him? What if he and Mama had stayed together and I'd grown up with him as my papi? Would we have loved each other?*

But Celina did not voice her thoughts aloud. "I know," she whispered, meeting his eyes with a hesitant gaze of her own.

Martie started to say something else but stopped midsentence. "G'night," he said again, leaving the room without another word.

Celina put her head in her hands and closed her eyes tightly. *I don't want to know him. I just want to go home! Will I ever go home for real?* Head aching, she crawled under the quilts and tried to sleep.

The next morning, Celina awakened to sunshine streaming in her window. Following a shower, she dressed quickly in a blue denim skort, her favorite, fitted, pink t-shirt and denim sneakers. As she was brushing her thick black hair, a soft knock sounded at the bathroom door.

Jenita smiled, cheeks flushed, barely making eye contact. "I didn't really notice much last night," she mumbled an apology, "but I do now. You're very beautiful, Lina. Your eyes are so like your father's. And your hair—" she reached out as if to touch it. Celina stepped backward. Jenita blushed and looked down again. "Breakfast?" she whispered.

Celina did not acknowledge the compliment. "No *gracias*. Where's Martie?"

"Downtown with the *vaqueros*. They're riding motorcycles."

Inwardly, Celina rolled her eyes. "Don't he got no job?"

Jenita hesitated. "He does . . . odd jobs."

Celina did not question further. *It's weird the way she stares at the floor when she talks.*

"Well, I'm gonna head out for a while and see what's around. I'll be back later."

When Jenita disappeared into the kitchen, Celina stepped back into the bathroom. She stared critically at her reflection in the chipped, oval mirror above the sink. Her eyes, wide, dark, and deep-set, were undeniably the spitting image of Martie. Her oval face and gently pointed chin came from Mama and her olive skin was a combination of both. She ran her fingers through her thick head of naturally messy curls, also like Martie's. She chewed her lip.

I'm not beautiful like Mama and Sol. If only I could wear makeup like Lissy and my other friends, then maybe I'd be pretty. I mean, I'm almost a woman. Except for Mama, women wear makeup! She sighed as she turned to one side and then another and shook her head. *When am I ever gonna get boobs? Lissy's already a B and I've been stuck in these dumb bunny training bras for almost a year now.*

As Celina strolled down a quiet, dusty back street adjacent to an alley littered with various trash, she took in her surroundings. Small houses with dirt yards, littered with brush and leaves, and a few somewhat old-fashioned stores and buildings lined the streets. She smiled as she gazed out at the highway, such a combination of modern city and more traditional Mexican regions.

This is gonna be interesting. She touched her growling stomach. *Maybe a soda and a popsicle.*

As she headed out of the air-conditioned convenience store, the boiling dry heat from the sun nearly took her breath away. She sucked her popsicle quickly as it started to melt almost immediately and gulped her soda. Sitting on the pavement sidewalk in the shade, just outside the store, chin in hand, she smiled at a traditionally dressed family as they exited the post office adjacent to the convenience store. The eldest, a girl wearing a peasant skirt and white blouse with a *rebozo* over her head, appeared to be about her own age. Carrying an infant strapped to her back, she smiled shyly in Celina's direction. As the family climbed into their pickup, she said something to her father then headed back in Celina's direction,

"¡*Hola, mí llamo* Josefina Juarez. ¿*Cómo te llamos?*"

"Lina Montoya."

"I've never seen you around before, and I know pretty much everybody in this part of town."

Celina shrugged. "I just got in yesterday. As much as it sucks, I'm being forced to spend the summer with my biological father. Who I just found out about."

Josefina's dark eyes widened. "What's his name? I don't know any Montoyas around here."

"Not Montoya, Pancorro. Martie Pancorro."

Josefina did not reply to this, only smiled tightly and glanced away. Celina wanted to ask what was wrong but refrained.

She quickly changed the subject. "Wanna hang out? I don't know anyone here."

Josefina smiled. "Kinda' what I was hoping for when I came over. I only have a couple of friends since I take care of *mí* papa and the little kids."

"You don't got a mama?"

Josefina's eyes darkened and she shrugged. "Let's walk. Would you like to come to my house? I gotta keep an eye on the kids. "

She then waved to her father who waved back and climbed into his truck.

As the girls strolled in silence, Celina furtively studied her companion. Josefina was several inches taller than she and round like Elizaveta. Long, coal black hair, glistening like a raven's wing in the brilliant mid-morning sun, was braided tightly and her dress was a white peasant top with a colorful, red and orange, knee-length skirt edged in black and white trim. As they turned down a dusty, back road, Josefina kept kicking up little clouds of sand with her worn sandal. Celina wished she would stop but said nothing.

Senor Juarez, happy that his eldest was spending time with a friend her age, enlisted eleven-year-old Cesar to look after three-year-old Aquino and the youngest, beautiful, thirteen-month-old Leticia. He then sent Ignatius to bring the girls cool lemonade as they sat at the farthest end of the dirt yard and talked.

"So, where you from? I'm from Culiacan in Mexico."

"Santa Fe. I'm a city girl. You ever been there?"

Josefina blinked and stared hard at her hands for a moment.

"What is it?"

Josefina shook her head and sighed, deeply. "My-my mama lives in Santa Fe. I've never been there."

"Your mama doesn't live with you?"

"Nope," Josefina replied, matter-of-factly, "took off with *mí* papa's kid brother right after my sister was born. That was a year ago, and we ain't heard from her since. I take care of Papa and the kids. I'm old enough."

Celina did not know what to say. *Mothers just don't do that, do they? Even when parents get divorced, mothers don't just go away and leave their kids forever . . . do they?*

"I got five kids to take care of," Josefina countered, sadness in her eyes. "I wish Mama was here to help me, but she doesn't want us anymore." Josefina's voice hardened. "It's Leticia she doesn't want. Before she left, she said a defective baby isn't worth raising."

Celina gulped her lemonade to avoid a rush of tears. *Poor Leticia, poor Josefina and the boys. Maybe Mama didn't love me at first, but she never abandoned me! She never forgot she was my mama.*

Josefina did not appear to notice Celina's discomfort as she continued. "It's rough on Papa, but he works hard. He'd work harder if the asthma weren't always givin' him the devil. What about you?"

"Well, I'm the eldest of ten," Celina replied, still a bit distracted. Her expression suddenly troubled, she turned and stared off toward the horizon. "I-I didn't want to come here. I mean, Martie's *mí* papa, I guess, but I don't even know him. I kinda hate him. I'm scared, Josefina," she turned to her new friend, dark eyes wide and worried, "I don't know what's gonna happen."

The other girl placed a hand on Celina's shoulder. "*Yo sé*," she whispered, meaningfully. "*Yo sé.*"

And Celina, often skeptical of the true intentions of others, knew in her heart that Josefina spoke the truth. The motherless girl most certainly did know.

Celina spent the rest of the day at Josefina's. The immigrant family welcomed her with open arms. Two years earlier, Julio Juarez, his pregnant wife and then five young children left their central Mexican village and settled in Los Alamos. Celina instantly liked Señor Juarez and Josefina's four young brothers, Cesar, Ignatius, Romero and adorable Aquino. The youngest of the Juarez children, beautiful Leticia, was blind.

Despite their poverty, Celina couldn't help but smile to herself, watching them interact as a family. While Señor Juarez held Leticia on one knee and Aquino on the other, he told them stories and sang them songs. Josefina and Cesar cooked supper, declining Celina's offer to help. During her time with them, Celina was able to forget her homesickness and truly enjoy herself. After visiting for a while, she and Josefina played hide and seek with the boys and took turns pushing them on a homebuilt tire swing.

At five-thirty, she fully intended to head back to Martie's, but Señor Juarez and the children insisted she stay for supper. During the evening meal, Josefina's father told stories of his childhood in Mexico. Julio Juarez was a gifted storyteller, and even little Aquino listened eagerly. As they visited, Celina fed Baby Leticia for her older sister. The sweet baby turned her thoughts to Diego.

Will I ever see him again; will I ever see any of them again?

Lost in thought, Celina touched her gold locket with Papi's picture. As she silently reminisced, the thought once again came to her about who's picture belonged on the other side. No matter how she tried, Celina could not settle on the right person. It seemed it would forever—

"Lina. Lina?"

Celina started and turned. Josefina smiled. "Want to help me with cleanup?"

Before Celina could reply, Señor Juarez turned to his eldest daughter and offered her Leticia. "How about Tish joins you and Lina outside, and the boys and I will take care of the clean-up? That was a beautiful supper, *nena.*"

Josefina kissed her father's cheek and she and Celina hurried outside. As they chatted, Josefina rocked Leticia in her arms. Finally, a lump in her throat at the thought of Baby Diego, Celina held out her arms.

"May I?" she whispered. The tiny child responsively rested her head on Celina's shoulder and as she rocked her, it was not long before Leticia was fast asleep in her arms.

"I had a great time, Josefina. *Gracias*. I hope we can hang out again soon."

"Come over tomorrow if you can. I have to watch the kids, but we could all go to the park."

"For sure," Celina smiled, "Besides, Martie's probably sleeping one off in jail by now." She rolled her eyes and waved goodbye.

Upon arriving home, Celina found Martie surprisingly not very drunk but upset. "Where the hell ya' been all day?"

"I-you-well— Celina stammered, taken off guard.

Slamming his left fist into his right palm, Martie shouted, "Ya' tried to run, didn't ya'? Just admit it!"

Celina shouted back, "Is there some medication you forgot to take today: like a CHILL PILL! I didn't do anything wrong, and I'm not gonna sit in your house all day, doing nothing! So, get over yourself!"

Martie was so taken aback that he didn't even attempt to respond. Celina took advantage of his silence to explain.

"You were gone this morning, so I got a soda at the convenience store and walked around town. Made a new friend too. Nothing to give yourself a stroke over! Dude, you're wound tighter'n a drum!"

Martie rolled his eyes but did not reply as he started for the kitchen, then turned so suddenly that Celina took a step backward.

"Who's her papa?" he demanded.

She blinked. "Uhm, Juarez . . . I think. *Si*, that's right. Julio Juarez. His oldest girl's my age and—

Celina was less than prepared for Martie's reaction. "Julio Juarez!" He bellowed; fists balled at his side. "What the— can't trust ya' outta' my sight for a second? Don'tcha ever go there again, and ya' can forget being friends with that kid! The family's trash and no kid o' mine's gonna' hang around trash like them! Ya' friggin' understand me?"

Anger boiling inside her, Celina shoulder-checked him out of the way as she started for her room.

"Why you little—get yer'self back here!"

"*¡Vete al diablo!*" Celina shouted at him then stomped down the hall, slamming her bedroom door so hard the walls vibrated. She flung herself onto the bed and lay, glaring at the wall.

If Martie thinks he can pull this crap, he's got another thing coming! I'll be friends with whoever the heck I want to!"

For a long time, Celina lay on her bed, staring at the open locket containing Papi's picture. It was now two years since Giac Montoya had passed away, yet to his daughter, it seemed like yesterday that she had lain beside him on the bed, wrapped in his arms.

"Oh, Papi," she whispered, tears trickling down her cheeks and dripping onto the pillow, "You'd have never let all this happen, would you? I bet you wouldn't have."

Celina never learned what caused Martie to hate Senor Juarez, however, he finally agreed that the girls could hang out together if he didn't have to see Josefina's father. Julio Juarez worked six days a week at a snuff factory downtown, "a sweatshop," Josefina called it. Cesar was nearly twelve, old enough to look after Ignatius and Romero on his own while his sister and Celina cared for the littlest ones. Most often, Celina and Josefina stayed near the Juarez home or the schoolyard, but sometimes, the two babies in tow, they walked downtown to window shop and eat popsicles.

"So, I think I'll head out tomorrow," Martie leaned back and put his feet on the table. "*Amigos* and me haven't rode motorcycle in a while. I—

Between bites of her supper, Celina glanced at Jenita who cleared her throat and gave Martie a pointed look.

Martie nodded and turned to Celina. "So, Lina, what say you and yer' ole' papa ride motorcycle tomorrow? Want to?"

Celina's mouth broke into a broad grin. "Sure thing," she could not hide her excitement, "I'd love to. Tío doesn't have a motorcycle."

"Yeah? So, ole' Gonzalez don't got ever'thing, now does he? Wonders never cease. So, what would 'Lexei say if she knew you was ridin' bike?"

"Wouldn't allow it."

"Then It'll be our secret."

Celina grinned again. Her heart raced joyfully. *I've always wanted to ride a motorcycle! And he even wants to do something with me instead of always hanging around downtown.*

The next morning, she awakened earlier than usual. She smiled broadly at the bright, sunny day outside. After dressing in jeans, tennis shoes, and a pink spaghetti strap tank, she rushed out to the kitchen. Her heart sank when she saw no sign of Martie. Jenita was sitting at the table. She smiled when she saw Celina.

"Lina, it's so early. Your papa's not up yet."

Celina slumped into the chair closest to her. "Gee, I just wanted to get on the road. I've never rode motorcycle before."

Jenita reached over and lightly touched her hand. "Soon, my *nena*. Have patience. He'll probably be up in a few hours. In the meantime, breakfast?"

Jenita talking and Jenita whispering are like totally the same thing. Hope she loosens up soon. It's not like I'm gonna bite or something.

Motioning to the empty speedway, Martie grinned down at Celina, "Here we are. Just me and you today, Kid. The vaqueros are all sleeping one off somewhere."

"Cool! Are we ready to go?"

"Hey! Hey, Kid, take it a bit slower, or I'll have to put the training wheels on!" Martie shouted, jokingly.

Within half an hour, Celina no longer needed Martie pressing his hands over hers on the handlebars. "I got it!" she cried, laughing, as she revved the engine and took off for another spin, even faster this time. "I *got* it!" She yelled again as she passed Martie who stood by, a lit cigarette in his hand, laughing as he called out.

"That's my girl!"

He motioned for her to stop. Reluctantly, Celina pulled up in front of him. She pushed her windblown hair back out of her eyes, still laughing.

"Best high there is, huh, Kid?"

Still sitting on the bike, Celina gasped out, "Exactly! It's like you're flying, and nothing bad can touch you. Nothing at all."

Martie nodded. "The endorphins don't suck either, do they? Here, move over, Kid, Let ole' daddy show you how it's done."

Still giggling, Celina playfully punched Martie's shoulder. "Here, gimme' one of those." She motioned to the cigarette in his hand.

"You smoke, Kid?"

"Keeps the appetite down," was Celina's only explanation as she took the offered cigarette. She was glad Martie did not press further.

He narrowed his eyes at her as he lit it. "One's fine, but iffn' I catch ya' smokin' more'n one or two a day, I'll—

"I know, I know, you'll kick my ass!" Celina laughed as she grabbed his hand, "let's do some more riding."

On the way home that evening, Celina asked, "Can we ride again tomorrow?"

"Well, I'm with the *vaqueros* tomorrow, and I think we're headin' into— At the disappointment on her face, he paused then smiled. "We can ride early for a few hours 'til my *amigos* come to."

"Yeah, just *you* don't get wasted and blow our chance."

Martie laughed at the playful scolding as they climbed into the jeep and headed home.

That night in bed, Celina could hardly stop smiling. *He's actually real fun. And he doesn't judge me either. I'm like-I'm starting to like him.*

After Celina and Martie's early motorcycle ride, Martie told her and Jenita that he was off to Fort Worth for a few days but wanted to take Celina to a rock concert in the middle of town when he got back.

"It's not *Diamante Rio* or anything that big, but they're still pretty awesome. Local band outta' La Paz called *Trial by Jury*. They were on the *X-Factor* a year ago, and Sharon Osborne was for sure blown away by 'em, especially since they did their best song *Legacy*. They've been in town a few times a couple years back. Their music's off the hook!"

"Well, that's the juice. Don't be gone too long, buddy."

Despite her wonderful friendship with the Juarez children, her growing friendship with Jenita and the fun times she was having with the father she barely knew, Celina could hardly shake her homesickness. She missed laughing and sharing private jokes with Chaim and Javier. She missed having to remind the motherly Yacqueline to mind her own business. She missed caring for Diego and Elian, and she yearned for the heart-to-hearts she and Mama often shared over hot cocoa.

Heck, I even miss Sol. Little brat that she is.

When she had been in Los Alamos for two months, Celina decided to write a letter home. She had about an hour before she was to meet Josefina's family. They were going into town to watch a Spanish parade that was coming through.

I can mail a letter there without getting caught.

She knew that part of the temporary custody decision was that she was not to contact her family in Santa Fe except through the court's family liaison.

Who's never shown up, by the way? Not my fault she's like a total ditz.

She simply could not tolerate how much she missed her family anymore. Because Martie was home, Celina locked her bedroom door. As their friendship grew, anymore he would simply stroll into her room without even knocking.

Tonto.

Laying down on her bed with her personalized stationery and gel pens, she stared at the wall for a few minutes then began to write, trying hard to spell correctly:

The Music of What Happens

Dear Mama,
I no I'm not sposed to write to you all, but I'm homesick and I don't care. Martie is aktualy cool, and we're havin a lot of fun. I like him most of the time but it's not as good as being home. I hope Eli is doin okay. I bet Diego is getting big. I made a new frind here named Josefina. You wood like her a lot. I miss you all. I love you. Love, Lina.

Tears ran down Celina's cheeks as she folded the letter and kissed it before sealing the envelope. After scribbling on the address, she tucked it into the pocket of her overall shorts. After a quick word to Jenita, she ran off down the dusty road to Josefina's. Señor Juarez was loading a large picnic basket into the family's '64 GMC pickup. As soon as he saw Celina, Aquino let out a glad cry, wriggled out of his sister's arms and ran to her. After a hug, she carried the toddler back to where his family was waiting.

As they arrived in town, Señor Juarez dropped the children off at the corner of Main Street to await the parade while he took Leticia and went to take care of some business. Celina gave him her letter to mail. She and the Juarez children had been waiting on the sandy knoll above the street for just a few minutes before the parade came into sight. Josefina and Celina kept a sharp eye on the smaller boys as the number of people arriving to watch the parade grew. Holding Aquino up on her shoulders, Celina watched with rapt attention. Colorfully attired flamenco dancers whirled and twirled down the dusty street. Little Mexican children, on hay wagons, waved colorful streamers and threw confetti, candy and chewing gum into the street for the spectators. Guitar and mandolin players, riding in the back of old pickup trucks, entertained with both old and contemporary Spanish tunes. Celina, Josefina and Cesar rushed around with the excited little boys helping them fill their paper sacks with the candy and gum that littered the streets and sidewalk. Because they were poor, Celina knew this was a special treat for the Juarez children.

When the parade had disappeared down the next street, the little group settled on the grass, amid other picnickers, to enjoy their lunch of refried bean and salsa sandwiches, lemonade and cookies. The food was simple but delicious. Celina left for home shortly after. Martie had promised to take her for another motorcycle ride and then swimming in the large lake north of town.

"If it rains fer' a few days here soon," he had told her, "We'll take the jeep and go mudding."

Celina sighed contentedly as she strolled home. *If I do get to go home, I'll totally miss all the fun I've had here with everybody. I don't wanna stay for good, but I'm not mad anymore that I came.*

Three days after the parade, Josefina appeared at the front door while Celina and Jenita were enjoying their lunch of sandwiches and Pepsi. The look on Josefina's face worried her.

What's she doing here? Martie'll have a fit if he gets back and she's here.

"Josefina, what're you doing here?" Celina whispered, glancing back behind her and then to her left at the road leading up to the small, brown house. "You know Martie'll totally freak if he sees you. What's up?"

Without a reply, Josefina grabbed her friend's arm and hurried her into the woods just out of sight of the road.

"I have to go to Santa Fe."

"What? Why?"

"Juanita, *mi* mama, she wants me and Cesar and the little boys to come visit her and my *tío* Leo." Josefina sighed and stared at the leaves covering the forest floor. She kicked at a small pebble with her sandal. "I don't wanna go. I haven't seen her in a year, and she won't see Tish at all, still calls her defective; she just wants to see me and the boys. And *Tío* Leo's a creep. I don't like being around him. He calls me Jojo and once, he tried to grab me—she motioned to her developing chest. Her cheeks flushed, she looked away and shrugged. As she talked, Josefina sat down on a fallen tree trunk and held her head in her hands. Celina sat down beside her on a bed of warm moss.

"What does your papa say?"

"He doesn't have a choice. If he's gonna keep us, he must do what she says. She threatened him."

"Threatened him?"

"That if he doesn't let her see us whenever she wants, she'll go to court and tell the judge to let her have us all the time. That means we wouldn't live here anymore. I dunno' why Juanita wants us now anyway. She didn't care when she left. I hate her! I wish I didn't have to go."

Celina touched her friend's hand. "For how long?"

"Like ten days. That's what she said. W-would you watch Aquino and Leticia while Cesar and I pack our stuff?"

"Hey, *muchacha,*" she patted Josefina's hand, "maybe it won't be all that bad. Maybe it'll be like me and Mart. I hated him at first but now we're sorta' friends. Maybe that'll happen."

Josefina surveyed her dubiously but did not comment. Celina stood and brushed the dust off her bare legs. She grabbed Josefina's hand and pulled her to her feet.

"Let's go. I'll watch the kids."

As Celina sat in the living room at the Juarez home, cuddling beautiful, sweet-tempered Leticia who looked so much like her older sister, anger at a woman she had never even seen steadily grew. She held the baby protectively. "You'll be okay, Tish. As long as I'm here, I'll help take care of you. Baby, don't be sad. Your mama doesn't know what she's missing not knowing you. *Te quiero,* little one, and so does your papa and Josefina and all your brothers too. Don't you see? You're loved, *malaynkia.*"

As Leticia's beautiful sightless eyes traveled toward the sound of her voice, her delightful mouth turned upward in a most precious smile, showing off her adorable dimples. Celina's heart tore a little.

Early the next morning, Senor Juarez and his children climbed into their old truck for the long drive to Santa Fe. When he heard that Martie was away for a few days, Julio asked Celina to take Leticia home with her until he returned the next day.

The next evening, Martie unexpectedly returned from one of his frequent motorcycle trips and was immediately taken with the good-natured, blind baby.

As he held her on his knee, he studied Leticia's sweet little face. "I-I wonder," he began, hesitantly, without looking at Celina, "what ya' looked like at her age?"

"I have a baby picture in my duffel. Wanna see?"

"*Si!*" Martie exclaimed, "*por favor* bring it."

When Celina handed the picture to Martie, he gazed at it for a long time, his eyes growing misty at the face of the adorable baby he had never known existed.

"Lina, this is-this is . . . you?"

"*¡Claro está*. Why?"

Without a reply, he stood and made his way down the hall to his bedroom. When he returned, he handed Celina a small, faded, black and white photo. It was a picture of a beautiful nine or ten-month-old baby girl . . . or was it a boy? Celina had no idea. Wild, black curls covered the child's head, and the eyes, deep and wide, were almost midnight black. The last thing Celina noticed was a darling grin and dimples in the small child's cheeks. Suddenly it dawned on her. She picked up her picture and her eyes widened in astonishment when she saw that the two babies were nearly twins.

She looked up at Martie in amazement. "This is you, isn't it? We're like twins!"

"Like family. Like father, like daughter, *si?*"

"Wow!" Celina marveled, again examining the photos.

"It hit me, Kid," Martie replied, eyes downcast as he handed her Leticia, "was as if I was lookin' at myself there fer' a minute." Finally, he looked up, dark eyes pained. "I missed so much." Sadness edged his voice. "I-I don't wanna miss more. Please, Kid, tell me it ain't too late. Please say ya'll stay, like stay with me fer' good. Ya' can have anything ya' want; you can do anything you want. I'll-I'll get you yer' own little dirt bike so ya' can ride all you want, and I'll even get ya' a phone like 'Lexei won't let'cha have. I won't sleep so late so we can do more stuff. You can even come on some o' my runs with the *vaqueros*. They'll love ya' like I do. *Por favor,* stay here with me." Martie suddenly choked and fell silent.

Celina shut her eyes momentarily. "Martie, don't— she began.

I'm growing to like Martie, but I like him as a friend, like Elizaveta and Lincoln. I don't wanna hurt him when he's been cool lately but—

"Mart, I can't stay," she finally said after a long silence, "I can come spend a few days here sometimes, but this isn't my home. I miss my fam—"

"Dang it, Kid, what about me?" Martie exploded, slamming his fist down on the sofa arm. Celina's eyes went wide, and she scooted backward, holding Leticia close. "I'm yer' family too! Yer' so selfish ya' can't even think about me too! Kid, I need ya'! Yer' my little baby girl, and I barely even know ya'!"

On her feet, Celina flung the pictures onto the floor and screamed back, "You shoulda thought of that before you ran my mama off!" With that, she rushed down the hall to her bedroom. Holding the baby close, she sat on her bed for a long time, sobbing.

I just can't do another three weeks of this, and have it go on til I'm eighteen. Martie's cool one minute and yelling and throwing a fit the next if he doesn't like something. I can't stay here! I'd go bananas living with him all the time. He's a total dumb bunny when he's mad or drunk!

"Oh, Leticia," she wept, "I wanna go home so bad; I miss my mama and the kids!"

A knock at the door startled her. "Lina," Jenita's voice called out gently. "Señor Juarez is here for the baby."

Slowly Celina opened the door and, without looking into Jenita's, sympathetic eyes, marched to the front door. Julio Juarez, sober and faraway, graciously thanked Celina for her time and handed her four dollars.

"No, no, señor," she pressed it back into his hand. "Keep it. It was my pleasure for real."

For a moment, the man hesitated then nodded and walked back to his truck. Celina stared after him. *He's gotta be so sad right now.*

When she had shut the door behind him, she caught sight of Martie watching her from his open bedroom door, his gaze almost as sorrowful as that of Señor Juarez. Not allowing herself to feel sorry for him, Celina turned on her heel and stalked back to her room, slamming the door behind her. For a long time, she leafed through the scrapbook she and Mama had made together last year. She thought the pictures of her family would make her feel better, however, she only felt more lonesome. She stared hard at the closed door in front of her.

I gotta talk to Martie alone, and I gotta do it soon.

The next evening, Celina waited until Martie went into his bedroom and closed the door. The day had not been a good one. Father and daughter had not spoken to each other since their last fight. Now that Jenita was out of the house, grocery shopping, Celina knew what she had to do. Her feet felt like lead as she trudged down the hall and stopped at Martie's bedroom door. She tapped gently on the hollow-sounding door.

"It's open."

Taking a deep breath, Celina pushed open the door, stepping into the soft light of the nightstand lamp.

"Kid!" Martie exclaimed, pleasantly surprised. He sat up from where he lay crosswise on the bed. Tapping his cigarette over the ashtray on the floor beside his bed, he looked up, expectantly.

"It's *Lina,*" she corrected him, calmly but purposefully. "Montoya. I am the daughter of Giacamo Montoya and Alexei Gonzalez." Celina choked as tears welled up in her dark eyes and she continued, determinedly, "and I want to go home."

Without another word, she shut the door behind her and ran down the hall to her room, unable to push Martie's stunned face from her mind. How she hated to choose! He had been nice much of the time, and she had to admit that she no longer hated him.

I like him a lot, but it's just not enough. Mama and the kids love me. Martie doesn't love me like a real family, and I don't love him like that either.

Suddenly a soft knock sounded on her door. "Go away, Martie. *Por favor*, I don't wanna talk to you right now, please just go!"

"Lina, it's I," came Jenita's whisper, "may I come in?"

Sighing dramatically, Celina swung open the door and turned away silently. Jenita hesitated a moment before she followed her over to where she now sat on the bed. Jenita waited for her to look up then spoke, gently.

"Lina, I-I know it's been hard for you here away from your other family. But in God's time, you'll come to love Martie as much as you loved your other papa."

"No," Celina replied, softly but stubbornly, "I won't. Don't get me wrong, Jen. Martie's a pal and a good one when he's not drinking and acting the fool. But he's not my papi. I care about him, but I can't love him like he was."

"But *nena*, he loves you so much. Martie's never had the privilege of being a father until now. Do you really want to take that away from him? Lina," Jenita sighed, deeply. "your papa has had such heartbreak in his life. *Por favor* give him a chance; just a chance. It would make him so happy."

"You're in love with Martie, aren't you? Like very much?" But it was more a statement than a question.

Jenita blushed and looked down at her hands. For a long time, she said nothing, and Celina did not press her.

Martie doesn't deserve her. She's so kind, and he can be such a dumb bunny when he's drinking. I wish she could see that. But Mama couldn't see it either.

Jenita finally glanced up with a nervous smile, "Your papa and I are engaged."

"You're joking!" she exclaimed, half hoping it wasn't true but knowing it was.

Jenita shook her head. "I speak the truth, Lina. We've been together for three years, and I've loved him more than I could ever say. He finally asked me last week. But Lina, do you know what else? We both love *you.*" Tenderly, she drew Celina into her arms. "We could have a good life together, the three of us. You-you won't be lonely either. Martie and I will have children, so you'll have little brothers and sisters to love and play with. I know he'll let you see your other family sometimes if I talk to him. Think about it, little one. Think of the good life we could have together as a family." Jenita kissed Celina's forehead and with a parting smile, disappeared down the hall.

She's trying to make me feel bad for wanting to go home. I have to go home! And," she added aloud, with new resolve, "if Tío will let me, I *will!*"

Late that night, Celina was roughly shaken awake.

"Lina? Celina!"

Blinking several times, Celina sat up. "Morning already?" she mumbled, stupidly.

"Naw," Martie's low voice replied, "it's only mi'night, but Lina, I gotta talk to ya'." He paused. "I s'pose Jen's told ya' about-about us?"

"Yeah," Celina replied, sleepily, "that's way cool. I'm happy for you two."

Martie smiled his thanks and continued, "You jes gotta' believe me when I tell ya' how much Jen and I love ya' and want ya' here. I-I know ya' don't love me now, but ya' could later, right? You and me and Jen could be a real tight family."

Without asking, he impulsively reached over and hugged her close. Celina's body went rigid. She had never been hugged by a man before except for Papi and, on rare occasions, Marcos. Before she could pull away, she apprehensively returned the embrace. She liked his scent. Minus the ever-present odor of cheap tequila on his breath and clothes, he smelled of cologne and faint cigarette smoke, like Marcos.

Momentarily, Celina broke the embrace as well as the silence. She tried to swallow the rising lump in her throat, "Martie, please try to understand. I like you and Jen, honest; I like you guys a lot. But I don't belong here. I belong at home with my family. I can-can come visit you guys sometimes, I'd love that, but I have to go home. Can't you see?"

Martie Pancorro's eyes clouded just then, and he stood. "I see Gonzalez filled yer' head with all kinds of smack about me!" he spat through clenched teeth, eyes narrowed in anger. "And if he thinks he can take my kid away from me, he'd jes' better think again! That rich bird can't have everything he wants jes' cuz he's drownin' in cash!" Without warning, Martie grabbed Celina's shoulders, causing her to cry out. "Kid, I jes' found ya'! I-I'll do anything!"

Celina choked back tears, "Mart, no—

At that, Martie flung her away from him so quickly she flinched. "All right!" he roared, sticking his finger in her face, "I'm through being nice! I'm through! This here's gonna' be settled in court, and I know jes' whose side that judge'll take! 'Lexei and Gonzalez can't have ev'rything they want! *I'm* yer' papa, he ain't! Get used to it!" With that, Martie stormed out and slammed the door so hard the room rattled.

Shaking uncontrollably Celina buried her face in her quilt and wept. Figuring Martie would go out and drink until dawn; she locked her door and tried to sleep. Hidden under the quilt, she prayed fervently that Marcos and the judge would let her come home.

"Dear God," she prayed softly between sobs, "*por favor, por favor* let me go home!"

CHAPTER 10

The Thunder Rolls

"Aw, jes' shutup, Martie! All you do is talk smack, and I'm not listening anymore!" Celina stormed out the door and headed down the road with quick, firm step. She sighed, deeply as she hurried toward Lincaro Boulevard to the convenience store.

I swear, that dumb bunny is driving me bananas! I'm through listening to him shoot off his mouth about Mama! Next week can't come soon enough!

In one week, Martie was scheduled to head for Santa Fe for the final custody hearing. The judge had decided that Celina would not be present. It had been five days since the exchange in the bedroom and ever since, Celina and Martie spoke to each other only when necessary, and those few words usually started yet another fight.

His face looks dark like a thundercloud. If he didn't go off like a bottle rocket every time he doesn't get his way, I might think about coming around regular. But not like this, no way!

The only time Martie seemed at all happy was when he was with Jenita. It was as though the shy, young woman held some sort of mystical power over Celina's, birth father.

Leaving the convenience store, sucking down a Jones soda and licking her favorite popsicle, a red, white, and blue, bomb pop, Celina stopped at the park where she, Josefina and the younger children had spent many afternoons that summer. Sitting on a swing in the nearly empty park, she swung slightly back and forth. She held one chain and rested her cheek against her hand.

Oh, Mama. I don't wanna stay here. I like Martie most of the time, but I love you and the kids.

Sucking hard and deliberate on her bomb pop, she stared straight ahead at the back road beside the park. An occasional car passed, but the park remained empty. Celina was glad for the quiet.

I miss Josefina.

Her friend was still in Santa Fe but had telephoned Celina the other day to say that she hoped her mother and uncle would soon send her and the boys back to Los Alamos.

If only I could apologize to Tío. If only I could make him understand. I don't hate him, but I'm so afraid he hates me now. Why couldn't I just have acted better?

Almost before Celina knew it, Martie was leaving for Santa Fe for the hearing. Judge Freeman had requested that Celina write a request detailing her views on the custody situation. This would be read aloud during her absence as she would remain in Los Alamos with Jenita for the time being.

Right now, Celina rested contentedly in the big, faded, corduroy rocker, watching a Spanish soap and drinking Pepsi as she tried not to think about the custody request she had been unable to write for court. Besides the fact that she could not spell intelligently, she knew it was pointless. Who listens to a fourteen-year-old? *Whatever they're gonna do with me was already decided last May. Nothing I say's gonna' make any real difference.*

Celina sniffed the air and grinned to herself. Supper was going to be chicken/cheese enchiladas, her all-time favorite!

I'd better go make the chocoatl. Jen might forget, and chicken/cheese enchiladas just aren't at their best without hot chocoatl with plenty of cinnamon and Mexican vanilla.

When Celina appeared in the kitchen, Jenita was bent over the oven, checking on their supper. The delectable aroma permeating the air caused her mouth to water.

"Hey, Jen," she asked Jenita's back, "can I make *chocoatl*?"

Jenita grinned as she picked up the clay pitcher filled with steaming *chocoatl*, topped with melting marshmallows and generously sprinkled with cinnamon. Celina giggled.

"You're smart, Jen," she teased.

Jenita giggled, *"Si. Yo sé."*

Minutes later, Celina and Jenita were biting into warm enchiladas, oozing with small chunks of chicken, melted cheese, refried beans and sour cream. Celina closed her eyes as she savored every mouthful.

Enchiladas are the best food in the world, but no one makes them as good as Mama. It's weird, Mama's not even Mexican, but she makes some of our foods better than any of our tías do.

As she ate, Celina's thoughts traveled back home. *I wonder what they're doing right now.*

"Lina?" Jenita's voice brought Celina out of her reverie.

"Yeah?"

"You were miles away, *nena*. You must finish your supper before it's cold."

No matter how she tried, Celina could not stop thinking about Tuesday's hearing. How she hated not being there!

I mean, like the whole thing's about me, isn't it? I'm more than old enough to handle a dumb custody hearing. Of all the stupid crap!

That evening, Celina and Jenita curled up on the couch watching *El Diablo*, a Spanish comedy and eating ice cream. During the movie, she glanced across the couch at Jenita.

I feel guilty. They've tried. I wasn't expecting to like either of them, but they've really tried, and I do like them both a lot. I'm just so homesick.

As if reading her thoughts, Jenita turned in her direction and smiled understandingly. Celina chewed her lower lip as she quickly blinked back tears and looked away. She gulped when Jenita took her hand, but she did not pull away. Jenita turned off the show and motioned for Celina to move closer. She knew she was showing her that, even though she might be leaving, there would be no hard feelings. They could always be friends. Glad she wasn't angry with her for making Martie upset, she moved closer as Jenita wrapped her arms around her.

He's not sad, Celina tried to convince herself. *He just wants to get back at Mama for leaving him like that! If I stay, I'll be out on my butt as soon as he gets sick of me and my mouth. Someone as bipolar as Martie can't stay in the same mind for two minutes. I hate how mad he gets when he's drinking. Mama and Marc never act like that.*

"*Gracias,* Jen, it's been way fun," Celina thanked her once the show had ended.

Jenita hugged her tightly, and Celina easily returned the embrace. "You're welcome," she replied. Even as she spoke, Jenita's eyes were troubled. "Are you sure you won't change your mind about . . . you know?"

Celina looked at the floor and sighed deeply.

Jenita continued, "If you stay, you'd come with us to Mexico for our honeymoon. It could be such fun. Please consider."

Celina shook her head. "I've made up my mind, Jen. I won't be swayed." As she spoke, Celina's dark eyes scanned Jenita's face, silently pleading for understanding.

Gentle eyes mirroring a love and tenderness that reminded her so much of Mama, Jenita touched Celina's cheek. "You're so like your papa, so stubborn and independent. He wouldn't have been swayed either. Oh, that man," the deep love in Jenita's eyes as she spoke of her Martie caused Celina's breath to catch, "he's like a wild pony, one that runs so fast against the wind and will never be tamed. But no matter, I do not want a tame husband. I love him just as he is. And I love you too, Lina—she smiled and touched Celina's face again—but since it's your wish to go, I'll ask the Blessed Virgin tonight to let you return to your family."

Just minutes later, Celina was asleep, the smiling faces of her family floating through her dreams. What she did not know was that the Juarez children had returned from Santa Fe earlier that evening.

The next day, all came over to play, even the boys. After a few rowdy rounds of Freeze Tag, Josefina, sweat-soaked hair plastered against her face, plopped down on the ground, and Celina lay down beside her, panting. Aquino jumped on her stomach.

"Good grief, Kid, you need a diaper change."

As Josefina lifted her brother off Celina, Cesar came rushing over from where he and Ignatius had been building a swing in the only tree Martie had in his trash-littered, dirt yard.

"Let's get Leticia from Papa and go swimming! It's too hot out to keep playing like this."

For hours, the children swam and played in the cool waters of St. Delores. Celina enjoyed swimming with Leticia. The baby took easily to water, and Celina helped her float. Her heart-melting giggles floated on the breeze as Celina dipped her again and again in the water. After a time, Josefina took over, and Celina joined the older boys on a floating dock in the middle of the lake. For hours the children jumped off and climbed back on. When the August day began to grow cool, they walked into town, dripping and barefoot, to buy popsicles.

"That was so much fun," Ignatius enthused, his green popsicle dripping down his bare chest. "We should do it again tomorrow."

"That's the cutest bikini, Lina. I wish mí papa was okay with me wearing one." Josefina complimented, enviously, glancing down at her own shorts and t-shirt. Celina giggled.

"Martie bought it for me. My mama would have a fit if she knew. I'll never be able to wear it at home. Heck, Mama would have a fit if she knew half the stuff Martie lets me do here. He doesn't even judge my smoking."

Josefina's eyes widened but she did not comment, just shook her head. Celina bristled. What was her problem anyway? She didn't have to wait long to find out. Josefina, soaked hair plastered against the sides of her head, turned to her, and Celina was surprised to see tears in her friend's eyes.

"Lina, mí papa's sick because of all the smoke where he works. All the snuff and tobacco and his coworkers all smoking around him. That's why he's so sick. I'm scared of him dying. And now I'm scared for you too. Please don't; please stop. I don't want to lose my friend." She gulped back more tears and awkwardly turned her attention to Aquino. Blue popsicle juice drooled down his chin and all over his bare stomach. Both girls giggled at his chubby, messy face. The toddler was sticky from ear to ear.

That night, after obtaining permission from Señor Juarez and Jenita, Josefina came over to spend the night. As they painted each other's toenails and ate the chocolate cupcakes they had baked, Celina popped in the CD Martie had bought her at the last *Trial by Jury* concert they had attended.

"Oh, wow," Josefina approved, banging her head to the music, "Wish I'd been able to go to the concert. Juanita never does anything except Tío Leo. All we did was sit around, watching TV and those two making out on the couch. It was boring as heck."

Celina nodded then grinned. "Well next time you're in Santa Fe, call me and we can all hang out and you can meet my brothers and sisters too."

"I'll do that," Josefina smiled back, "that place is total dumb bunny!"

Celina laughed, "Hey, you sound just like me!"

Long past midnight, the girls lay in bed, giggling and without a care in the world. Celina finally spoke, seriously, "So I've been thinking about what you said about smoking. I'm kinda addicted, but I'm gonna try to kick. I don't want to get sick like that either."

Josefina reached over and hugged her friend, "*Gracias*. I don't want to lose you, Lina. You're the coolest, you know. I wasn't judging you, just so you know. I was super worried is all. I worry every day about *mí* papa. I don't want to worry anymore. Makes my stomach sick. What about you, *amiga*? Do you worry about stuff?"

Celina sighed. "*Si*. I do. I worry I won't get to go back home."

"You're worried that Martie'll get to keep you here?"

"Not really. I'm worried Tío—I mean, my stepdad—won't let me come back; that he'll tell Martie he can just have me."

"He wouldn't really do that, would he? I mean, that would be awful."

"That's just it," Celina mumbled, "I was awful to him after he married Mama. I missed my papi, and I just wanted Marcos to stay our pal like he'd always been. Then, all of a sudden, there he was telling us what to do and what not to do all the time. Like a papa. He's never been mean, but he's strict and him and Mama have all these rules for us. That's what I like so much about Martie. He never judges me, and he lets me do all the things that Mama and Tío won't let us do."

"I see. *Mi* papa has rules for us, but Juanita doesn't care about rules as long as we leave her and Tío Leo alone. I hate it. I hardly knew which end was up while we were there. Lina, Martie wants to be cool 'cuz he wants you to stay, but I think your mama and stepdad love you, and that's why they have rules. Martie just wants to be your pal, right?"

"I guess. He plays with me, like PlayStation and riding motorcycle and concerts and stuff when he's not with the *vaqueros* downtown. I like it a lot, so why do I miss Mama and the kids so much? Why do I want to go home so bad?"

"I dunno. But you'll probably miss Martie too if you leave."

The hearing was to be concluded on Tuesday, but by Thursday morning, Martie had still not telephoned to tell her and Jenita the outcome. Every time Celina thought about it, her stomach tightened. She did not know how long she could bear the suspense. Where was he? He should have been back by now.

Just moments after they had finished breakfast on Thursday morning, there was a knock at the door.

Expecting Josefina, Celina called out, "I'll get it." Her heart thudded in her chest when she opened the door and saw who stood there. She opened the door wider and stepped back. Celina looked up at her mother, unaware that her heart was in her eyes. She swallowed hard and forced herself to speak.

"Have-have you come to say g-goodbye?"

Mama shook her head, her tender, familiar smile gently lifting her lips. "*Nyet, dochka.* I've come to say, 'welcome home.'"

Celina could not hold them then. Tears filled her eyes, and her hand flew to her mouth. Alexei instantly stepped forward and gathered her daughter close. Celina clung to her and sobbed.

"I-I'm s-so sorry, Mama," she gasped at one point, but she could not regain control.

"It's all right, *malaynkia*," Alexei's gentle voice whispered into her hair. "E-everything's going to ball right now."

"T-tío," Celina barely managed, "I have to talk to—

"You will," Mama reassured. "He wants to see you too."

Celina raised her head and looked at her mother through astonished, tear-filled eyes. "He-he does? Oh, Mama, you don't understand! I was so mean!"

"*Da,* I do understand. Marcos finally told me. I can't deny that I was sad and disappointed and that he was hurt, but—well—let's speak of it no more. You and he can talk when we get home. Yes, my Lina, he *does* want to see you. When I say we've had a miserable three months, I don't mean maybe. Baby, you're coming home now."

"*Pravda,* Mama?" Celina wiped her eyes with the back of her hand. She had never realized how wonderful it felt to speak Russian.

"*Da. Pravda.* I was given full custody. Martie and I will figure out visitation but at our discretion."

Celina shook her head determinedly. "It's okay, Mama. Martie and Jen are my friends. I'll be sure to stay in touch."

"Then we'll leave right away, yes?"

"Didn't Martie come back?" Celina inquired.

Alexei's expression was one of deep compassion as she shook her head, "Martie was upset after the judge's decision. He left the courthouse before anyone could speak to him, and I think he was crying. Knowing him as I do, he'll be gone a month if not longer. He never learned that you can't run from disappointment, but that you must face it. Rise above it. Martie missed *so* much; he missed knowing you. Now, do you see why I hold such high standards for you children?" Alexei shook her head again as she continued, "Remember, *dochka*, you can never turn back time. Once it's over, it's over. Always remember that."

"Lina, who's this?"

Celina started and whirled around when she heard Jenita's voice. "Oh, Jen, this is my mama, Alexei Gonzalez. Mama, this is Jenita Marquez, Martie's uhm fiancé."

Alexei's eyes widened at the word fiancé, but she greeted the other woman courteously.

"Are you here to take Lina home?"

When Mama replied affirmatively, Jenita nodded and quickly returned to the kitchen. Celina led her mother to her room. As they packed her duffel, Mama wanted to know how she had fared during the summer visit with Martie.

"It was pretty cool, actually. Martie was nice mostly, and I became friends with Jenita. We went to this super cool concert twice, and he got me this CD and a t-shirt." She handed Mama the *Trial by Jury* CD to look at. Not wanting to upset her mother, Celina was careful to omit the motorcycle riding and Martie's drinking and explosions of anger. She was also careful not to mention that the so-called court-appointed, family liaison had never once shown up to check on father and daughter. Instead, she went into detail about hanging out with Josefina and her siblings and the concerts, fiestas and rock climbing she had enjoyed with Martie.

Mama smiled thoughtfully, "You seem to have had such fun, *malaynkia*."

Celina's expression grew serious, "Yeah, I guess I did. It wasn't half bad, but I need to come home now. I don't know much, but I know where I belong."

Mama had tears in her eyes just then. She reached for her daughter and pressed her close. Celina sighed contentedly. How she had missed her mother!

The Music of What Happens

"Oh, my Lina," Alexei wept, "I lost your father, and I thought I'd lost you too!" When she finally drew back, Mama wiped her eyes and Celina did likewise. "So, what do you think, Baby?"

"I-I think it's time to go home!" Celina choked.

"And I think you're right. Let's be on our way."

Carrying the heavy duffel between them, mother and daughter headed for the front door. When they reached the door, Mama took the duffel and told Celina to say goodbye to Jenita. "I'll be in the car."

When Celina arrived in the kitchen archway. Jenita sat at the kitchen table, watching her sadly. "So . . . you're going home?" But it was more a statement than a question.

"*Si,*" Celina replied, breathlessly, "Please understand. *Por favor* tell Martie goodbye for me, and tell him . . . Celina sighed, eyes far away, ". . . just tell Martie I said thank you."

Jenita nodded, understandingly. "I think he knew it would turn out this way. I-I suppose it's for the best. You need to be with the family that raised you. I see that now, and I think-I think Martie does too. Don't be a stranger though. Visit us, and call whenever you like." Fighting tears, she hugged Celina hard. "You-you'd better go," she choked.

Celina left the room without a backward glance. As she climbed into the passenger seat of the Gonzalez's Escalade beside her mother, Celina turned and waved to Jenita who stood watching them from the window. As they drove away, she was sure she saw tears in her eyes.

As they headed toward the highway that would take them back to Santa Fe, Alexei reached over and squeezed her daughter's hand. "So good to have you back, *malaynkia*," she whispered.

"It's good to be going home. How are the kids and—she hesitated— *Tío.*"

Alexei seemed not to notice the mild edge in her daughter's voice when Celina mentioned her stepfather. "Everyone is well." Mama stated, eyes on the road, "but they've all missed you terribly. Javier wanted to write back when we received your letter. He was so disappointed when we had to say no. I must say though, we read it many times over. Eli's also been sad without his "second mother," and Yacque—

"How is he?" Celina interrupted, "Eli, I mean. Is he doing okay?"

Alexei replied, vaguely, "He's missed you very much, but now that you're home, he should be in better spirits."

"Mama."

Alexei nodded reluctantly at her daughter's one-word message. "Last week, we took him in for his monthly. Dr. Grosvenor says he's not responding to the new medications the way we'd hoped. He's recommending a complete heart and lung transplant. Marc and I saw another cardiology specialist for a second opinion. He confirmed that the transplant is what he needs but after examining Eli, he told us his body would never stand the strain of such an operation. They want us to wait until he's stronger. But," Mama glanced at her, "he's not getting stronger."

"So?" Celina inquired, sharply.

Mama sighed, "Marc and I are talking; but when we know, we'll tell you older children." Alexei then changed the subject. "Now about that bikini I saw . . .

Celina laughed. "Yeah, Mart bought me that."

Mama shook her head but was unable to restrain a chuckle. "Great, now I have him to worry about too."

The next several hours were spent in lighthearted conversation. That evening, both tired, Mama and Celina stopped at a nice hotel for the night.

CHAPTER 11

Home Again

The next morning Mama and Celina got a leisurely start for Santa Fe. Every mile behind them, Celina's excitement mounted. How she longed for the sight of her family. Finally, she spotted the familiar *Welcome to Santa Fe* sign in the distance.

"We're home!" she squealed. It was a mere twenty minutes before Mama turned the Escalade into the Gonzalez's circular driveway.

Before Celina had even stepped from the vehicle, the front door opened and Jackie and Soledad came rushing down the porch steps shouting excitedly, "Lina! Lina! Lina's home!" In a matter of seconds, both were in their older sister's arms, hugging her so tightly Celina could barely breathe. At that moment, Chaim, Yacqueline, carrying baby Diego, Javier and Evangelo appeared around the car door. Marcos came hurrying down the porch steps, carrying Elian.

Little Man was right behind his stepfather, shrieking in delight, "Oh, Lina, you're home!"

Celina had never been hugged so many times at once. Finally, Marcos reached her. Celina's breath caught.

How do I tell him I'm sorry? I was so awful to him.

Unable to think of something to say, Celina started toward him, and he moved toward her at the same instant. Anger, fear and mistrust melting away, She held tightly to her stepfather, and tried not to cry. It didn't work.

"I-I'm so sorry, Tío," she sobbed into his shirt, "I was aw-awful to you! I'm so s-s-sorry!"

Marcos hugged her close, tears in his eyes as well, and gently kissed the top of her curly head. "It's all right, Lina. I'm here, and it's all right now. This is your home. This is where you belong."

Celina gulped and stepped back. "It-it's not that. I'm sorry for how m-mean I w-was before I left. You didn't d-deserve any of that. I feel awful!"

Marcos reached for her again and held her tightly to him, Celina wrapped her arms around his waist.

"I forgive you, Lina," he said, tenderly, "you were afraid, afraid I wouldn't let you come back. I realized that. *Si*, your words hurt, but that's all in the past. You've apologized— He held her from him and with a sincere and loving smile, concluded, "and I forgive you. Now," Marcos turned and glanced behind him. "There's somebody who's simply going to burst if I don't let him say welcome home to his big sister."

Celina leaned to the right so she could see behind Marcos. Elian waited there, tears trembling in his wide, sunken, dark eyes, filmy from frequent fevers and illness. Her heart nearly broke at the sight of him. Her little brother had turned eight while she was in Los Alamos, yet six-year-old Little Man still outweighed him. Every ragged breath seemed to drain his frail body. Fighting emotion, Celina forced a smile and dropped to one knee on the grass.

"Hi, Eli," she said, softly, "I'm home, Sunbeam, home for good."

Choking on a sob, Elian threw himself into Celina's open arms. Crying into her shoulder, he hugged her as hard as he could. "Lina, Lina!" he cried, "I thought you-you-oh, Lina, I thought he took you away for-forever."

Celina was crying too. "No, Eli," she whispered into his dark curls, "I could never like stay away forever. I love you guys way too much."

Elian's response was to hug his sister tighter and bury his damp face against her neck.

The Music of What Happens

Though everyone was in high spirits now that Celina was home, she sensed that something was troubling Mama and Marcos. Celina longed to know what it was, but also dreaded the truth whatever it might be.

Martie better not be causing more problems. If he's planning to make another mess of things, I'll never speak to him again—no, no, it can't be anything like that, I—oh, stop being a dumb bunny and take a chill pill, she scolded herself, *I'll talk to Chaim and Javier tonight. If something's up, they're sure to have got wind of it.*

However, Celina was exhausted after the long trip and quickly fell asleep, forgetting her plan to talk to her brothers. The next day's trip to the beach was as much fun as she had had all summer. Strangely though, even with the wonderful time they had, she could not erase from her mind the tense and worried look Marcos had worn on his face ever since yesterday.

"So, you three haven't heard *anything*?" Celina pressed. She was sitting cross-legged across from Javier on his bed. Chaim lay on his bed, listening intently, and Yacqueline sat on the floor. All three shook their heads.

"But we've noticed what you're noticing now." Yacqueline put in, "Mama and Marc have been acting weird, and they seem stressed out. What do you guys think it is?"

Chaim shrugged. "Heck if I know, but I've heard Tío talking to his brother, Martino in Washington state. He's a lawyer too, you know."

Celina nodded. "I wonder if Martino's like moving here to join Tío and Mr. Dugan in their law practice?"

"I think it's a new baby," Javier chuckled.

"Or a divorce."

"Oh, go fly a kite, they can't keep their hands off each other so there's no way they're getting divorced, and just *how* many babies does our family need anyway?"

"Well, whatever it is," Yacqueline added, "I hope they tell us soon if they're going to. It's making my stomach hurt seeing them so worried and secret-keeping."

"Maybe 'cuz it's none of your business," Javier retorted, smugly, "I have a feeling they'll tell Lina, Chaim and me, but not you. Only us oldest ones can handle the truth."

"Like I can handle it just as well as you guys. Geez, I'm eleven. What do you think I am?" Yacqueline snapped, uncharacteristically offended.

"Don't worry, sis," Celina cast a withering glance at Javier, "I'm sure we'll all figure it out eventually."

The next morning, after helping Yacqueline and Soledad with the breakfast dishes, Celina climbed on her bicycle and rode the seven blocks down the street to Elizaveta's. As she rode, she smiled to herself.

Dear old Martie. I do kinda' miss him already, and especially miss riding motorcycle together. Wish I had one here, or even just a dirt bike. If only Mama weren't so strict about it.

Elizaveta Allende was thrilled to see her best friend again. Basking in the summer sunshine, they munched homemade cookies, sipped ice-cold lemonade and talked.

". . . and Jade had her baby last month, a little girl, and I don't think Cal's having anything to do with it. Mayor Ainsworth probably wouldn't allow it anyway even if Cal wanted to. I heard the mayor's paying big money child support to keep Jade's mama shut up. You know how Mrs. Bridger is; mouth, mouth, mouth, that's what my mama says. What a total scandal! *Everybody* in town knows It's Cal's, but even Staci's pretending that no one knows. Boy, Lina, that's some serious-butt denial that family's in. Oh, and then Lincoln was caught hotwiring Mr. Gallagher's car to go joyriding. Man was he *ever* in trouble! Mr. Gallagher was like so mad . . .

Celina smiled to herself as she stared up at the sun, though her heart raced at the mention of Calvert Ainsworth. Elizaveta loved to share school gossip, and seldom required a response.

Finally, Celina broke in. "We should hotwire a motorcycle and go riding. Did you know my biological dad taught me how this summer? And how to ride too."

Elizaveta's dark eyes widened. "No way! He sure sounds like fun. I'd love to. When Ramos gets his back from the garage, maybe we should take it for a spin. He never lets me touch it; it'll serve him right for being so stingy. If you know how, I'm game. Speaking of Ramos, let's see if he'll top off the pool for us. I'm so sticky hot in this nasty bra." Elizaveta fanned herself with an empty paper plate.

"At least you can fit a *real* bra," Celina muttered, more to herself than Elizaveta. "Come on," she added, louder this time, "let's go find him."

The Allende's enormous backyard swimming pool was pure heaven and Celina was glad to sink into the cold water, a stark contrast with the boiling sun beating down on everything below.

"Oh, this is better than se—"

"No way," Celina interrupted, bobbing up from where she had been soaking her hair. "Lissy," she grinned, "do you mean what I think you mean? You lost your—"

Elizaveta cocked her head, momentarily and then realization filled her eyes. "Oh, oh, no. Not me. Heck no. It's just something Asayra says a lot when something feels good. She's a total tramp."

Celina laughed and dove under the water then popped back up. "Hey, won't she get mad when she gets home and we're in here? Doesn't she swim laps after work?"

Asayra Allende was the eldest of Elizaveta's four siblings. A hot-tempered seventeen-year-old, she worked as a seating hostess at the local Ihop and had zero patience with her younger siblings, especially Elizaveta who was the second eldest.

"Oh, yeah, she'll be pissed all right, but we're not getting out no matter how loud she screams, right?"

Celina high-fived her friend. "Race you to the end?"

"Lissy!" came a sudden shrill yell.

Celina and Elizaveta's heads popped up above the pool rim at the same instant. There stood Asayra, home from work. She was impeccably dressed in a red silk halter top, a black mini skirt, and glossy black stilettos. Waist length, raven black hair glowed in the evening sun, and flashing brown eyes were defined with heavy black eyeliner, Asayra was a flawless beauty even when she was mad.

"Lissy," she shouted again, "you know the rules! Get yourself outta' that pool right now. I need to swim my laps, and you," she added, pointing at Celina, "get lost! I'm not babysitting you *and* my moron siblings all evening!"

Elizaveta stuck out her tongue as she reached behind her and grabbed Celina who was now climbing up the pool ladder to get out.

"What the— Celina choked on water as Elizaveta yanked her back into the pool from behind.

"Well, speak of the devil! Mom ain't here, loser!" she hollered back, "there's no one to run freaking out to when you don't get your way!"

Asayra stamped her foot and swore at the two girls as she stalked up the walkway to the front door.

Ducking low, Celina and Elizaveta shook with laughter as they secretly watched Asayra stomp up the walk to the house, cursing in Spanish.

Celina couldn't resist calling out, aggravatingly, mimicking their elderly priest, Father Yvano Domingo's, shaky, gravelly voice, "Ohhh, thy foul temper; ohhh, thy foul tongue! God will surely punish thee for thy tantrum!"

Elizaveta burst into laughter, and Asayra whirled around angrily. "Shut up, you snot-nosed, little brat! And GET OUT OF THAT POOL!" With that, she stalked into the house and slammed the door so hard it shook. Through an open window, the girls could hear her screaming at Vito, the Allende's youngest child, for daring to leave his crayons on the table. Moments later she had found some reason to holler at Ramos.

"*Ay mierda*," Elizaveta exclaimed, exasperated, "That diva wannabe is driving me up the friggin' wall. See, Lina, Ramos, Vito and I are the result of clueless parents and bad childcare arrangements. I *think* I hate her!"

"And why should *you* be an exception just because she's your sister? Let's take Ramos' dirt bike." She pointed in the direction of the Allende's garage. "I'll teach you to ride."

"Lissy!" Asayra's enraged voice echoed from the open kitchen window overlooking the pool.

"Rats! What now? I suppose she just found out I borrowed her *Gucci* hoodie. Sorry, Lina, the PMS queen demands my attention—

When Celina arrived home, Mama and Yacqueline were preparing sauerkraut soup and *pirozhki* for the evening meal, and Soledad was setting the table. Alexei quickly assigned her eldest to change baby Diego's diaper before supper.

During supper, Marcos and Mama kept exchanging looks that seemed to communicate some form of message. Sensing that their parents wanted quiet, the children ate their meal in silence. Mama did not even have to reprimand Jackie for requesting seconds before they were offered. And Little Man finished his supper without sneaking the *pirozhki* shells to their golden retriever, Pedro, who often hid under the table, hoping for discarded morsels.

After supper, Marcos beckoned his family into the living room. When all were seated, he spoke to them seriously, "My kid brother, Martino, is establishing a new law partnership in Washington and he's invited me to join him. That will mean moving our family to Washington State. Washington, as Martino has told me, has a great need for multilingual lawyers like the two of us who can save the firm the cost of interpreters. For the last two months, your mother and I have been looking through real estate magazines. We're ready to put a down payment on a house in a nice neighborhood close to some high-quality schools. Maybe we should have let you children in on this earlier, however, with Lina gone all summer, we figured it best to wait until we could speak to you all together. So, feedback?"

Celina was speechless. She stared down at her hands. *Leave Santa Fe? Do we have a choice?* Though she had been born in Texas, Celina had never been further from home than Los Alamos for as long as she could remember. Now, Marcos was planning to take them to Washington State! *This is mucho loco! This is the only home we've ever known! How can Tío do this?*

"Well," Yacqueline ventured, after a long, stunned silence, "It'll be kinda hard to leave our friends and some of Papi's family, but we'll get used to it. Maybe this is what God's wanted for us all along."

Celina stifled a groan. Yacqueline was mature and wise beyond her years. Chaim hesitated then added simply, "We can handle it, Marc."

I don't wanna move. I don't want things to change. Yacque's probably right though, she finally concluded to herself, *maybe it'll be good for us. But I'll totally miss Lissy and Lincoln and some of our cousins. I totally doubt Washington has many Mexican kids.*

A few minutes later, sensing the children's reaction to the impending move was positive, Marcos dismissed them and tuned in to the evening news.

Needing to be alone with her thoughts, Celina locked herself in the upstairs library. Lying on the velour chaise, she stared unseeing up at the ceiling for what seemed like forever when the landline on the end table rang. She grabbed it. "Gonzalez residence, this is Lina."

"Lina?" came the muffled voice on the other end.

"Yeah, that's me—Lissy! Hey, *chica, qué pasa*? Huh? For gosh sakes, talk normal, Lissy, I can barely hear you."

"Can't," came the still muffled voice, "I'm calling from the linen closet. I'd get shot if Mama and Papa overheard me, but I just had to spill the juice: 'Cruella De Vil' got busted this evening! Mama and Papa came home early, and Vito was crying because she wouldn't let him out of his room. She had her boyfriend over. You know, Jovon's not allowed here when the parents are gone."

"Right. And?"

"Well, let's just say they were on the couch, getting all hot and heavy, when Mama and Papa walked in the door. Man, I've never seen Papa so pissed off! He grabbed that smart-mouth, hippie zebra right off the couch and tossed him out by the seat of his baggy, gangbanger pants. Then Asayra was sent to her room in tears. And then-you're gonna love me for this-I finally told Papa about all the times she's come home strung out. Well, now she has to quit her job and help Papa with the bookwork at the factory so Mama can stay home with us again. She also has to go to early Mass every morning before school for four months, perform the Stations of the Cross daily for the next two weeks and get drug tested every week. Man, I *almost* feel sorry for her!"

By now, Elizaveta and Celina were giggling uncontrollably. "Well, don't go all soft on me now," Celina managed, weak from laughter, "that dumb bunny sister of yours is a total psycho, and a double dose of religion might just be what she needs to get straight!"

Elizaveta abruptly changed the subject, "Any news on your end since we parted today?"

"Well, yeah, actually there is."

"What? Oh, what? Spill the juice."

"We're moving, Lissy."

"What!" Elizaveta spat out, "Oh, *por favor* tell me your kidding!"

"If only."

"I don't believe this shiz," Elizaveta groaned, "when was all this decided?"

"It's like been in the cards for a while, but tonight's the first I've heard."

"Where the heck are you going?"

"Washington State," Celina sighed, "can't remember the name of the city."

"Dammit!" Elizaveta exclaimed boldly, "well, at least we can email and whatever, right?"

Just days later, Marcos received a phone call from a family wanting to purchase the house. "The Martinson's want to move in in two weeks," he informed the family.

Alexei smiled as she hugged him. "God is good."

CHAPTER 12

Everything I've Ever Known

The days following the sale of the house were a blur to Celina. The family finished packing and then cleaned the house from top to bottom. "No one will ever be able to criticize my housekeeping," Mama said.

The day they were scheduled to leave, Mama awoke the children earlier than usual. For once, they did not dress immediately but ate breakfast in pajamas. Barely had Celina finished her breakfast when Mama appeared, carrying a tousle-headed Diego on her hip. "Lina, I just pumped a bottle, please feed your brother for me."

Celina eagerly took her smiling baby brother in her arms. Diego gurgled as he grabbed a handful of his sister's dark hair.

Just as she finished feeding the baby, Javier came rushing into the kitchen in his bathrobe. "Lina, *hurry!* Mama wants you upstairs now. Our plane's coming in two hours now instead of three, and some of us haven't even showered yet!"

"Dammit!" Celina shouted, not caring that she would probably be scolded for swearing. Cradling Diego against her chest, she ran up the stairs behind Javier.

Mama met them at the top and took the baby. "The plane is coming early," she explained. "Wake Marc, Javier. Lina, for mercy's sake, jump in the shower now. Oh, and send your sisters to me so I can fix their hair."

An hour later, the children were sitting in the family room, carefully dressed and groomed as though going to Mass. Mama was determined that they would all make a favorable impression on her husband's family whom she had never met. Diego was especially adorable in a little sailor outfit and white shoes. In Celina's opinion, if their precious, curly-headed grandchild was unable to impress their stepfather's parents, they might as well all give up.

It was still dark as the Gonzalez family left the house for the last time and drove down the quiet, early morning streets of Santa Fe, New Mexico for the last time. Celina gazed wistfully out the window at the familiar streets and buildings, the schools she had attended since kindergarten, Aleman's grocery store where she had worked when Papi was alive. She noted absently that *Gonzalez* had already been removed from the *Dugan and Gonzalez, Attorneys-At-Law* sign that hung over the entrance to Marcos' old law office. Celina sighed.

I'm leaving behind like everything I've ever known and loved.

Papi was buried here, as was his mother Abuela Auria Gutierrez and his only half-sister, Carlena Palancia who had died at just one-year-old. Marcos' first wife and daughter were interred in this cemetery, as well. Celina wondered if Marcos was thinking about them.

When the family arrived at the airport, to their pleasant surprise, the Allende family and Konroy Dugan had arisen early to say goodbye. Celina and Elizaveta sat away from the others. Both girls barely held back tears.

"*Por favor amiga*, message me when you can," Elizaveta choked.

"I will, and whenever I visit Martie, I'll come see you too."

A voice suddenly came over the loudspeaker announcing that all passengers for flight 758 to Seattle were to report to the ticket counter. As the two friends stood, Elizaveta reached into her purse and pulled out a heart-shaped necklace that said *Friends Forever* in Spanish. She fastened half of it around Celina's neck and the other half around her own. The girls hugged tightly.

That afternoon, the plane set down at Sea-Tac. Mama frantically brushed at and smoothed her children's clothes and hair. She took Diego from Yacqueline.

"Stay close to Tío and me," she instructed them all, "Tío's parents are meeting us, and I fully expect you all to be on your *best* behavior. Don't speak until they speak to you first, and be careful to speak *straight* Spanish. I don't want my new in-laws thinking, 'Oh, Lord, *what* did our son marry?' Celina, Chaim, and Javier, if I hear a single swear word out of any of you three, you'll be punished until the next century. You all know your manners. Make me proud."

As Mama turned to follow Marcos, the muscles in her lovely face were drawn tight, and her lips were set in a firm line. Celina knew her mother was worried sick, not only about what her husband's parents would think of her but more importantly, how they would receive her children.

When they entered the terminal, several people turned and stared at the family of twelve. Their stares annoyed Celina. She was sure she would hate Washington if this was how they would be received everywhere they went just because their family was so large.

Suddenly a softly accented, female voice called out, "Marcos?"

Marcos turned quickly. A stout, smiling, elderly woman and a tall, serious-looking man were coming toward them from somewhere in the crowd.

"Mama!" His voice was excited. "Papa!"

Gently setting Elian down, he hurried to the older couple. Celina inhaled sharply and glanced up at Chaim. He met his older sister's worried gaze with one of his own, and she knew they were both thinking the same thing. She smiled slightly as she watched the elderly couple throw their arms around their tall son and shower him with kisses, speaking rapid-fire Spanish. After a moment, Marcos turned and motioned for Mama and the children to join him.

"Mama and Papa," he said, proudly, "this is my wife, Alexei, and our children." He pointed to each child in turn as he introduced them. "And this," he finished with a broad grin, "is my son, Diego."

The Music of What Happens

Señor and Señora Gonzalez gasped almost simultaneously as Marcos placed the baby in his grandmother's arms. Happy tears filled her eyes as she hugged the baby close, "Oh, my son, he looks just like you. Such a dear cherub. And the others," she smiled at the Montoya children, "such lovely children. He," Señora Gonzalez motioned to Chaim, "looks just like Giac did at that age, do you remember?"

Chaim beamed at this, and Mama appeared to relax a little as the elder Gonzalez's hugged her.

"Kids," Marcos finally said, "these are my parents, Arturo Sr. and Genecia Gonzalez."

"*Buenos tardes*, Señor *y* Señora Gonzalez," the children chorused softly.

"Exquisite manners," Señora Gonzalez commented in English. "Alexei, I must commend you for raising such mannerly children in an age when the behavior of young people is often in an unfortunate state. But *por favor*," she added, now speaking to the children, "we're Abuelita and Abuelo to you all. After all, you're our son's new family and a most welcome addition to the Gonzalez's. Well," continued Señora Gonzalez, whose English was even better than her son's, "the whole clan is at our house, eager to see their brother again and meet his family." She stood on her toes and kissed her son's cheek. "It's been too long, Marcos, far too long."

Señora Gonzalez took Evangelo and Little Man by the hands and led the way to the exit. It was already growing dark, so Celina was able to see little of Seattle as they climbed into the senior Gonzalez's van and started down the highway. Following a three-hour drive, they arrived at a large, stately home in a quiet neighborhood. Carrying Diego in one arm and holding Evangelo's hand, Abuelita Gonzalez chatted with them as she led the way to the front door. Abuelo Gonzalez, though reserved by nature, quickly warmed to his new grandchildren and was especially taken with the smiling, talkative, and good-natured Little Man. Carrying the curly-headed six-year-old on his shoulder, the elderly immigrant and little boy, laughing and talking together, appeared totally at ease with each other.

When they arrived inside, the family was greeted by a huge crowd waiting in the family room. Marcos had scarcely taken off his shoes when he was grabbed in a bear hug and passed from one pair of loving arms to the next like a newborn baby. Celina blinked, surprised.

Papi's family was never like this; most of them didn't even like us.

After he had been greeted and hugged by nearly everyone in the room, Marcos introduced his own family and then began the monumental task of introducing his six siblings, their spouses, and children. When introductions were complete, the adults left the family room and headed down the hall to the parlor room. Celina followed them from a distance. She was amazed at the unusually elegant room that met her eyes. Even with the presence of two, large, dusty rose sofas, three forest green armchairs and a lovely, rosewood piano, the room was remarkably spacious. The off-white walls were decorated with framed, family photographs and a few, well-chosen decorations. Celina couldn't help but smile when she caught sight of a photograph of Marcos as a boy. About her age when the photo was taken, a young Marcos posed with his guitar, dressed in a white shirt and Hispanic breeches, sporting the widest grin she had ever seen. Suddenly, the man himself spotted her and motioned her into the parlor. As he did, Marcos leaned over from where he sat beside Mama and whispered to his mother. Abuelita then hurried to Celina's side.

"Celina," she whispered, "Marc just told me that you're an accomplished pianist. Would you do us the honor?"

Celina was horrified. She had never played in front of strangers. Despite her misgivings, she saw no polite way out of it, and acquiesced, courteously, "I-I'd love to, Abuelita."

Flashing Marcos what Martie had called her "look from hell," Celina sat down at the piano and began to play *Pie Jesu*. Everyone stood nearby, mouths open in amazement. When Celina played *Panis Angelicus* followed by *Ave Maria*, Abuelo, standing close behind her, closed his eyes and began to sing, voice pure, strong and resonant just like his son's. It was but a moment before the entire family had joined in. As Celina played, Elian sat down on the bench beside his sister and rested his head on her shoulder.

When the song was finished, Celina looked down at him and read the request he was communicating with his wide, expressive eyes. "*Da,* Eli," she answered in soft Russian so that Marcos' family would not understand them, "I'll play Papi's song."

Elian's smile was magical. "*Spiseeba bolshoye,* Lina," he replied in kind.

As Celina played *Si Volvieres a Mí,* she heard Marcos' voice soaring above the rest. *Si,* she told herself, *this song means as much to him as it does to us.*

One hour and many songs later, Tía Aletta, always cautious of children staying up long past their bedtime, insisted that all should be asleep. Among the children, there were no faces less than gloomy at the pessimistic announcement.

As everyone stood, Marcos commented, in passing, "It's too bad Eli's violin is packed. You'll all have to hear him play sometime."

"Don't tell me we have *another* musician in the family," Abuelita gushed. "Elian," she turned to him, "we Gonzalez's are a music-loving family, and the addition of two more musicians is nothing short of a miracle!"

Like his late father in displaying little, outward emotion, Elian merely smiled. "I'm not very good, Abuelita, I mean, not like Lina, but I try."

Glancing at his mother, Marcos snorted, disbelievingly. "The boy's amazing; pure, natural talent."

At that moment, Abuelo who had been sitting across the room, in thoughtful silence, whispered in Elian's ear. The child's peaked face glowed with enthusiasm, "*Si, si, Abuelo, m-muchas gracias!*"

Abuelo grinned as he strode into a den, adjacent to the parlor. Momentarily, he returned, carrying a black violin case. Celina glanced at Elian. Her brother's eyes radiated eagerness, and she heard his ragged breath catch. Carefully, Marcos' father placed the instrument on the pinewood coffee table and stepped away. Elian lifted it gently from its case and stroked the strings with the bow as if they were made of the finest crystal. Celina nearly choked. Elian was so fragile that the violin appeared almost too heavy for him. He managed the instrument perfectly, however, as he began to play *Yerushalayim Shel Zahav*, a Jewish song. Murmurs of 'Jesus, Mary and Joseph' and '*Ay Dios mío*, listen to the child!' echoed softly around the room.

As the strains of haunting, Hebrew music filled the air, leaving Elian's audience spellbound, Tía Aletta's eldest daughter made her way hesitantly to where Celina sat and sat down beside her. She smiled, brightly.

"*¡Hola,*" she whispered, "Mama says I should introduce myself. I'm Justinia Walsh, one of your *many* new cousins."

A bit guarded, Celina returned the smile, "Lina Montoya," she whispered back, "pleased to meet you."

In silence, the girls sat side by side until Elian finished his performance. Everyone clapped vigorously as he set the violin back in its case, thanked Abuelo and bowed to his audience.

"*Ay Dios mío*, he's cute," Justinia commented, "how'd he learn to play like that? He's just a baby, but he's almost as good as Abuelo."

"He's not a baby," Celina forced herself to be polite. "He's eight. He's just small because he's sick."

"Sick? Sick how?"

But Celina quickly changed the subject. "He's a music natural for sure, born that way. He's been playing since he was like three. Someone gave us this garage sale violin, and it was as if he knew what to do with it from day one."

Justinia shook her head in amazement as she continued. "You're *awfully* good on the piano too. I've been taking lessons for six years, but I don't know *anyone* who plays that well except our Tía Kyle, and maybe the pianist at Little Mother of God."

Before Celina could reply, Tía Aletta called out over the din as everyone made the rounds of hugging Elian and congratulating his performance. He responded politely to the compliments but was overwhelmed. He had never been left in doubt of his musical abilities by his parents but, because of his health, Elian had never performed in public and was not accustomed to such admiration from strangers.

"All right!" Tía Aletta called out yet again. "it's high time everyone was asleep. In case anyone cares, the grandfather clock reads midnight!"

Gasps emitted all over the room, and mothers hurried their children upstairs to prepare for bed.

"Know what, Lina?" Justinia explained as she and Celina ran up the stairs together, "None of us are going back home until the day after tomorrow. We get to spend two nights here, all of us."

"Cool."

"*Si*," Justinia clapped her hands as she spoke, "and that's not the best part. Tomorrow, Abuelita and my mama and your mama and all our tías are going to cook a huge, fiesta dinner, as big as on *Los Posadas*! Oh, Lina, Abuelita's dinners are so much fun. Come on, I'll show you where us girls will be sleeping."

The next morning, the two girls awoke somewhat early, considering the late hour they had retired the night before. After they had dressed, Celina brushed her hair in the bathroom while Justinia applied her makeup. Celina shook her head as she watched her cousin, envious.

"You're *so* lucky," she complained, "Mama won't even let me touch the stuff, and I'm only seven months younger than you. Not fair!"

Justinia held out the gold and pink tube of lipstick, "Wanna' try some?"

"Do I want to be grounded for a month? No, *gracias*."

Justinia giggled, "But your clothes are so much cooler than I'm allowed to wear. I love that skirt. Mine have to reach my knees. I think you're pretty lucky. Plus you have perfect curls and my hair's straight as an old stick. Mothers, they can be a pain sometimes, *Yo sé*. So, what's your mama's problem with makeup?"

"Beats me. Look, I love my mama, but sometimes, she's way too Republican for my taste."

"Republican? What's politics got to do with it?"

Celina shook her head. "Not politics. That's just what it's called when you're strict about stuff."

Justinia burst out laughing. "Oh, I think you mean *conservative*!"

Celina rolled her eyes and laughed at herself. "Yeah, that's what I mean."

"Too conservative, huh? Man, I'd have to like kill my mother if she ever came up with a lame excuse like that. Hey," Justinia suddenly changed the subject. "I've got an awesome idea. Do you like boats?" Without waiting for a reply, she continued, "Let's ask Abuelita if we can take the peddle boat out on the lake."

"Yeah let's!" She and Justinia rushed downstairs and into the enormous kitchen where the women were already hard at work, preparing the fiesta feast the family would partake of that evening. Mama, her unruly curls tumbled forward in her eyes, looked up from the tomatoes she was slicing for the salsa dip. She smiled, brightly, at her daughter and new niece.

"*Dobraye otra, d'vochkee*," she said cheerily. Celina returned the greeting in kind while Justinia stared, in bewilderment.

"Oh, Abuelita," Justinia asked, hurriedly, "can me and Lina take the peddle boat on the lake?"

"*May* Lina and *I*," Abuelita corrected her, "and, well— she turned to the girls' mothers, "do you ladies mind if the girls go on the lake?"

Mama eyed Celina, dubiously, "It won't do your cold any good," she countered, slowly, "so only for an hour. Do not get wet."

"Oh, Mama, can Eli come too? He looks bored just lying on the divan. I know he'd love to go on the lake."

Mama's eyes widened in horror, "Absolutely not! He'll catch a cold and be in the hospital!"

"But I'll put his wool coat and scarf on. He'll be okay."

Mama was unyielding, however, "I said no, Linochka," she reminded, gently but firmly, "we can't risk him getting sick. You and Justinia have a good time."

"Be sure to wear life vests," Tía Aletta cautioned.

"And don't go past your abuelo's ¾ buoy line. It's not safe further on!" Abuelita called out.

"And Lina, put on your gray cardigan and button it up all the way. I don't want that cough getting worse."

The two girls looked at each other and hurried outside before they could be issued any more stifling instructions. Although the sky was gray and overcast, there was no wind, and the temperature was cool. Celina and Justinia ran down the gently sloping, grassy hill to the shed and dragged out the little pink and black peddle boat.

"How beautiful," Celina breathed, admiring her new grandparents' watercraft.

"Isn't it though? Hey, let's ask Les if she wants to go too. Les!" she shouted, "wanna' come in the peddle boat with me and Lina?"

Celestyna Gonzalez had been sitting on the porch swing, reading, however, she came running at the invite. Sixteen years old, Celestyna was the eldest of Senor and Senora Gonzalez's grandchildren. Despite her lack of makeup, she was, in Celina's opinion, extraordinarily beautiful. Celestyna smiled and shook her new cousin's hand when Justinia introduced them.

"Pleased to meet you," Celina said, sweetly, "I know Marc introduced us all last night, but there were so many people, I can't remember everyone's name."

"Pleased to meet you too, cuz. And just call me Les."

Justinia sat in the back while Celina and Celestyna peddled away from the dock. They peddled slowly through the water, enjoying the cool, sparkling stillness of calm, gray morning. The sapphire blue water sparkled from a faint ray of sunshine peeking through the dark clouds above. An amusing bullfrog hopped from lily pad to lily pad as if in search of a bit of warm sun.

That evening, the entire family went to their rooms to dress for dinner. Justinia had told Celina that welcome-home dinners in the Gonzalez family were always dressy but still lots of fun. When Celina, Celestyna and Justinia came downstairs together, they stood and stared, in awe, at the banquet table. Covered food dishes laden down the middle and Abuelita's fine black and gold china from Mexico was laid out.

"It's gonna be so yummy!" Justinia enthused, patting her stomach.

There were enchiladas, taco fixings, salsa dip and pitchers of lemonade. There were trays of deviled eggs, cakes and pies of several kinds, molded ambrosia and piping hot rolls. As the family joined hands around the table, Abuelo said a special grace in Spanish. He prayed to God to bless the food and asked for rich blessings on each family member by name. When their grandfather prayed for healing and health for Elian, Celina glanced across the table at her mother. Mama held her young son's hand protectively. Tears welled in her dark eyes, and her lips were moving.

As she and Celestyna helped their *tías* fill plates for the smallest children, Celina did not even notice Marcos and his parents leave the room. Marcos suddenly reappeared in a colorful, black, red and yellow *sombrero*, playing a catchy, Spanish tune on his guitar. Everyone laughed, but then paused as Abuelita and Abuelo appeared, in traditional Mexican costumes, and began dancing a remarkable flamenco. As they whirled and twirled around the living room, Celina grinned at Justinia sitting beside her.

"They can really dance," she commented.

"Oh, *si*," her cousin replied, "they were dancers in Old Mexico, they dance at all of our fiesta parties."

When the dancing was over, everyone clapped enthusiastically and then turned their attention to their food. How delicious it all was. Celina bit into an enchilada filled with cheese, beans and Abuelita's famous salsa dip. She sipped her lemonade. The conversation was light-hearted as Abuelo told stories from his childhood in Mexico, and also his children's. Celina smiled around the table. What a merry time spent with a family that truly loved each other.

We've never had an extended family like this. I'm so glad we do now. This is fun.

There were boisterous shouts of laughter as Tío Arturo Jr. teasingly offered tequila to both Chaim and Javier. Mama was offended but tried to hide her feelings and be a good sport.

There was even more laughter, mostly from the men, when cousin Igracio belched loudly during a brief conversation lull, leaving his mother mortified.

Celina fell asleep late that night, no longer afraid of the unknown. *I like our new family. I think I'm gonna like this town and tomorrow we get to see our new home.*

CHAPTER 13

Songs of My Soul

The next morning after a breakfast of Mama's delicious *blini* and jam, the families prepared to leave for their homes.

Celina, Justinia and Celestyna hugged each other and promised to keep in touch. "I don't know how close our homes are, but we live here in town too," Justinia told her. "We'll get to see each other a lot."

Celina was not even given a chance to respond before Tía Arabella stole her away for a hug. She and her siblings were passed from one pair of loving arms to the next.

Finally, Marcos broke in above the din, "All right, gang! We've got a new house to check out. We're burning daylight!"

Mama handed Diego to Yacqueline as she helped Little Man with a stuck zipper. The children once again thanked their new grandparents for their hospitality before heading out the door. Marcos skillfully maneuvered his father's van through the maze of cars backed up in the long driveway and pulled out of the neighborhood and onto the highway. It wasn't long thereafter before the Gonzalez's were pulling up in front of a beautiful, three-story brick home.

"*Ay Dios mío*," Jackie gasped as they parked. "Marc, Mama, it's awesome! Wow!"

As Marcos turned off the car, the Montoya children practically climbed over each other to get out. Helping Elian from his booster seat, Marcos laughed as he called after them, "I believe you forgot something!"

The Music of What Happens

Chaim turned and caught the key his stepfather tossed him. "Oh, oh, yeah . . . gotcha!"

When the children reached the front step, Soledad turned and called out, "Come on, Eli, you have to see this too!"

Elian nearly broke into a run, but Marcos caught his arm just in time. "Slowly, son," he reminded, "you can go, but walk *por favor.*"

The other children waited for their brother next to the front door for a moment until Javier, clearly out of patience, rushed down the long walkway, scooped Elian up into his strong arms, and they all hurried inside. Celina's breath caught. The real thing was so much better than the realtor's pictures. The house consisted of a large kitchen and dining room, an enormous family room, six bedrooms all on the second floor, two bathrooms, an office, playroom, laundry room, several closets and two large bonus rooms on the third floor. The children rushed from room to room, exclaiming with delight at everything they saw.

"Sol, this is a perfect house for hide-and-seek!" Jackie called out from upstairs. "Evangelo, get up here, you *gotta* see this cool, cubby hole!"

Nearly barreling Celina over, Evangelo rounded the corner, coming from the family room, raced down the hall and up the stairs without a backward glance.

"Lina, come see the kitchen," Yacqueline called out, enthusiastically, "there's so much room! I can cook anything in here."

Celina peeked around the corner, obligingly. She herself had never enjoyed cooking and took little pleasure in a kitchen. Yacqueline was right; however, the room was much larger than their kitchen in Santa Fe.

"That's awesome, Sis. I'd like to put in an order for Danish pastry and Eggs Benedict for breakfast tomorrow. It's been like forever!"

Yacqueline laughed and linked arms with her sister as they hurried upstairs, "With parsley in the Hollandaise? You got it."

For the first time, Celina had her own room. Sitting on the bed one afternoon, she stared out the window down onto a carefully manicured lawn partially concealed with hedges. She smiled to herself at the sight of Chaim, Javier and Jackie playing street hockey on inline skates in front of the house. Yacqueline sat some distance away under an apple tree, her nose in a cookbook, as usual. Celina cupped her chin in her hand and leaned out over the windowsill. She sighed, perfectly content. The unknown still lay ahead of her, yet she had no fear of it. A whole new life waited to be embraced.

In the days that followed, the family was so busy getting settled in their new home that Celina scarcely had time to think. Mama and Marcos wasted no time in assigning chores to the children, such as unpacking boxes and putting things away. They painted, laid new carpet and finally purchased furniture.

Just three weeks after moving into their new home, the family was completely settled, and instead of a regular public school such as the one they had attended in Santa Fe, Alexei and Marcos decided that the children would attend Ronald Reagan Academy K-12, one of the city's private schools. Celina had no idea when she had been more nervous. Mama was especially glad to hear that the school had small class sizes and an excellent, remedial reading program.

"That's embarrassing," Celina protested when Mama told her she had enrolled her. "Everyone'll see how dumb I am."

"You're *not* dumb, Lina, not in the slightest, but you're *going* to learn to read. We're getting you and Javier tested so you'll have the help you need through this program instead of being pushed through grade to grade. We're going to make this happen."

Celina leaned back against the couch and sighed, dramatically. "I'd rather not learn to read at all than have everyone in my grade thinking I'm a moron."

Of course, she had no choice in the matter, and when the children were enrolled in school, Mama and Marcos signed both her and Javier up for extensive testing for learning disabilities. When she came home after the tests, a week before school started, Celina was exhausted and nearly in tears.

I hate this crap, she thought, angrily, I just want to go to school like normal. I can't read, and I want to be left alone about it.

A tear ran down her cheek as she stared at the report she was supposed to give to Mama. She could only read a little of it, but her skills in reading had been recorded at a first-grade level.

I am dumb.

That night, alone with Mama and Marcos, they reviewed Celina's scores with her on the couch. "But look at your math skills, and your knowledge of history," Marcos pointed out, "You wouldn't test in at a *tenth-grade* level in math if you were stupid. It's called dyslexia and as far as these notes go, it's pretty severe. But let's try and see how this reading program helps you. It's better than those intensive resource classrooms in Santa Fe that never really helped you, right?"

Celina reluctantly nodded. "I don't want to, but I guess I'll try."

On the first day of classes, the Montoya children boarded the bus and were off.

If only we could have stayed in public school; I don't know anything about private schools, and this uniform is downright dumb looking.

Little Man, looking as though he did not have a care in the world, sat beside her, clutching his lunchbox.

Almost before Celina realized what was happening, the bus pulled up in front of the Academy. This school was much smaller than the public schools they had attended in Santa Fe; and unlike public schools, all grades attended school in the same building.

"We're doomed," Chaim said softly to his siblings as they climbed off the bus. Celina shot him a warning glance, silently reminding him that he must not frighten Evangelo and Little Man.

Celina took her youngest brothers by the hands, "Come on," she said, firmly to the others who stood staring ahead at the doors, eyes reflecting their uncertainty.

When they arrived inside, students of all ages were milling around in the hallways, catching up with friends and collecting supplies from their lockers. Many of their new classmates turned and stared at the Montoya children. Celina noticed a couple of glares, but for the most part, they just seemed curious. Celina and Chaim exchanged long-suffering glances.

Total rich kid, gringo school. Why can't we just go to a normal school with normal kids? Celina turned her back and motioned for her siblings to follow her. Whispers and a few giggles followed them as they made their way down a long hallway. First, they arrived at the eighth-grade arithmetic class, and Chaim remained. Finally, Celina found the tenth-grade math class which was on the second floor. Like she always had in Santa Fe, she had tested a grade above in math.

I miss Lissy so much. We were like really looking forward to taking on Santa Fe High together.

When she arrived, no one was in the room except the teacher who was writing algebraic expressions on the blackboard. Celina cleared her throat, and the stern-looking, middle-aged woman turned to survey her critically.

"Uhm, you *can't* be the new girl we're expecting from Boston, the heir to the *Post-It* fortune, the Kennedy relation?"

Celina looked at the ceiling and nearly snorted. Just in time, she remembered her manners and replied, "No, ma'am. My name's Lina, and I'm the heir to the Trojan Man fortune." She grinned, mischievously.

The teacher flushed red at this and gritted her teeth; however, she did not reply as she thumbed through a stack of file folders.

"Ah, here we are. Celina Zagoradniy, correct?"

"Legally. But I only answer to Lina Montoya."

The teacher lifted an eyebrow and pursed her lips. "I am Mrs. Lawton-Kent, your arithmetic teacher. I understand you're actually a ninth grader. Excellent work testing an entire grade ahead. Your desk is number 18. Also, Celina, I see from your dossier here that you've only attended a public school until this year. Please understand that we are an elite, private school with higher academic standards and especially social graces. Vulgarity is not tolerated at the Academy. I don't know what barn you were brought up in, but that includes crude conversation about any item for which the word "protection" is a euphemism. Is that clear?"

"Yes, ma'am, loud and clear." She barely resisted the urge to ask, *What the hell's a euphemism?*

"Oh, and Celina," Mrs. Lawton-Kent continued as her new student turned away, "please let your parents know that we offer optional elementary Spanish three times weekly for ninth-grade students."

Celina smiled, condescendingly. "I pass. Spanish *and* Russian are my first languages. I'm an ESL student. It's in the *dossier.*" She knew she had been rude, but she didn't care. It was apparent she had left the hoity-toity teacher stunned, and that left Celina with a sense of real satisfaction.

The other students were now beginning to arrive. Celina noted that besides three African-American students, she was the only student of color in the entire classroom.

I just know I'm not going to like it here. I bet they have a lot more Staci's than Santa Fe Middle did.

Finally, Mrs. Lawton-Kent pointed to the arithmetic problems on the blackboard. The teacher scanned the sea of pupils all gazing up at her expectantly. She tapped her chin. "I would like Griffin Arkwright, Shania Webley-Marcum, Celina Zagoradniy and Jamal Delaney to please come forward and find the solutions to these sets of problems."

When the chosen students were ready, the teacher continued: "The equations are in groups of four. Each of you choose a section and begin. Be sure to show all your work. You others pay close attention because a new set of volunteers will be asked to explain, in detail, how Griffin, Shania, Celina and Jamal found their solutions or were unable to reach the correct answer."

Celina glanced around as she picked up a piece of new chalk. *Of course, only us non-white kids would have to prove ourselves. Flippin' racist bunny!*

The problems were difficult but as math had always been her strongest subject, she finished first. On her way back to her seat, she momentarily leaned over Mrs. Lawton-Kent's desk and said in a voice low but firm, "The name's Montoya."

Surprised at how quickly her newest pupil had completed the assignment, the teacher made her way to the blackboard. She forced a smile. "W-well done, Celina," was her only comment as she scrawled 100% above the row of equations. Celina grinned to herself.

There's academic standards for you!

After what seemed like forever, it was time to meet for lunch in the cafeteria. Because they knew no one yet and felt a little shy, the Montoya children ate together at the back of the room and recounted the morning's events.

"This school's not as bad as we thought this morning," Chaim gave tentative approval, "I thought it was just gonna be full of gringos with shotgun mouths like the Ainsworths', but most aren't half bad. And my teachers seem cool so far. Oh," he added in disgust, "only real problem is, no one here says my name right. They say dumb bunny stuff like Chime and Chame. But," he grinned, "Mr. Dunn, my world history teacher, finally gave up trying to say it right and nicknamed me C-Man. I totally dig it! How about you, Lina?"

"Well, my math teacher's a racist, and a *total* prude," She laughed. "That snooty thing went all red in the face when I mentioned condoms. But as for the rest, I'm thinking it's not going to be half bad either. We'll see."

"I was told there's a drama club here," Soledad broke in, "they get to do plays. I'm gonna join if Mama and Tío'll let me."

"Drama?" Javier rolled his eyes, "Sol, your middle name is drama. You sure don't need any help. Wait 'til everyone hears about—

"Don't dare say it, Javier," Chaim warned, "Or I'll let the whole school know *your* dirty, little secret, and you'll never make any friends here."

"And that would be . . ." Javier challenged, narrowing his eyes at his brother.

Before Chaim could reply, Jackie moved so that he and Javier were nose to nose and said, sweetly, "Bedwetter."

Javier's piercing, dark eyes grew wide at this, flashing angrily. "You- you— he sputtered.

Peacemaker, Yacqueline intervened, gently, "Chaim, Jackie, you both know better. Teasing like that is totally not okay."

"What the—what in heck are you all speaking?"

The Montoya's turned abruptly to see a red-haired girl Celina recognized from Bio. Celina stood and smiled as she extended her hand. "Hey there, I'm Lina Montoya and these are my brothers and sisters. I know we have Bio together, I'm sorry, I don't remember your name."

Instead of taking Celina's hand, the girl wrinkled her nose. "I asked what you were speaking. I didn't like come over here because I needed a *friend*. Not that you're even in my league, but— The girl looked Celina up and down and sniffed. "Not from around here, are you? Was that Spanish?"

Celina took an instant dislike to the tall, blue-eyed redhead, but she simply shrugged. "Some of it."

"I knew it. So, I'm guessing you all's father is the one that made that big donation last month."

Celina furrowed her brow at this, and Chaim cocked his head, "What big donation?"

"The one that let you people in here. Otherwise, you'd have all gotten waitlisted."

Hillary! That's her name.

No longer friendly, Celina stared hard at the other girl, "Listen, Hillary, I suggest you move on. We got nothing to say to each other."

Instead of leaving Hillary smirked, "You'll never be like me, Lina. Donations from your father will be the only way you get through life without cleaning houses and picking fruit."

Celina chewed her lip, determined not to get in trouble for fighting on the first day.

"Now your father—

"Okay, creep," Soledad broke in, "enough with this donation crap. By the way, Marc is our *step*father, and well, he wins the prize then.

Betcha' the only crappy thing *your* father ever donated to this school was *you*!"

Celina turned back to her siblings, unable to restrain her laughter as they all joined in. Soledad smirked at Hillary. "Just move on, creep."

Hillary stood stock still, eyes flashing angrily, mouth set in a firm line. "If I were you, Lina, I'd shut that mouth of yours before you really get it. You don't belong here, you beaners think you're so smart and funny, but there's no way you all have connections. Now *my* dad—

"Oh, Hillary, grow up! We're in ninth grade; we passed the "my dad can beat up your dad" stage years ago. Can't you think of any new material, or are you just another dime-a-dozen racist? Get over yourself."

"She's like Staci, Lina," Evangelo commented, innocently.

Celina ignored the remark. "Like my little sis said, move it along, creep."

Hillary gritted her teeth. "You all better watch it; you'll soon see what it's like being in *my* school."

"Ohhhhhh, a threat!" Celina mocked her, "how original. Can't you do just a little better than that?"

"Oh, absolutely," Hillary narrowed her eyes, menacingly, "don't say you all weren't warned." With that, she turned on her heel and stalked off.

Javier whistled, "Man, what *is* her problem? Lina, you're gonna have to like to beat her dumb bunny butt, I think. Evangelo's right. She's so much like Staci."

Celina rolled her eyes. "Rich snobs are everywhere. Don't pay any attention, guys. I'll deal with her if I have to. Let's finish lunch."

Obediently, all resumed eating their sandwiches and fruit except Little Man. "Lina, why'd she call us beaners? That's mean."

Before Celina could respond, Yacqueline patted his hand. "*Si*, it is, *hermano*. And she's a mean girl for saying things like that. But we don't have to be like her, do we?"

Little Man shook his head, vigorously.

"*Ochin kharasho,* now let's finish lunch." She smiled, reassuringly as she patted his curly head.

The Music of What Happens

Celina shook her head to herself. *I just want to put my fist in her nasty mouth. Why is Yacque always so perfectly good?*

Celina's last class of the day was Advanced Musical Performance which Mama had wasted no time enrolling her in.

"Hello, *malaynkia*," the instructor issued a cheery greeting when she saw Celina standing in the doorway. "Come in; you're on time, I see. Unlike the rest," she muttered more to herself than Celina. "I am your piano instructor, Miss Kropotkin, and you are—

"Lina. Celina Montoya." She could already tell that she was going to like Miss Kropotkin. As the teacher wrote her name on the attendance list, Celina looked around the room. Two, lovely pianos were positioned against some of the white walls, and bookshelves filled with sheet music lined the other walls. Six desks were lined in rows of three in the middle of the classroom directly in front of Miss Kropotkin's large desk.

"Lina, what instructors have you studied under?"

Celina cocked her head. The woman's musical European accent had aroused her curiosity. She turned back to her teacher. "I taught myself. I've never had a piano teacher before now. But I'm looking forward to learning a lot from you."

The music teacher's head snapped up; her emerald-green eyes mirrored shock when she realized her pupil had replied to her question in perfect Russian.

Instinctively, she replied, in kind and asked her the rest of the questionnaire in Russian. Celina grinned as she answered the questions.

Miss Kropotkin then switched back to English. "*Wherever* did you learn Russian?"

Celina laughed as she explained.

"Oh, my goodness, you're the first— she was interrupted when two more students walked in. Smiling, she leaned over and whispered, in Russian, "Desk four, to your left."

As Celina sat down, her eyebrow raised when she saw Hillary Oswald saunter in, as though she owned the place, and sit down across from her. Hillary glared balefully at her new classmate and smoothly flipped Celina the bird as she laid her music folder neatly beside her chair.

Celina rolled her eyes and mouthed, "Grow up!" She then opened her theory book and pretended to be deeply engrossed in Lesson 27.

This fool isn't worth five minutes.

When all six students were assembled, Miss Kropotkin stood. "Good afternoon, class. My name is Dunyasha Kropotkin. I moved here six years ago from my hometown in Ukraine. Before I Immigrated to this country, I taught piano and voice at conservatories in Kyiv, Moscow, and Yalta. This is my first time teaching American high school students, however, regardless of who or where I teach, I hold *very* high standards of diligence and discipline. When I speak, my students remain silent and attentive. All assignments are to be completed on time without fail, and lastly, I have a zero-tolerance policy for bullying others and *especially* interrupting. My rules are simple and reasonable, and if you have a problem following them, then you cannot remain here. This is an elite class, as you can see, there are only six of you, and trust me, that number will decrease as the school year progresses. Now," she faced her small class, squarely, "Who would like to be first to show off what they can do at the piano? Everyone has prepared a piece and brought a copy of the sheet music for me, am I correct?"

Celina gulped when she heard Miss Kropotkin call on her.

She swallowed hard and stood. "Y-yes, ma'am?"

"Would you care to be our first volunteer?"

Not really.

"Yes, ma'am. The piece I'm gonna play is called *Taken Too Soon*. It's a composition I wrote about my father after he died." Celina blinked hard as she moved to the piano closest to her.

"Thank you, Lina. May I have a copy of your sheet music please?"

Celina shut her eyes, heat rising in her cheeks. She grimaced, apologetically, "I'm sorry, ma'am. I-I don't know how to read or write notes."

The Music of What Happens

Miss Kropotkin's eyes widened, but she motioned for Celina to be seated at the piano.

Hillary's mean voice broke in. "Guess we all know who's going to be first to get her butt kicked out of class."

Sierra Markwell and Owen Dodge snickered behind their hands at this. "This class is *way* outta' her league anyway," Sierra whispered back. "What's she even doing here?"

"Hillary and Sierra, this is your only warning!" Miss Kropotkin snapped and then turned back to Celina, "Go ahead."

For a moment Celina was silent, but the giggles from Hillary and Sierra behind her gave her courage. Closing her eyes, she began to play.

Papi, can you hear me? This is for you. I know you didn't mean to, but you took so much away when you left. You left a hole in the world and a hole in my heart. Please hear me, please love my song. I love you. I miss you as much now as I did then. My heart still hurts, but I hope you haven't forgotten me even though you're with God now.

Almost before Celina realized what was happening, she had played the last eight bars and the composition ended with a gentle close. Swiping at her eyes and cheeks, Celina barely smiled and nodded to her teacher as she returned to her seat. All was silent, and Celina was unable to swallow the lump in her throat. She stared down at her desk.

Hillary, tall and slender, wavy red hair flowing down her back over her emerald cardigan, stood and made her way to the piano. "And now, "children," she made sarcastic quotations with her fingers as she spoke, "now that *that's* over, let's hitch our wagon to a star. I'll be playing Beethoven's *Moonlight Sonata.*"

Celina was astonished. She had to admit that *Moonlight Sonata* had never sounded quite so perfect to her. As Hillary stood, brimming with confidence, she sauntered back to her desk, gloating down at Celina as she did. Celina forced a smile as she leaned over and whispered, sincerely, "That was beautiful."

Hillary's nose was immediately in the air. "I know. I've been in music training in New York and Chicago since I was six. On my way to the conservatory in Seattle when I graduate. And you?" she sniffed, clearly holding back laughter.

When each student had performed, Miss Kropotkin dismissed one girl, telling her kindly, "You are improving, and I hope you'll try again next year."

Celina drew a ragged breath. Miss Kropotkin handed out single sheets of paper that she had filled out with notes on each student's performance. Celina's stomach dropped when hers simply read in Russian: *See me after class.* Her heart sank.

Just like all my spelling assignments back home. 'See me after class.' She sighed deeply as she watched her classmates exit the room. A tall, olive-skinned boy with clouds of thick dark curls turned and winked at her on his way out. Celina couldn't help but smile. This was the first real encouragement she had received all day.

Who is he? He's adorable.

When the last student had departed, Miss Kropotkin pulled up a chair beside her and sighed deeply as she looked into Celina's eyes. Celina nearly squirmed under the teacher's unwavering gaze.

"You know you're the best one here, don't you?"

Celina hesitated. She did not want to lie, but neither did she want to seem braggy. "Well—

"It's just us."

"I know. But-but the others are-are good too, especially Hillary."

"Lina," Miss Kropotkin leaned back in her chair, "you're completely self-taught, and yet you make a piano sing like an angel. That's raw talent, my girl. The rest will come with study. I want to give you this." She held out a piece of paper. "It's a bit early, but this is the form I want you to fill out for the Winter Musicale in December. Everyone in this school can perform, however, in this class, I only send my three, best students. I'm holding auditions in October, but you've already auditioned. Will you represent my class there? It's the biggest holiday event of the season in this town. Some people even come all the way from Seattle to see it. A few hundred people, for sure."

Celina's eyes widened. She began to shake her head then paused. *What is she saying? I've never played piano in public. And now she wants me to play in front of that many people. I'd probably pass out dead on the floor. At the very least I'd pee my pants! What the heck?*

"Uhm," she couldn't believe she was hearing herself say, "I'll think about it. Can I go now?"

The bus ride home was not a long one and within half an hour the children were rushing into the house, excited to tell Mama and Elian about their first day. Over molasses cookies, they chatted about the new school.

Amid the conversation, Elian awoke from his nap on the couch and joined his siblings at the breakfast bar. He grinned at Celina and wrapped his arms around her neck. Her heart tore. Despite the two-hour nap, Elian was exhausted. His eyes watered as he coughed hard into a napkin.

"What was your new school like, Lina?" He helped himself to a molasses cookie.

She winced at the husky sound of his voice. It was hard even to look at her brother anymore. He was so thin. Elian's body struggled to maintain weight, though he had a decent appetite much of the time, and Mama fed her family quality, home-cooked meals. Celina tried over and over to deny to herself what was happening to him. Although he had been ill most of his life, the terrible weight loss, debilitating exhaustion and loss of almost all physical strength were the final struggles Papi experienced in the three months before he died.

I can't lose my brother. I can't! What do we do?

Nevertheless, she managed a stiff smile, "Fine, Eli, the new school wa-was just f-fine."

Elian didn't appear to notice his sister's worry over his deteriorating condition. He grinned with genuine enthusiasm. "I hope I'm well enough to go to school with you all next year."

Celina turned away, fighting tears. Chaim, sitting near them, bit his lower lip and glared out the window. She knew they were both thinking the same thing. *Would little Elian even have a next year?*

Alexei, sitting across from her children, seemed to sense, as only she could, that something was bothering her two eldest. Leaving Javier and Yacqueline to supervise the younger ones, she motioned discreetly for Celina and Chaim to follow her. Together, they made their way upstairs to the master bedroom. Mama closed the door, and the three sat down. For a long time, no one spoke.

Finally, Mama took their hands in hers. "You're both worried about Eli," she said. However, it was more a statement than a question.

Celina nodded, tears filling her dark eyes as she tried not the think about last Friday when Elian had been too exhausted to even play his beloved violin. Chaim woodenly stared straight ahead out the window behind them, though Celina knew it took much effort on his part not to show the depth of his pain.

Mama continued, "I want you both to know that Marcos and I have been conferring with his new cardiologist, Dr. Peters, and a couple of specialists. Because he's so frail, it's incredibly risky, but they all agree it's your brother's only chance. Corrective surgery is scheduled for next month."

CHAPTER 14

To Live With Fear

"So, what do you think?" Celina asked Mama over the breakfast bar a week later. Mama was in the kitchen, seasoning the pea soup for supper. She smiled as she turned to her daughter.

"You're procrastinating on the grocery list, my love."

"No, really, Mama, what do you think about me performing in that big music play?"

"I think it's a great opportunity, Linochka. Remember that this is a whole new place. No one knows us here, and you can-can totally reinvent yourself if you want. Your gift is meant to be shared. I'm sorry you never had such opportunities in Santa Fe. But like I said, we're in a whole new place. I say go for it, *dochka*."

Celina leaned forward resting her cheek in her hand. "I love my music, but—" she hesitated, "what if other people don't?"

Mama nodded, understandingly. "Well, Miss Kropotkin's a professional, isn't she?"

"PH.D."

"And she didn't even ask you for a real audition for the winter musicale. She called it raw talent. Listen to her. You can go real distances with your music if you decide to. Now," she changed the subject, "back to that Costco list. Please add garlic powder and . . ."

Celina sighed as she carefully spelled out the words on the piece of paper. Her head ached as she slowly added each item Mama listed.

One of her ongoing homework assignments was that she was expected to do whatever real-life writing, reading and spelling practice Mama and Marcos could come up with.

"I'm sure you've noticed Lina uses her siblings to read and spell for her," Mrs. Bates had mentioned the week before at the student-teacher conference, "That must stop now. Practice, practice, practice. Every time you can find such assignments for her: grocery lists, helping her youngest brother with his spelling etc. etc. No more avoiding these subjects. She'll be doing better in no time."

Celina gritted her teeth as Mama named another item to put on the list and reminded her that she would be checking her spelling when the list was complete.

I hate this! It's too hard. Why can't I just play music? I understand all that. Chaim and Yacque don't mind spelling and reading for me. I've always helped them and Jackie with math. I don't "use" them! It's a two-way street! Mrs. Bates just doesn't get it. She—

"Lina. Lina?"

Celina started and looked up, sheepishly. She glanced down at the list, hoping she hadn't missed any of the words Mama had listed.

"You were far away," Mama smiled. "Can I check the list now?"

"So why the second thoughts?" Miss Kropotkin asked Celina after class one afternoon. "You're afraid, aren't you?"

Celina bit her lip and looked down at the floor. She reluctantly nodded. "Very. I love this class, I love playing, I love everything I'm learning. But like who am I trying to kid? I'm not a performer. The others have all been taking classes here for years, haven't they? They all play so much better than me. I'm afraid to screw up in public in front of everyone—" her voice trailed off.

"Lina," Miss Kropotkin pulled up a chair beside Celina's desk and motioned for her to sit. "Listen, *malaynkia*, I'm going to be honest with you: you have a gift the likes of which I've never seen. You moved me to tears with that composition to your father. I see you; I see your heart. In your music, creativity, love, passion, these powerful and beautiful emotions all come out. Don't hold back your heart, your feelings when you play. Like me, the audience will be deeply moved when they hear the song of your soul. You can do this, Lina. But ultimately, it's your decision."

Celina nodded as she excused herself. As she headed for the door, Hillary sauntered in, pausing only to wrinkle her nose at Celina.

"Miss Kropotkin, here's my form for the Winter Musicale. I—

"You're performing in the musicale?"

"Naturally," Hillary stared down her nose at the much shorter girl, "I've won the last three years in a row. I intend to do the same this year. Wait a minute-what's going on here? Don't tell me Miss Kropotkin's actually considering *you* as my competition?"

"But I am, Hillary. I most certainly am."

Hillary smirked at a silent Celina then scoffed, "This'll be the easiest competition I've ever won. Excuse me," Handing Miss Kropotkin her paperwork, she shoulder-checked Celina out of her way as she strode out the door. Celina glared at her back. She turned when Miss Kropotkin cleared her throat. She arched an eyebrow. Celina couldn't help but smile at the unspoken dare. She nodded with a confident grin she did not feel.

"Ma'am, I wouldn't miss this chance for anything."

As she left the classroom, Celina ran smack into Fulgencio Matlock who was arriving at the classroom with paperwork.

"Oh-oh, ¡hola," she stumbled backward, staring at her shoes. "*Lo siento.*"

"No *problemo*," Fulgencio replied, easily. Celina glanced up at him. Fulgencio and his sister, Maieh, were the only other Hispanic children at the Academy. Like Celina, Fulgencio was a pianist, having studied the instrument since he was six. Celina had just learned that he too had been chosen to represent Miss Kropotkin's class in the Winter Musicale. Fulgencio was a tenth grader, curly-headed, dark-eyed and already 6 feet tall, a star basketball player on the Academy's Eagle's Team.

He smiled down at her. "Wait for me?"

"W-what? Why?"

"Walk home with me?"

Celina sucked in her breath, feeling her cheeks grow warm. "I-I guess so."

Just moments later, they were heading down the sidewalk up town. For a while, the two walked in silence. Celina's heart was thumping. She loved the scent of his cologne and felt the heat rise in her neck when she realized how she would love to run her fingers through his dark curls. She glanced at the ground.

You weirdo; what's wrong with you?

"I've been wanting to talk to you. I love hearing you play. Can't hardly believe you've never performed before. Where you from anyway?"

"Santa Fe. Far as performing goes, just never had much chance for that. We were poor when my papi was alive. We had to work hard just to survive. Our mama did her best but—" Celina's voice trailed off.

I can't believe I'm telling him these things. Geez, I barely know him.

When Fulgencio reached hesitantly for her hand, Celina took it readily. She smiled up at him.

Ay Dios mío, he's so cute.

"You used to be poor? That's interesting."

"Why?"

Fulgencio shrugged. "I dunno. I guess I've never known what being poor is like. My dad's a lawyer."

"My tío—I mean my uhm—my stepdad's a lawyer too. That's why we're okay now."

"Lina, I-I was wondering if you-you'd like to go out with me sometime?"

Celina's eyes widened. She felt momentarily faint. *Out of all the girls in this school, he like wants to date me?*

"I-I'd *love* to," she heard herself reply, hoping she didn't sound over-eager, "I'd have to see what my mama and stepdad say, but I'd like to. What you got in mind?"

The Music of What Happens

"Basketball game. Orioles are playing the Cardinals in Seattle."
"But neither of us are old enough to drive yet."
"My dad'll drive, but he's cool. Nothing to worry about with him."
"Ok. When?"

"Well, I'm way crushing on him, and I totally think he likes me," Celina confided the next afternoon to Edie, her newest friend. "He finally asked me out. Three weeks it took him, but I'm excited. We're going to the Cardinals-Orioles game on Oct 15. Can hardly wait."

"You're sooooooo lucky," Edie complained, "my parents won't let me go out with Logan until I'm a junior. Two whole years. It sucks!"

Celina shrugged. "Uhm, I-I haven't asked my parents. Honestly, I don't know how they feel about guys. We-we've never talked about it."

"Lina Montoya, you mean to say you're gonna sneak out?" Edie giggled, passing her friend a copy of *Seventeen*, "Look at this rad sweater. Don't you think that would look great on me?"

"Sure, it would. And no, I'm not gonna sneak out. I'll talk with Mama and Tío, just haven't found the right moment. They're pretty worried about my little brother. He's doing bad right now, and he has surgery in two weeks."

"Hey," Edie slipped on her flip-flops, "let's go to the park."

As the girls headed past the community basketball court, Celina halted at a familiar, male voice across the way at the courts. *Fulgencio*! Edie heard it too, and the girls turned simultaneously. Celina felt as though her knees turned to jelly as she watched tall, handsome Fulgencio move with ease around his opponent, dribbling the ball. Sweat beads glistened on his tanned skin. His incredibly black, curly hair tumbled forward attractively. Celina was speechless as she gripped the diamond-shaped holes in the chain link fence, separating the sidewalk from the courts. Fulgencio moved fluidly past the other boy and slam dunked the ball into the hoop. She grinned.

At that moment, he caught sight of the girls watching him. "Lina! *Qué pasa, muchacha?*" Fulgencio easily jumped the fence. "Be back in a sec, Jayce," he called over his shoulder, "So," he continued, easily, falling in step alongside the girls. "Ready for our date?"

Celina grinned. "For sure."

It feels like I'm dreaming. The hottest guy in the Academy, the high-school basketball star wants to go out with me. And he's even a sophomore! Why me? I'm like nobody.

Celina knew well that practically every freshman and sophomore girl except Hillary Oswald would willingly give up their allowance for a date with the beautiful Fulgencio Matlock, yet he had asked *her*.

"Well, I gotta get back to Jayce, but I'll pick you up Friday at 6 in two weeks, *si*?"

"*Si, yo sé.*"

"See you Monday." Without waiting for a reply, he turned, and with long strides, hurried back to the basketball court. For a long moment, Celina stared after him. She turned to Edie.

"Told you."

Edie threw her arms around her friend. "Well, I didn't catch a word of that conversation, but it's wonderful. You're so totally lucky!"

The two girls squealed simultaneously as they hugged each other, both trying to talk at once. He hadn't forgotten. He had meant it. Her head was spinning; her *first* date.

The next afternoon after school, Celina and her siblings, except Elian and Diego, spent the afternoon at the Driscoll's with Edie and her brothers and sister. After a snack of cool milk and gingerbread cookies, the two eldest girls climbed up the tree house ladder to escape the rowdy, younger children. Edie kicked off her flip-flops as usual, and the girls thumbed through back issues of *Seventeen* and discussed Celina's upcoming date.

So thoroughly were they enjoying themselves that they did not immediately hear Edie's mother calling frantically from the front yard. "Edie! Lina? Girls, where are you?"

When they finally realized they were being summoned, the girls slid down the tree house pole to the ground to find Mrs. Driscoll searching for them.

"Oh, Lina, thank God. Marcos just phoned. Your little brother's been rushed to the Children's Hospital. I'm to drive you all there. Edie, find Sharon and your brothers and go inside until I come back. Quickly, Lina, come with me. The others are already in the car."

Frightened, Celina rushed on ahead. She glanced back only once when Edie called out, "I'll be praying for him, Lina!"

The next blurred fifteen minutes felt like hours as they sped off uptown to the Children's Hospital. Celina mumbled prayers the entire time. She barely realized that she was combining Latin prayers from church with Hebrew prayers from Mama's, old, Jewish devotionals.

No, Eli. No, you can't die! You just can't! Silent tears rolled down her cheeks as she pleaded with God. *Oh, please don't take him away. Hang on, Eli, hang on! Your beautiful spirit is your strength. You can do this, little brother. You can make it. Don't die, Eli, don't die like Papi did!*

Minutes later, Mrs. Driscoll pulled up in front of the hospital and hurriedly escorted the Montoya children inside. When they located the waiting area, Celina and her siblings stood in stunned silence for several minutes before they spotted Mama and Marcos together in the far corner, holding tightly to each other. As soon as he saw his stepchildren, Marcos motioned for them to come close. Mama was sobbing, quietly, into his shirt.

"Mama?" Chaim gently patted his mother's shoulder. Alexei was too choked to speak for a moment. Finally, she looked up at him, wiping away the tears rolling relentlessly down her cheeks.

"Your-your brother went into a cardiac arrest."

"No!" Celina whisper-yelled, in horror.

Mama reached for her hand and Chaim's. "He's in emergency surgery now." Again, she burst into tears. "My baby! Oh, Marc, they wouldn't let me stay with him! He-he'll be so afraid!"

Marcos gathered her close again. He couldn't understand his wife's, desperate, rapid-fire Russian, and he knew at this point, she would not be able to understand him either. Over her shoulder, he closed his eyes, and his lips were moving. Following his example, the children dropped to their knees. For a long time, they prayed and then just sat.

Oh, Eli, you can do this! I know you can. You gotta' fight, little brother. Please fight. I love you so much; it's not time for you to go.

Celina suddenly jerked awake and sat bolt upright. The waiting area was nearly dark, their only light coming from a small table lamp at the other end of the room. She had no idea how long she had been asleep. The other children were sprawled all over the floor, cuddled close to each other. Celina shifted uncomfortably, feeling the all-too-familiar sensation of wetness beneath her. Her cheeks flushed, thankful that her pants were dark.

Ay mierda!

Celina unceremoniously pushed Evangelo off her lap and moved away from where she had been lying. She looked around, fuzzy. Her stepfather was the only one still awake, though clearly by willpower alone. Little Man was fast asleep in his arms, and Mama, face tear-streaked and hair wild, was slumped against her husband, her head on his shoulder, undeniably hard asleep.

"Tio, what time is it?" she whispered. Marcos yawned and looked at his phone.

"It's after midnight. Here, help me lay Little Man down." Celina gathered her brother in her arms and laid him beside her. He hardly even stirred. She then stood and helped Marcos lay Mama carefully on the floor beside him. "I had them give her a sedative earlier," he explained, "and she's out like a light. I gotta' stay awake," he stretched hard and stood. "That coffee's not doing the job."

"Mr. Gonzalez?"

Celina immediately stood, and Marcos stopped pacing. A man in green scrubs stood in the doorway.

"*S-si?*" Marcos' voice betrayed his fear and concern.

The surgeon smiled. "Mr. Gonzalez, you can see your stepson now."

"How-how is he?"

The surgeon spoke, reassuringly, "It was touch and go for quite a while, but he made it through. With rest and careful care, Elian's going to be okay."

CHAPTER 15

First Date

Two weeks following his dangerous operation, Elian came home. The doctors told Marcos and Mama that, although he would always be physically frail, the surgery had been a partial success.

As Celina pulled a pan of molasses cookies from the oven, Little Man's eager voice rang out, "Eli's home! Eli's home!"

Celina lifted Diego from his highchair and followed as the others hurried to the front door. Marcos entered first, carrying Elian in his strong arms. Mama was beside them, holding her son's hand as though afraid to let go. Drained and exhausted, Elian appeared to be made of crystal. As a result of the difficult operation, his weight had plummeted to thirty-two pounds. Despite all, he was still the same sweet-natured Elian come home to his family. Marcos set him on the sofa, and Mama placed an afghan around his bone-thin shoulders and another over his lap. Everyone gathered around the sofa, all trying to talk at once, relieved and joyful to have their brother home again.

Fleetingly, Celina's mind wandered to her upcoming date with Fulgencio. *You dumb bunny!* she mentally kicked herself. *I haven't even mentioned it to Mama and Tío in all this craziness. Oh, they just have to say yes!*

That night, Celina helped Elian get ready for bed. "What story do you want tonight?" she asked, examining the titles in the bookcase. Elian sighed contentedly. Her back to him, Celina closed her eyes and smiled to herself. She could not recall the last time she had heard him breathe so easily.

"Well," Elian said, after a moment's deliberation, "it's Christmas in a few weeks, could you please read *Toliya and the Christmas Train?*"

She grinned. "Great choice, Sunbeam." Celina, herself, still loved the folktale about a little, Russian boy who wished for a toy train for Christmas. She pulled the worn volume from the shelf and sat down on the bed beside him.

"Once upon a time," she began, in Russian, thankful she knew the story by heart, "in a tiny village called Katyk, there lived a poor little boy named Toliya . . ."

When the first chapter was finished, Elian sat up and wrapped his arms around his sister's neck. "*Te quiero*, Lina," he said softly.

Celina raised an eyebrow, surprised that he had spoken Spanish instead of Russian, which he preferred whenever possible. "*Te quiero mucho*, Eli, You like-you like have no idea how much."

When they broke the embrace, Elian looked seriously into Celina's eyes. "Marc loves you too, Lina. He wishes you loved him back."

Celina looked away. "Eli," she finally said, slowly, "I was very wrong to be so mean to Tío all last year when he was so good to take care of us and Mama. I'm sorry for that; Tío knows I'm sorry too. But he-he's not our papa, you know? Right?"

Elian nodded. "I know that, Lina. I know Tío's not our real papa, but Papi's dead." Elian's dark eyes suddenly filled with tears. "I-I get so scared, Lina. Sometimes I can't even remember Papi's voice anymore." He gulped back tears and continued, brokenly, "Would it be very wrong to have *another* papa, Lina? Would that be wrong?"

Celina stared down at her hands. She had no answer for her brother. Sometimes it seemed like Elian was far more perceptive than an eight-year-old had any right to be. He had backed her into a corner. Marcos had asked her practically the same thing over a year ago now. What *was* wrong with having another father whom she loved and who loved her?

Celina's smile was strained as she said, softly, "It-it's late, Sunbeam. Go to sleep now."

Elian smiled, almost knowingly, as he snuggled down beneath the quilts. Within minutes, he had been lulled into a sound sleep, amid the sweet strains of *Holy Water* sung in his sister's, soft contralto.

Back downstairs, Celina was thrilled to see that the other children were nowhere in sight, and Mama and Marcos were alone in the family room, talking.

Here goes nothing. Make it good.

"Hey there, Kiddo," Marcos greeted her, "have a seat."

Plopping down on the loveseat across from her parents, Celina was quiet for a moment. "Uhm, Mama, Tío, there's something I need to ask you guys."

"Course, Lina. What's on your mind?"

"Well," Celina hesitated, "do you know Fulgencio Matlock?"

Marcos leaned back in his recliner and shook his head. "No, I—why does that name sound familiar?"

"His dad's a lawyer like you, Collier Matlock, that's why I thought you might know him."

"Oh! Oh, yeah. He works in the firm below mine. Good egg, Collier is. He's married to a Mexican woman and has a couple of kids, I think. Now, what's this about his son?"

"Uhm," Celina hesitated again, "he goes to the Academy with us, and he's asked me to go to the Orioles-Cardinals basketball game with him on Friday; the big one in Seattle."

At this, Marcos winked, knowingly, at his wife. She in turn rolled her eyes at him. Celina's stomach tightened. She was sure she had blown it. "Can-can I go?" she finished, timidly.

Mama sighed, but Marcos understood. "Hmmm, you like this Fulgencio don't you?"

Celina grinned, nodding vigorously. "He-he's so cool, Tío! And gorgeous!"

At this, Marcos threw back his head and laughed, heartily. Celina cringed.

The Music of What Happens

Oh, why did I say that?

Marcos sucked in his cheeks, "Well, you're only fourteen, Lina. Your mother and I have discussed dating lately, and we agree that fourteen's too young, and we would prefer you wait until you're a junior. Rushing it only leads to things a girl your age isn't ready for. *But,*" he continued, "since it's just a ballgame, I'll allow it *if* one of Fulgencio's parents is going, as well. I don't mean dropping you two off alone in Seattle either. I have briefs to prepare on Friday night for a trial Monday, and your mother has Elian and the baby to take care of, so if one of them can't make it, I'm afraid you won't be allowed to go. I don't plan on agreeing to more than supervised outings until you're a little older, so if you want to go, I suggest you call Fulgencio, and get a game plan together."

"Oh, Tío, *gracias!*" Celina jumped from the sofa and gave her stepfather a rare, voluntary hug before rushing from the room.

"So perfect," Celina smiled to herself that Friday evening. Chin cupped in her hand, she stared, dreamily, out the window into starry, romantic darkness. Her sisters and Edie were in the bedroom with her, almost as excited as Celina herself, as they tried to help her decide what to wear and how to fix her hair. After much indecision, Edie curled the ends of Celina's hair off her shoulders with a faux red rose clip tucked and pinned in her hair above her ear. She also opted to wear her short, fluttery, blue skirt, white and silver sneakers with white socks and a gray and blue sweatshirt. Finally, she was ready, and according to Yacqueline and Edie, looked totally "to die for."

"Oh, Lina," Soledad gushed, "Fulgencio will *never* date another girl after tonight."

"Shhhh, don't be a dumb bunny!" Celina glanced over her shoulder at her closed bedroom door, "and keep your mouth shut. Tío read me the riot act yesterday! He gets wind I'm calling this a *real* date and he'll pull the plug for sure. He's already double-checked to make sure Mr. Matlock will be staying there with us. Totally embarrassing!"

Soledad paused. "Well, anyway, you like look so-so— she halted, searching for a grownup word, "sexy!"

Celina and Edie burst into laughter, while the proper Yacqueline gently reprimanded her younger sister for using "that word."

Edie reached over and flung open the bedroom door, yelling out into the hall, "Mrs. Gonzalez, come and see Lina! If looks could kill!"

A moment later, Mama appeared, a finger over her lips, reminding the girls that Elian and Diego were already in bed. She surveyed her eldest carefully. "You look quite nice, *malaynkia*," she countered with an approving smile. "Just remember, pretty is as pretty does." She turned to leave and did a double take. "Celina Montoya! Are you wearing *makeup?*"

Celina's heart skipped a beat. "I-I-uhm-well, I mean sorta'. Edie brought some for me to try. *Puzhalste* Mama, just this once? It's just a little bit. This is a very special—

"Absolutely not! There's no occasion special enough for a daughter of mine to look like a painted china doll. Wash your face immediately! You shan't leave this house until that awful stuff is gone. *Ponyala?*"

Celina sighed and looked at the ceiling.

"Answer me, Celina," came her mother's calm but unyielding voice.

"*Da*, Mama."

In the meantime, Edie, her back to Celina and Mama, was desperately fighting giggles. When Mama left the room, she fell on the bed, clutching her stomach as she howled with laughter.

"Yeah, I know," Celina said, sarcastically as she scrubbed her face clean, "never did join us in this century, need I say more?"

"I guess not!"

"Lina!" came a sing-song voice from downstairs, "your boyfriend's here!"

"Ohhh," Celina growled, snatching up her purse, "if Marc hears him . . ." She rushed frantically downstairs and into the family room. Marcos was sitting in the recliner, reading the newspaper. He smiled, brightly, at her. At that moment, a knock sounded at the front door.

The Music of What Happens

"Lina's boyyyyyfriend!" Jackie teased, loudly from behind the sofa.

Celina marched over to the couch, grabbed a handful of her brother's curls and yanked them hard. "*Cállate!*" she hissed, "and get a life!"

"Ow! What the—

Without looking up from his paper, Marcos intervened, quietly, "Lina, I'd like to meet your friend. Giacamo, that'll be quite enough out of you. *Comprende?*"

Celina nearly burst into laughter. *No one* called Jackie Giacamo unless they seriously meant business.

The dumb bunny! At least Tío gets it.

Once out of Marcos' sight, Celina fairly flew down the hall to the front door. Her breath caught in her chest. Fulgencio stood there, dressed in a handsome red and blue *Orioles* tee shirt and brand-new blue jeans. The vibrant colors of his shirt set off his tanned skin to perfection. *Hot* was the only word Celina could mentally formulate. Looking into his wide, velvet brown eyes made her feel as though her heart was melting into a puddle.

"*¡Hola*, Celine," he smiled shyly.

"*¡H-hola*," she replied, trying to keep her voice steady. She loved the way he called her Celine. "P-please come in. Tío-I mean my-uhm-my stepdad would like to meet you."

"No problem, we've got time to kill."

Celina showed Fulgencio into the living room where Marcos still sat in his recliner, engrossed in the newspaper. She glanced at Fulgencio. His dark eyes reflected nervousness while they stood, waiting for Marcos to notice them. When he did, Celina introduced them.

"Tío, this is my friend, Fulgencio Matlock. Fulgencio, my stepfather, Marcos Gonzalez."

Marcos stood and extended his hand.

"*¡Buenos tardes*, Señor Gonzalez," Fulgencio greeted Marcos as he took the proffered hand in a firm, masculine handshake.

"Lina," Marcos turned to her, "*por favor* leave us a moment."

Reluctantly, Celina left the room. She paused and ducked around the archway where she could still hear what was being said.

"Son, you're quite young, and Lina's even younger. I know your father's going along. I'll still say this: treat my Lina with respect, decency and consideration. Be a gentleman. Think of how you want your sister treated when she becomes friendly with boys."

Out of sight, Celina furrowed her brow at Marcos' words. *My Lina. Sometimes I wish that were true. Tío cares about us, I know. But I— he called me my Lina. He must actually love me. Why else would he say that?* She smiled slightly then started when she heard Marcos call her name.

When Celina rounded the corner, Fulgencio's dark eyes brightened, and he stared as though seeing her for the first time. Marcos chuckled.

"Okay, you two, scoot, or you'll be late for the game. Behave and have a good time."

Fulgencio awkwardly offered his hand and Celina took it after a glance at Mama, who now sat near Marcos, watching them warily.

When they reached the car, Collier Matlock shook hands with Celina, surprised to hear that she was the stepdaughter of his acquaintance and fellow lawyer. Pressed against Fulgencio's side, Celina rested her head on his shoulder as he wrapped an arm protectively around her shoulder.

I really like him. Like really. I wonder if . . . her thoughts trailed off.

"Whatcha' thinking, Celine?"

Celina leaned her head back and looked up at him. She smiled, softly. "Just that it's like really nice being here with you. I'm real glad you asked me to go."

"You ever been to a basketball game?"

"Nope. I don't know much about basketball."

"I'll tell you all about it."

As they talked and snuggled, Celina was surprised at how comfortable she was with Fulgencio and how much she enjoyed their conversation.

What felt like just a short time later, Mr. Matlock pulled up in front of the huge Seattle gymnasium.

As Fulgencio, Celina and Mr. Matlock found seats on the bleachers, the game began. In no time at all, Celina was lost in the excitement of the game and found herself cheering hoarsely with the rest of the crowd. During the break, Fulgencio bought them nachos and root beer which they shared while watching the second half of the game. For some time, Celina was engrossed, yet when she finally glanced over at Fulgencio, she was surprised to see that he was no longer watching the game, but her. Heart pounding, she, at first, pretended not to notice, but when she glanced back a few minutes later, he was still watching her. When their eyes finally met, he smiled, she smiled, and the basketball game was forgotten.

On the way home, Collier Matlock talked incessantly about the scores. He probably would have been somewhat less than pleased had he known he was practically talking to himself. Celina and his son, in the back seat, whispered together and shared peppermint, crème-centered chocolates Fulgencio had brought along as a gift for his date, oblivious to the lawyer's chatting.

Too soon, or so it seemed to the young couple, they were pulling up in front of the Gonzalez home. Celina politely thanked Mr. Matlock, as she stepped from the warmth of the sedan into the chilly night air.

"May I walk Celine to her door, Dad?" Fulgencio asked his father.

"You may. Hurry back. Your mother's expecting us home."

Fulgencio leaped from the vehicle, wrapped his woolen coat around Celina's shoulders and reached for her hand as they meandered up the stone walkway. When they reached the porch, they stood in the glow of the porch light, smiling at each other, shyly.

"I had fun," Celina whispered, gently squeezing his hand. "*Gracias.*"

Fulgencio blushed and stammered, "Oh, it was n-nothing. I-I'm just so glad you could come. You're way cool, Celine. I n-never thought freshman could be cool 'til I met you."

At the bold declaration, Celina flushed crimson and grinned, despite herself. Awkwardly, she touched his arm as she opened the door. "G'nite F-Fulgencio."

CHAPTER 16

Challenge Accepted

In the days that followed, Celina felt as though she were walking on air. She had little time to think about Fulgencio, however. Her biggest concern was the fast-approaching Winter Musicale, and Celina practiced her three pieces feverishly and frequently. She was determined to show the stuck-up Hillary Oswald a thing or two.

I really don't expect to win, but if I could just place higher than Hillary, that would be enough for me. She needs her nasty nose knocked out of the air, and I want to be the one who does it! At least Fulgencio will be performing, as well. I don't think I could get through this without him.

The next week, Miss Kropotkin gave more details about the musicale. Children from all grades would be performing with songs, readings or instruments. Trinity Chapel downtown had organized an elaborate nativity scene which would be one of the program's main highlights.

That same afternoon, in late November, Miss Kropotkin approached Celina as the latter gathered up her books in preparation to go home.

"Lina, would you mind waiting a moment? I see your bus doesn't arrive for another twenty minutes."

Celina followed her music teacher down the long hall. Once inside the classroom, Miss Kropotkin sat down at her desk and opened a thick file, filled with folders, and marked MUSICALE.

The Music of What Happens

"Lina," she finally said, thoughtfully surveying the papers, "our program is timed at approximately two hours. All is ready except for a very strong closing number. I would most prefer a violin or viola, the two instruments we sadly lack, but I suppose I could make do with a second cello number." At the mention of the violin, Celina's eyes widened.

"I'm asking if you have suggestions because I know Marcos Gonzalez's family is quite musical. Nearly every child in this school is involved in the program somehow, but we simply have not been able to come up with an acceptable closing number. It can't be just anything either. It must be impressive, able to pass as a professional performance."

Celina's knowing grin was hard to hide. "Impressive and professional?" she repeated. "With a violin?"

Miss Kropotkin nodded.

Again, Celina grinned. "Consider it done," she told her teacher, proudly, "I'll have your violinist here in an hour and a half for his audition."

As she strolled out of the room and down the hall, she thought, *Sunbeam, you're about to be discovered.*

That afternoon, over an afternoon snack of milk and maple butterscotch brownies, Celina broached the subject of Elian performing the closing number for the winter musicale. Elian was excited, but it took more than a little persuasion for Mama, who had become even more protective of him since his difficult surgery just a month ago. She finally called Marcos to get his opinion, and he gave the green light for Elian to perform with his violin. It was a happy duo that Mama deposited at the Academy on her way downtown to do the weekly grocery shopping.

Miss Kropotkin smiled a cheery hello when the children entered the classroom. Her eyebrow lifted, however, at the small, sickly-looking child her star pupil was recommending for the violin number. Celina knew Elian only looked about five or six years old, but she also knew his gentle, solemn, dark eyes and air of natural intelligence would tug at Miss Kropotkin's curiosity.

Miss Kropotkin motioned for Elian to come close. "What's your name, little one?"

Not understanding the English words, Elian turned his palms upward and remained silent. At the teacher's confused expression, Celina said, with a shrug, "Speak Russian."

Miss Kropotkin's eyes widened; however, she did not question and repeated her words.

"My name's Elian Montoya, madam."

"And you're how old?"

"I'll be nine in June," he replied, gazing, in distracted awe, around the music room.

"All right then, Mr. Montoya, let's see what you can do."

Flashing Celina a sneaky smile, Elian opened his violin case and turned a piece of music just enough for her to see the title. She rolled her eyes at him, affectionately.

Why does he always think he has to show off?

Elian had chosen, by far, the most beautiful, not to mention, the most complicated piece he knew. Trying, with little success, to hide his cheesy smile, he arranged his papers on the music stand and began to play.

Celina glanced at Miss Kropotkin. The teacher could not conceal her amazement. Her jaw dropped, and she could not take her eyes off the small boy. Elian played with his eyes closed, not once looking at his sheet music. Celina too closed her eyes. The passion and feeling her brother put into his music was breathtaking as always. His facial expressions and the deft speed with which he moved his little hands all spoke volumes for the beautiful composition he played.

As Elian moved, with apparent ease, through the Hungarian, love song, Miss Kropotkin stood and turned her back.

He's got this. He's made her cry. I've never even made her cry, and neither have any of the others here. He's totally got this.

Moments later, Elian completed his audition with a dramatic finish. Miss Kropotkin took a moment to compose herself before she turned to face him.

The Music of What Happens

"That-that was beautiful, Elian," she said, inadequately, "simply gorgeous. *Da. Da*, you'll make a perfect, closing musician. Can you play *Pas De Deux*? It's a most lovely piece and a favorite of our Dean of Students."

Elian barely glanced at the music. "*Da*, madam, I can do it." His eager voice trembled. "It-it looks so pretty." In his excitement, he nearly forgot to speak straight Russian as his sister had previously told him.

"All right then, the part is yours. Here's the sheet music for you to practice, but I have a good feeling you won't need it," Miss Kropotkin smiled. After giving the spelling of Elian's name and thanking Miss Kropotkin, the children took their leave.

Besides the musicale, the holidays were drawing near. Thanksgiving was spent at Abuelo and Abuelita Gonzalez's house. Several of Marcos' siblings were there as well, and Celina and Justinia were excited to see each other again. After the meal, the younger children disappeared downstairs to play, and Justinia, a plate of pie in her hand, motioned Celina to a small cubby room, next to one of Abuelita's spare bedrooms.

"Here, just be careful, you don't wanna get in trouble," Justinia whispered, handing Celina a small parcel containing a tube of lipstick, clear nail polish, blush, and eye makeup.

"Yeah, I'll wash it off after my performances before Mama sees it," Celina shrugged, taking a large bite of her pumpkin pie. "So, you coming to the musicale?"

"Children?" the girls suddenly heard Abuelita calling, "Children! Let's all meet downstairs in the parlor."

"I guess they'll want me to play piano again," Celina laughed as they climbed out of the cubby.

Justinia playfully punched her arm. "You know you love it."

For the next hour, the family sang around the piano. Celina and Tía Kyle took turns playing the piano while Elian and Abuelo accompanied on their violins, and Marcos played the guitar.

Shortly before Christmas, Mama began experimenting with Christmas baking, something they had never been able to do while Papi was alive. The Montoya children had never tasted such homemade, Yuletide delicacies as fudge or Mama's, melt-in-your-mouth, Russian teacakes. All watched with eagerness and curiosity as Alexei labored for days over these Christmas creations. Each day, Celina found herself willing the school day to fly by so she could hurry home and help. The first thing Mama made was creamy, peanut butter fudge. When it was set, Marcos cut it as the children gathered around the breakfast bar and kitchen counter. He handed Little Man the first slice. As the small boy bit into the soft confection, his velvety-brown eyes turned perfectly round with delight.

"Oh, wow!" he breathed, "it-it's so-so . . ." he halted, unable to find words to adequately describe it.

"Me next! Me next!" the others clamored, as Mama passed out individual slices. Celina closed her eyes as she bit into hers. She could not remember tasting anything so delicious.

"Christmas is going to be awesome!" Chaim declared, as he polished off his fudge in one bite and promptly cut himself a second piece.

Just days later, the children adorned the entire house for Christmas. Chaim, Yacqueline and Jackie decorated the windowsills and doorframes with silvery garlands, ceramic ornaments and candles. A tall tree stood in a prominent corner of the family room, decorated by the children, mostly with ornaments they had created in school. A lovely Nativity scene was placed on the living room coffee table. Finally, Javier and Celina hung mistletoe in the kitchen doorway, and the children lured Mama and Marcos beneath it. When they realized the trick, they kissed while the children laughed and clapped, approvingly.

CHAPTER 17

A Most Precious Gift

The night of the Musicale arrived cold, clear and just three days before Christmas. That evening, Celina dressed in a brand-new dress, an early Christmas present from Mama and Marcos. The dress was white with black and red trim and puffy short sleeves. It had a barely off-the-shoulder neckline, embroidered flowers on the bodice, and a full skirt that fell mid-knee. She curled the ends of her hair and wore a black headband with a red silk rose that was set just above her ear. Her neckline was just low enough to show Papi's crucifix, and she had lain off her locket for the evening.

A knock at the door startled her. Mama smiled as she opened a small blue velvet box. "Would you like to borrow these for tonight?"

Celina's breath caught when she saw Mama's diamond and ruby earrings glittering in the soft light from the bedroom lamp. It was the only piece of expensive jewelry Papi had purchased for her during their twelve-year marriage. Celina blinked back tears as she put them in, resolving to herself to be careful not to lose them. For a long moment, mother and daughter stared at their reflections in the mirror.

"Your papi would be so proud if only he could see you tonight, Linochka. You've become such a lovely young woman, inside and out." With these words, Mama enveloped her in a careful hug.

An hour later, the Gonzalez's, blue Escalade was pulling up in front of the city gymnasium. When they arrived inside, Celina, clutching her black folder of sheet music, hurried to the ladies' room to check her hair. Staring almost unseeingly into the mirror, she carefully wiped off the clear moisturizer Mama had given her for her lips and replaced it with the rose red lipstick Justinia had loaned her. When she had finished applying the borrowed makeup, Celina checked her earrings and tightened the backs.

"Hey, Lina," came a familiar voice from a sink on the other side of the bathroom. Edie stepped from behind a partition, grinning, excitedly. Her grin changed quickly to a look of amazement. "Lina, you look incredible! I just love your dress! Wait a sec—your mom's letting you wear makeup now? That's the juice!"

Celina giggled, "Nope, and I gotta make sure she doesn't see me up close before I can wash it off. I'm just so sick of looking like a little kid. You look terrific too!" she exclaimed, sincerely, changing the subject. "Wow!"

Edie, clearly unaccustomed to being complimented, mumbled a thank you and looked away, shyly. She wore a short, royal blue, velvet dress with a mandarin collar. Her long, thick, blonde hair was curled and piled on top of her head, princess style. Wide, blue eyes were lovely, accentuated with black liner and silvery blue eyeshadow. Celina had always thought her friend pretty, however, at that moment, she was simply stunning!

At that instant, the restroom door swung inward and in sauntered Hillary. Edie rolled her eyes over Celina's shoulder and muttered in her ear, "Entering, winner of last year's charm school award, prep division!"

Celina whirled around, her eyes widening when she saw the taller girl. "Who-*whoa!*"

Hillary smiled snidely down her nose. "Well, my, my," she countered, "if it isn't chocolate and vanilla, the perfect loser pair. Uhm, seriously, Lina, where *did* you get that dress? Like Amazon Mexico? It looks like you're about to dance for a mariachi band. Oh," she turned, showing off her dress. "What do you two think? Isn't it just to die for? My dad told my mom to order it straight off the London runway. It's a designer original. Let's face it, girls, which of your dads loves you enough to buy you a *designer original?* Oh, my bad," she smirked, cruelly, looking down her nose at Celina, "you don't even *have* a dad." Hillary did another turn as she admired herself in the long mirror. "You know girls, I can wear just about anything. Pilates, ladies, pilates will totally give you these thighs. It's not like normal women can have my— As Hillary droned on, Celina bit her lip hard, her back turned as she nonchalantly pretended to be blending her concealer. She blinked hard at the dad comment, determined not to smudge her eyeliner. Hillary's figure-hugging dress *was* stunning: ice blue and backless with a slim, micro mini skirt, and plunging, halter neck and all covered with glittering, silvery rhinestones. Her thick, auburn hair was curled and hung down her bare back like a shampoo model. Clear, glassy stilettos completed the ensemble. She was drop-dead gorgeous and at that moment, could have easily passed as old enough to get into clubs. Despite her own beautiful outfit, Celina had to swallow a pang of envy.

Mama would never let me wear a dress like that even though—Oh. em. gee, did she get implants?

Celina nearly burst out laughing when she realized Hillary was wearing padding in her strapless bra.

Hillary prodded, rolling her eyes. "What, no smart remarks, Lina? Like, of course, you're jealous, I get it, but I want an opinion. I mean, I've always wanted to look like that one influencer who's—

Celina turned back to face her. She sucked in her cheeks and looked Hillary up and down condescendingly. "Hillary, at least lose the fake tits, you're not fooling anyone, and that cheap perfume puts me in the mind of an angel on heroin! Now I'd like to stay and chat because I know *just* how much you love to hear yourself talk, but *I've* got a competition to win. Come *along*, Edie!" Without another word, Celina sauntered from the bathroom, shoulder checking a stunned and fuming Hillary out of the way. Edie dashed after her from the restroom stall where she had been hiding. She stuck her tongue out at Hillary as she passed her.

"Oh, for crying out loud, what a total dumb bunny!" Celina exclaimed when they reached the hallway." I think I just barfed in my mouth. If her nose were any higher in the sky, she'd achieve airlift. So, can we sit wherever we want?"

Edie's eyes widened as she tucked her black music folder under her arm. "Are you kidding me? No way. Miss Kropotkin reserves the whole balcony for us performers! Oh, Lina, you just gotta see the gym! It's all decorated for Christmas, and we're sold out! Standing room only! Come on."

Celina barely had a chance to snatch up her music folder before Edie grabbed her arm and excitedly dragged her through the big double doors into the gymnasium.

"Lina! Edith!" Miss Kropotkin motioned to them frantically from behind the stage. "Get to the balcony immediately! The program's about to begin, and for heaven's sake, don't let anyone see you!"

Celina and Edie rushed around the back way, up the balcony stairs and into their assigned seats. Barely were they seated when the Dean of Students, Errol Rodham, stood and addressed the audience. "I bid you all welcome to the fourth annual Academy Christmas Musicale. Our leading instructor, as well as the overseer of every inch of this production, is Dunyasha Kropotkin from Dnepropetrovsk, Ukraine. It's her devotion and unfailing dedication that has made this year's program possible. Without further ado, Dunyasha Kropotkin."

Miss Kropotkin, looking most elegant in a slim, floor-length, velvet, forest green dress, stood and bowed to the applauding audience. Because she did not believe in wasting words, Miss Kropotkin thanked Dean Rodham and said, "I'm sure you're all anxious for our program to begin. I thank you all for coming, and I certainly hope you enjoy yourselves. The first performers of our musicale are Fulgencio and Mieha Matlock who will be performing *Feliz Navidad*. Without further ado, please welcome Mr. and Miss Matlock."

From where he sat, across the aisle from Celina, Fulgencio stood, attired in a black suit and red tie. Music in hand, he strode easily down the steps and up to the stage. Mieha, in a short, red, mandarin-collared, silk dress, followed him. Although not nearly as tall, she strongly resembled her brother. Fulgencio played with gusto, and Mieha sang the upbeat Spanish carol beautifully, not making a single mistake. The applause was loud as Dean Rodham shook both children's hands before they bowed, simultaneously, and left the stage.

A lovely manger scene, presented by small children from Trinity Chapel, followed the Matlocks' performance. A six-year-old in the cast sang *Away in a Manger*, leaving many in the audience in tears.

"And now," Miss Kropotkin finally announced into the microphone, "I'm excited to present one of my own students, Celina Zagoradniy, playing *Dance of the Sugar Plum Fairies* from Tchaikovsky's *Nutcracker Suite*. Please welcome Miss Zagoradniy."

Edie squeezed her hand as Celina stood, gripping her sheet music tightly against her chest and moved feverishly down the steps to the stage. Miss Kropotkin smiled her encouragement as she sat down at the piano and glanced at her music. For one dreadful moment, the notes swam before her eyes, and Celina was sure she was going to be sick.

Breathe. Just breathe.

The room grew deathly quiet as she played a dramatic introduction that she had composed herself. Closing her eyes, Celina forced her focus to the music. As her fingers glided effortlessly across the keys, her smile grew wider. *Dance of the Sugar Plum Fairies. Make it waltz.* When she glanced into the audience at Mama and Marcos, she noticed that Marcos' eyes were closed, a soft smile on his lips. She pressed on. Harder, faster, softer, her fingers flying over the keys until the piece ended with a dramatic crescendo.

A stunned silence fell over the room, and for one terrible moment, Celina was sure her performance must have been awful, yet she could not recall having done anything wrong. Suddenly the audience rose to their feet. They clapped and clapped and clapped. Thunderous applause grew to a deafening roar as Celina bowed and left the stage, inwardly trembling.

When she reached her seat, she was hugged tightly by an ecstatic Edie. "Oh, Lina," she gushed, trying without much success to whisper, "listen! They're *still* clapping! Oh, you've won the instrumental prize for sure!"

Celina leaned over the railing to look down into the audience below. Grinning from ear to ear, Marcos looked up and gave her two thumbs up. Mama was in tears.

"Man, girl, don't you jinx me already," she reprimanded, "I still have that crazy, concerto to do. Can you believe it, it's not even a Christmas song! I'm gonna blow it!"

"Aw, Kropotkin just wants to show you off. Everyone knows you're her best student. And don't you dare blow it— I'm counting on you, girl. If that awful bimbo, Hillary, wins *again*, I swear—

"It is now my pleasure to present to you Miss Edith Driscoll and Miss Rivalee Ariesz performing *What Child is This* for piano and voice."

The program moved too swiftly after that, and Celina performed her other two pieces, between many other numbers, receiving virtually the same reaction as she had with the first. Almost before she realized what was happening, it was time for the closing number.

"And now, ladies and gentlemen, for the conclusion of tonight's performance, may I present Mr. Elian Montoya performing Tchaikovsky's *Pas De Deux* or the *Nutcracker* on the violin."

Elian looked excited yet, at the same time, a little nervous as he stood, dressed in an adorable vest and tie ensemble. Carrying his violin case, he headed confidently to the stage. Watching him, Celina tensed. Even the short walk to the stage had left him almost completely out of breath. Elian inhaled slowly and flashed his audience an angelic, if not tired smile. Carefully, he drew the bow across the strings, sending chords of crystal clear, resonant notes into the air. By the time he was finished, there was not a dry eye in the building. The applause was thunderous as Elian laid the violin back in its case and bowed.

The Music of What Happens

After closing words from Dean Rodham, Miss Kropotkin who had been conferring with the three judges, seated at a table a short distance from the stage, returned with their decisions written on the piece of paper she clutched nervously in her hand.

"Will the performers in this year's Winter Musicale please come forward and stand below the stage in neat rows according to performance category?"

Holding Elian's hand, Celina followed the large group of children moving carefully down the stairs toward the stage. They were quickly organized by Miss Kropotkin in order of height. The audience was almost perfectly silent not wanting to miss the announcements. Celina and Edie stood, side by side, holding hands for good luck. Celina turned to Fulgencio, standing behind her. A wide grin lighting his face, he winked. She smiled, weakly, her heart roaring in her ears, as she waited for the announcements.

After a pause for effect, Miss Kropotkin continued, "When your name is called, please come to the stage and accept your medal from Dean Rodham. All performers have delivered exceptional presentations. However, by the decision of our esteemed judges, awards in the reading and vocal music category are as follows: Third prize is awarded to Mr. Chaim Montoya for gracing us with such a stirring reading as *The Nights of Los Posadas*. I will have you all know that Chaim, just thirteen years old, wrote this incredible poem himself. Please give a hand for Chaim." After the applause had died down, she continued, "Second prize is awarded to the duet pair of Rivalee Ariesz and Edith Driscoll for the lovely song, What Child is This? First prize is awarded to . . ."

Celina missed the last part of the announcement as she threw her arms around Edie, who stood, stock still, in shock. "I knew it! I just knew it!" she whispered, excitedly, in her friend's ear, "you were *terrific!*"

Finally, it was time to announce the instrumental awards. Trembling in her shoes, Celina kept her eyes closed as Miss Kropotkin began: "Third prize is awarded to Miss Hillary Oswald for her lovely, proficient performance of *Carol of the Bells*."

Celina nudged Edie as they both began cracking up at the scattered applause from the audience. Hillary glared at them both, then forced a smile for the crowd as she made her way to the stage. "Second prize," Miss Kropotkin continued, "is awarded to Miss Celina Zagoradniy for her astonishing performance of *Dance of the Sugar Plum Fairies* from Tchaikovsky's *Nutcracker Suite.*"

At this, Celina felt her knees buckle. *No way!*

Fulgencio easily steadied her. "Don't pass out now, Celine. Second place! That's amazing! You did it; you really did it! Oh, Babe, I'm so proud of you. Are you gonna be okay? Do you want me to go to the stage with you?"

"*Gracias,* but it wouldn't look right to Tío. I'm okay," She squeezed his hand reassuringly as she made her way to the stage.

An ecstatic Miss Kropotkin hugged her hard as she hung the medal around Celina's neck. "I knew you would place! I just knew! You did an outstanding job, and I am *so* proud of you."

Celina barely heard her teacher's words; her mind was reeling: Second place out of twenty-one instrumentalists, she had beaten all but one. Who could it be? She could barely hide her cheesy grin.

It's like totally enough to have beaten Hillary! Merry Christmas to me.

Back beside her friends, Celina grinned as Edie hugged her, and Elian tugged at her other hand. When she bent down, he whispered in her ear. "You were the best. I love you, sis." In response, she wrapped an arm around his shoulder.

I bet Sierra Markham-Collins will get first. Edie said if it's not Hillary, it's Sierra. She sighed; she knew she should be happy with her second-place win and not wish for more.

Unable to hide her broad smile, Miss Kropotkin turned back to her crowd of students and then to the audience. "And finally, first prize is awarded to Mr. Elian Montoya for his stirring, astounding performance of *Pas De Deux* or *The Nutcracker,* performed on the violin. Elian's future in music is bright indeed."

Cheering wildly, Celina was amused at the startled look on her brother's face as he shyly climbed the three steps to the stage, eyes fixed on his shoes, to accept his medal.

The musicale dismissed, and as everyone crowded around the refreshment tables, she slipped into the hallway to be alone with her thoughts. Sitting on the steps near the foyer, she fingered the silver medal that read in black letters SECOND PLACE INSTRUMENTAL. Winter Musicale. The Academy. In tiny letters, at the bottom, the year was stamped in blue.

I can't believe it! I just can't believe it!
"Thought I'd find you here."
Celina started but relaxed when she saw Fulgencio. He held out his hand, she took it and they walked outside. The December night was cold and starry, but Fulgencio took off his jacket and put it around her shoulders. He grinned.
"For a moment, I thought you were going to faint dead away when Miss Kropotkin announced you took second."
"You're not the only one," Celina laughed, weakly. "I did *not* see that coming!"
Without another word, Fulgencio placed a small, wrapped package in her hand. "*Feliz Navidad,* Celine," he mumbled, shyly, looking at his shoes, heat creeping up his neck. Celina grinned to herself; her heart full.
"*Feliz Navidad,*" she replied, as she, in turn, handed him the tiny box from her skirt pocket that contained a gold tie clip. Upon tearing away the wrapping on her gift, Celina discovered a small, black velvet box. Inside was a beautiful gold ring with emerald chips.
"I wish it coulda been a real one," Fulgencio took the ring from its resting place, "It's a promise ring. Will you?"
Celina stared down at the ring for a long moment. When she looked up, her dark eyes were shining, in the glow from the streetlights, overlooking the parking lot, where they stood. "*Si,*" she whispered as he slipped it on her finger, "I will."

When Celina looked back up, Fulgencio's dark eyes seemed to pierce right through her soul. *It's like he . . .*

"Fulgencio, d-don't look like that *por favor.*"

Fulgencio shook his head, his eyes almost frightened as well. "I-I love you, C-Celine," he whispered, in a voice she had never heard before.

Celina shook her head, vigorously, "No-no, Fulgencio, you can't— her voice trailed off. When his lips found hers. Celina could have sworn she was floating. Fulgencio wrapped his arms around her, and they embraced tightly. Her head was spinning. The scent of *Eternity*. She was kissing him back now, running her fingers through his mop of black curls.

Without warning, Celina found herself shaking uncontrollably, but she could not put her finger on the strange sounds and terrifying sensations coursing through her body and over her skin. It was but a few seconds before her mind cleared, and she remembered. As though it were happening now. She clung tightly to Fulgencio and tried to push aside the awful memory of two years ago when Cal Ainsworth had followed her into the woods, but there it was, as plain as day. Her wrists in his vice grip, his fist connecting with her cheek, the smell of his sweaty skin and crusty lips pressed hard against hers. His awful strength. The secret she had never dared share. *And I was only twelve.*

Celina was hyperventilating; Fulgencio's gentle kisses which, moments ago, were so welcome and sweet, now seemed to be crushing and bruising her lips. It was as though she were suffocating.

I-I—

With a sharp cry, she pulled out of Fulgencio's arms and shoved him backward. Fulgencio stood stock still, mouth agape, expressive eyes reflecting hurt.

"C-Celine, what did I—

But she did not give him a chance to finish. Tears filling her eyes, she turned and rushed back into the gymnasium and into the ladies' room.

The Music of What Happens

Huddled in a corner behind the lockers, Celina sat, trembling uncontrollably. When she could finally stand up again, she covered her hands with soap and scrubbed her face over and over.

All they ever knew is he beat me up. I just couldn't tell the rest. I was so scared. I tried to forget— Celina shut her eyes hard, feeling his rough skin against hers, his weight—

This should have been like the best evening of my whole life, but now it's ruined! And I've lost Fulgencio!

When Celina left the bathroom, Mama, Marcos and the other children were looking for her. Glad that she had cleaned the makeup smudges off her face, she forced a smile as Mama hugged her, telling her over and over how marvelous her performance had been.

Marcos exclaimed, "I was speechless through all three pieces, especially that concerto. You were incredible!" He squeezed her hand and turned to look at the others. "You all did amazingly well. And you," he picked up Elian and spun him around once, "you were just phenomenal."

Celina stared unseeingly towards the double doors leading into the parking lot. Alexei's smile faded when she saw her eyes, suspiciously red and puffy. When Celina caught her mother's eye, she looked away again, and Mama refrained from speaking as Marcos led the family outside to the Escalade.

As they left, Celina caught sight of Fulgencio, standing just inside the double doors, off to the side, in the shadows. Their eyes met. Fulgencio averted his gaze and walked away. Celina blinked back more tears.

I've lost him; I've lost my best friend.

During the drive home, the other children chatted excitedly about the musicale and how much fun it had been. Elian leaned his head on Celina's shoulder and quickly fell asleep. Celina wrapped an arm around him protectively and stared unseeing out the window into the winter darkness. Several times, she caught sight of Mama glancing back at her.

Please don't say anything. I just can't do this right now.

When the family arrived home, Celina changed out of her new dress and took refuge in the library on the third floor. Sitting at the piano, she stared down at her hands for a moment before she began to play *Si Volvieres a Mí*, Papi's favorite. Tears filled her eyes and drooled down her cheeks as she played softly. Soft turned forte, she played harder and faster as the tears rained down, dripping all over her t-shirt. The harder she hit the keys, the harder she cried.

After what felt like forever, she flung herself across the keyboard as the music subsided with a discordant crash. Celina wept uncontrollably. "Oh, Papi, Papi, I needed you so bad! I called for you! I called for you over and over, but you never came!"

Celina did not see her mother standing in the doorway, tears welling up in her own eyes. She started when Mama sat down on the piano bench beside her. Wrapping her arms tightly around her daughter, she held her close, stroking her dark curls.

"*Nyet, nyet, malaynkia,*" she crooned, softly as Celina clung to her, weeping into her shoulder, "You mustn't cry like this, my Linochka. Tell mama what's wrong. Tell me everything! Who's hurt you?" She continued to hold and rock Celina in her arms until she was somewhat calmed.

"Oh, Mama," Celina sobbed, "it was awful! It was like so awful! He-he wouldn't let me go! He-he-he—"

"Shhh, shhh," Alexei soothed, "who, my darling? Who's so awful?"

"Oh, God, please don't make me say! You'll hate me!!"

"No, *malaynkia, no!*" Mama again drew her daughter in close, "Oh, Lina, no! *Nothing,*" she emphasized into Celina's hair, "could *ever* cause Marc and I to stop loving you. You are my precious daughter, and I will always *always* love you with everything inside of me. Now tell Mama everything."

Trembling the entire time, Celina finally managed to say the things she had wished she could say for the last two years. She was sobbing again, in earnest, by the time she was finished, yet this time it was different. She could feel her troubled soul being cleansed, cleansed by a river of her tears.

Now in tears, as well, Alexei whispered against Celina's head, "It's all right, *malaynkia*. He's gone now. He can never hurt you again. Never. But why, Lina?" Alexei's voice broke. "Why did you never tell me and Papi back then?"

Celina barely shrugged, wiping her eyes with the back of her hand. "I-I couldn't. I knew how upset Papi would be; he'd do something crazy and get hurt. And you, you'd already gotten blamed for me getting beat up. It was all so crazy. And he-he—" she gulped hard, "he s-said he'd do it again if I ever told. The worst thing was he said he'd do it to the girls too. I could-I couldn't let that happen. Not my sisters, they-they were so little."

Mama sighed deeply as she pressed her head gently against her chest. "Lina, baby, this was *not* your fault! Nothing about this is your fault. No matter what messages whirl through your mind, you mustn't believe them, you must believe the ones who love you. Real love doesn't die, my Lina. It's the one thing that stands for truth, no matter how many awful things happen in our lives. It's the hope we wouldn't have otherwise. And you have the love of your entire family." She sat back and cupped Celina's chin in her hand, lifting her eyes to meet hers. "Truly, my love, truly. And you're safe now. And I could never stop loving you. I'm so very proud of you for telling me. We're going to help you through this. We're going to get you help. You're going to be okay, my little one. Rest in that, oh, rest in that."

Celina nodded, slowly and smiled, in spite of herself. She knew it was true. Her family's love was unconditional. They had proven it over and over. Mama then took her hand, and they left the room together.

As soon as her mother disappeared downstairs and into the kitchen, Celina slipped away to Marcos' den to use the landline. All she could think of was her last glimpse of Fulgencio, staring after her, sad, hurt and confused. Heart thumping madly, she dialed his number.

"Good evening, Matlock residence?" Fulgencio's soft voice answered, politely.

"Uhm-uh, ¡hola, Fulgencio."

"Celine!" Fulgencio did not even try to conceal his excitement, "I hoped so much that you'd call. Listen, about tonight, I'm sorry. I-I should've asked first. I knew better. It-it's just that-well-I thought or rather . . . I hoped that you loved me too. I'm really sorry."

Celina's heart nearly broke at his forlorn words. "No, Fulgencio, no! It was me, it was all me. It's still me. I *do* love you, I *do*. And for the record, you're a totally awesome kisser. It-It's just that-well-something really bad happened to me two years ago, and I've been like-well-running from it be-because I was so ashamed. I thought it was all my fault. But what-what I was running from just ended up catching up with me that much quicker. And when you kissed me, I like remembered it really bad. It was my fault, not yours. Can you forgive me?"

"There's nothing to forgive! And I'm so sorry that you had bad stuff happen to you," Fulgencio replied without hesitation. "If I'd known, I'd have been more careful and gone slower. We cool?"

"We cool."

Her heart overflowing, Celina stared down at the emerald promise ring on her hand. "*Te quiero*," she whispered, with her hand over the mouthpiece as she hung up the receiver.

"Hey, Lina!" Soledad sang out as her sister entered the kitchen. "We're gonna eat all the yummies without you if you don't hurry it up."

Giving her younger sister a playful swat on the behind as she passed her, Celina snatched up a paper plate and filled it with Mama's homemade Christmas goodies. Marcos handed her a red, plastic cup filled with sparkling cider. How delicious it all was.

Two days later, on Christmas morning, Celina was rudely awakened by an excited Evangelo and Little Man bouncing up and down on her bed, shouting, "Wake up, Lina! Wake up! It's Chris'mas! It's Chris'mas! Hurry! We gotta' open presents."

"*Ay Dios mío*, you've *got* to be kidding me," Celina moaned when she saw the alarm clock beside her bed read seven-fifteen.

Yacqueline and Soledad were awake as well and pulling their robes and slippers from the closet. "Come on, Lina, come on!" Yacqueline pleaded. The older boys suddenly appeared, dark eyes shining with excitement.

"Oh, *fine!*" Celina grudgingly threw off her quilt. "I'll get Diego and you guys wake Mama and Tío. Don't blame me though if Tío grounds you all for waking him and Mama at crazy, stupid o'clock and makes us all wait 'til next year to open the presents. None of this dumb bunny business was any of *my* idea!"

When Celina entered the nursery, Diego was sitting up in his crib, a sunny smile plastered all over his angelic, baby face.

"*Feliz Navidad, hermano pequeño,*" Celina greeted the baby, brightly, lifting him into her arms. "You wanna see what's in all those presents?"

When Celina and Diego entered the family room, the other children were already waiting. Marcos looked like a skinny Santa Claus, in white pajamas and red robe, as he carried a plate of Russian tea cakes and a pitcher of hot *chocoatl* into the family room for a light, holiday breakfast.

When all were finally gathered in front of the tree, they tore into the presents. Squeals of excitement and glee accompanied the opened gifts. A short while after, Mama, accompanied by Yacqueline, went to the kitchen to feed Diego while the other children went upstairs to play awhile with their new toys and games before the family was to meet at Tía Aletta and Tío Jorge's house for Christmas dinner.

Marcos rested cozily on the sofa with a new, law book, however, he was not really reading. When Celina returned from the kitchen with the mug of coffee he had asked for, he patted the cushion beside him, and she willingly sat down. For a moment, he stared down at her hand where she clutched something firmly.

"I-I thought you should see this," she told him, slowly, "I finally decided . . . about my locket." Without another word, Celina opened it to show Marcos a small picture of himself in the tiny frame opposite Giacamo's. "I'll always love my papi," she continued, seriously, "but I can finally say goodbye. Elian was right. So were you."

Celina did not have to explain further. Marcos smiled, tenderly, and wrapped an arm around her. She, in response, laid her head on his shoulder.

"Merry Christmas, my Lina." He blinked away sudden tears as he leaned his head against hers.

"Merry Christmas . . . Dad."

THE BEGINNING

Made in the USA
Middletown, DE
09 October 2022